BURIED SECRETS

ALSO BY T.J. BREARTON

Dark Web
Dark Kills
Gone

THE TITAN SERIES
Habit
Survivors
Daybreak
Black Soul

TOM LANGE SERIES
Dead Gone

BURIED SECRETS

T.J. BREARTON

Bookouture

Published by Bookouture
An imprint of StoryFire Ltd.
23 Sussex Road, Ickenham, UB10 8PN
United Kingdom
www.bookouture.com

ISBN: 978-1-78681-215-5
eBook ISBN: 978-1-78681-214-8

This one is for my aunt Alison.

CHAPTER ONE

The shovel struck something hard.

Brett Larson moved his foot away and yanked the shovel from the ground. He stared down, sweat dripping from his face.

He plunged the blade into the earth again. It rammed some solid object about six inches deep.

He tried to lever the handle back – if it was a rock it might pop out, and he'd already encountered a couple good-sized rocks so far that day. Otherwise, the ground was soft. The property was an old cow pasture, lumpy and tufted with thick grass almost as high as his knees in places. Practically impossible to mow without a tractor, but rich as chocolate cake. God bless those cows.

Brett excavated around the object and scraped away some of the dark soil. He saw something white, but it might've been a nick in a rock caused by the sharp cutting edge of the shovel.

He took the handkerchief from his back pocket, wiped his brow, and blew his nose. He smiled as he wadded it up, thinking he was a real farmer now, and gazed across the deep, wide field at the house in the distance.

Their house. A little yellow farmhouse with white trim and shutters against a hazy blue morning.

Emily had disliked the color of the house when they'd first looked at it, but she had fallen in love with it anyway. Neither of them had gotten around to repainting yet. There had been other priorities.

Like a garden.

Brett surveyed his progress, trying to marshal a little confidence. He'd gotten up with the sun, just after 5 a.m. It had been cool then, misty, as the light spread over the mountains. Now the sun was really starting to beat down on the pasture he'd been turning over and plowing into rows.

He knew he needed a real rototiller – turning earth by shovel was hard going – but all good things started small. Plus it was already mid-June and they were up against time if they wanted to get seeds in the ground. The property had taken ninety days to go to closing, ninety days from the offer agreement to the handing over of the keys. Twice the usual time it took to buy a house, from everything he'd heard. Now they were doing a bit of racing against the season.

He stowed the handkerchief and rested his foot on the shovel's shoulder. He saw Emily in the kitchen window and raised a hand. She waved back.

She was barely the size of a child's doll from here. He smiled at her despite the distance.

He got back to work, deciding he'd remove just this last rock and then take a break. He was so anxious to sow seeds he figured he'd plant a little, dig a little, and go like this until he felt satisfied.

The fertile smell of the earth plumed up, the insects danced in the morning light, the dew on the grass evaporated. What a day.

He dug and picked and scraped with the shovel and tried to lever out the rock.

The more he worked at it, the more it didn't seem like a rock after all – the way the shovel hit it didn't make that metal-on-rock *chink*. It sounded like something else. Maybe some petrified piece of wood or an old tractor part.

He dug around a little more. As he carefully scraped the soil away, he could tell it wasn't round like a rock either. It was long, like buried wood, but white.

Like bone.

He circumscribed an even wider hole. No use trying to pop the thing out of there anymore. He thought about archaeologists digging up fossils, and how they would do it. He didn't want to damage the bone, if that's what it was, any further. He wanted to remove it intact.

It might've been from an animal, maybe a woodchuck or hedgehog.

Fresh sweat threaded between his eyes and dripped from his nose. He smeared it away with a dirty hand and kept going, boring out the hole a full yard deep and almost as wide.

The bone was too big to be from some backyard critter.

Maybe someone had buried their pet dog out here.

Maybe one of those old cows.

But he didn't think so, and his nerves were starting to crawl.

He glanced at the house again. Emily had left the kitchen and was approaching through the high grass. It looked like she was holding drinks.

Emily's own dog had died a year ago. Well, Cleaver had been *their* dog, she would've said, but it was really hers, far and away, a dog she'd had for twelve years, long before she'd ever met Brett.

Cleaver's death had left a hole in Emily's heart. Now the newlywed couple were trying for a baby. Married for just three months, in the house for just a few weeks so far, things were hustling right along. He wondered if Emily would get upset seeing the bone in the ground, if it would stir thoughts of her loss.

The dog had been cremated. The crematorium offered them a look at the bones, and Emily had opted to do it. Something about seeing the skeleton, she'd said afterward, was soothing. Cleaver had looked clean and un-suffering.

Brett went back to digging. The shovel banged into something else and he cleared away more cakey soil.

A second bone.

He stopped and stared a moment as his newlywed wife neared.

Then he went back to the first bone, carefully whittling away the soil until the far end of it was free. The thing was sixteen, maybe eighteen inches long.

One end was big and knobby, like the handle of a cane.

He suddenly considered throwing the dirt back, covering what was there. He'd burrowed down a good ways now, at least an arm's depth.

The bones made him anxious. But he left them exposed.

He leaned the shovel against the nearby fence and walked out to meet Emily.

She reached him and handed him the drink, ice cubes rattling in the glass. "How you doing, baby?"

He gave her a kiss on the lips and then took a sip. The iced tea was incredible, not too sweet, perfectly refreshing.

"I'm good."

Emily surveyed the work. "Wow. You're really going for it."

"We. *We're* going for it. This is garden number one right here."

She squinted. "Right at the edge of the woods? What about animals?"

He hadn't considered it. The oversight made him slightly defensive. "Yeah, yeah, I know. I'll put up a deer fence, totally…"

"You're going to get the garden hose all the way out here?"

"Yeah. Oh yeah." He had no idea if he had enough hose to reach. "Like I said, this is number one. The soil is something else here. Just so rich. I'll keep moving back towards the house as I go."

"Cool."

She was wearing high white shorts that showed off the thin taper of her legs and a light brown tank top, her skin already bronzed from the late spring sunshine. She'd been ovulating not quite two weeks ago and they'd had sex nearly every morning or night for a few days. She looked so good standing there, he wondered if she'd be up for an early-morning booty call, even if the window had closed.

But then her eyes drifted past him and she looked at the hole. "What's that?"

"Oh there's been bumps along the way," he said, catching up to her. It was stupid, he thought, but he really wished Emily wasn't out here, wasn't about to see this. "I thought it was just another rock."

She reached the hole and stopped, looking down, sipping her drink.

Brett fought the urge to grab her by the arm and lead her away, take her back to the house, make love, forget whatever was there in the dirt.

She lowered down to a squat and set the drink on the ground beside the hole.

The glass tipped over on the uneven ground, spilling the tea.

"What is that? Animal bones?"

"I don't know."

They fell silent, looking down. The crows were calling in the distance.

"Huh," she said.

He squatted beside her, grunting a little with the effort. He was by no means old, thirty was not old, but he was feeling the morning's labors. It was a hell of a lot different than driving a roller, sitting all day.

"That looks human," Emily said.

"No. No way."

But he thought so, too.

"Yeah." She pointed. "That's a leg bone. The femur." The aim of her finger shifted. "What's the other one?"

Just a piece of the second bone was visible, sticking out of the edge of the hole he'd excavated, down about half the depth.

"I don't know. The other leg?"

She glanced over, smiling but serious. She stood up and put her hands on her hips, the grin fading to a tight line. This was Pensive Emily, and it was a look he was coming to know as characteristic of his new bride.

She stared down at the bones. "Yeah, honey, I think that's a femur bone. See how the one end sort of has that little split? That's where it rests on the knee, the patella, or whatever. And the other end, that big knob, that's where it connects to the hip." The more she spoke the more she sounded confident. "Yeah. Holy shit. That's someone's leg, Brett."

The reality of it was sinking in. Maybe it was what he'd been hoping to avoid. With Emily's arrival and input, the possible implications were taking shape. Someone buried a body out here? Or just a leg? Had the person been dismembered? Where was the rest of it?

Brett was no archaeologist or physical anthropologist – tough to estimate the age of the bones. A basic grasp of decomposition, though, suggested they couldn't be *that* old because they were still pretty solid.

On the other hand, couldn't bones last for thousands of years? They called them fossils.

"I bet that's the tibia," Emily said, pointing again at the other piece.

Brett started for the shovel leaning against the fence. Emily squatted down again.

"Watch out, honey…" He moved to keep digging.

She stuck out her hand. "Okay, wait. Hold on."

"What?" He blinked away some more sweat. While she was thinking about things, Brett took off his T-shirt and wiped his face and neck. He tossed his shirt aside and waited, watching as Emily worked it through.

"Maybe we have to call somebody," she said.

"We don't even know what this is. Maybe it's a human leg bone, okay. But there's no emergency. Let me dig out the rest, see what's there."

She stood up again and rubbed her lips with the ball of her thumb, scowling down at the bones. Then she glanced around, as if someone might be watching.

"Watch out," he repeated, and edged closer.

When she stepped back, he resumed digging.

"Be careful," she said.

"I *am* being careful."

"Alright, you don't need to be snippy at me."

"I'm not snippy at you. Sorry."

He gouged fresh clods of dirt with the shovel and tossed them aside. Once he'd trenched around the second bone, he made more precise moves and slowly stripped away the soil. Emily was right, and his high-school biology was coming back to him – this was the tibia, the second part of the leg that went from the knee to the ankle. If memory served, there should be yet another, thinner bone that went along with it – the bottom half of the leg was two bones running parallel.

He made even softer, smaller digs, moving quickly and growing excited until he felt the subtlest impact. Now he put the tool aside and got down on his knees. He used his hands to scoop out the earth. Emily dropped down beside him.

As they dug, they glanced at each other, sharing a little frisson. Emily was a knockout for sure, and she looked her most youthful the way she was now, the lines in her forehead gone and the excitement shining in her eyes.

Their hands touched. They both grasped in the dirt and exhumed the small, thin bone. He didn't know the name of it. She probably did.

"I'm not sure about this one. Fibula, maybe. Tibia and fibula? Does that make sense? Or is it fibia and tibula? Look, be careful. This one is so thin. Man, Brett, we're touching it. Our fingerprints—" She let go and pushed away from the hole, rising to her feet.

Brett kept hold of the fragile bone. He could snap it like a twig if he wanted; there was nothing to it. Not knowing what else to do, he placed it back in the dirt.

He stood and dusted off his knees. "I'm going to keep digging. Maybe there's a whole skeleton here."

His words sounded strange – when did anyone ever say *maybe there's a whole skeleton here*? At least, anyone who didn't have a research grant and a string of letters after their name?

"I'm gonna call." Emily had paled, growing anxious.

"You have your phone?"

"There's barely service out here. Worse than inside."

They had yet to reconnect the landline which was already installed in the house. Sometimes they could find a spot upstairs where the cellular service came in nicely, but not always. There were rumors that a new tower was going to be erected in the area, but some of the locals had been fighting against it, calling it a potential "blight on the landscape." Brett and Emily had the internet wired in, though. They could contact someone that way if the phones didn't work. And they had the option of getting phone service through the internet, too. He just hadn't gotten around to it yet. Like painting the house.

"Well, head back in and give it a try," he said.

"Yeah. Yeah, okay." She wasn't taking her eyes off the bones.

Brett stepped close to her. Seeing her nervous made him protective, and he set aside his own concerns. "Hey. Honey, it's okay."

Her eyes found him and she seemed to relax a little bit, even smiled again. He noticed how she put her hands around her stomach, almost protectively. "Yeah. It's alright. Weird, though." She let out a breath.

"I'll be really careful. I'll dig around in a big wide area. Just like a scientist." He winked.

She smiled a little and then turned for the house. "Okay. Here I go."

Emily jogged back towards the house and Brett returned to digging.

CHAPTER TWO

James Russo saw the cops pull up in front of his house from the breakfast table. Felicia was in the kitchen with him. She had their little fourteen-month-old girl on her hip and was bouncing her, feeding her bits of eggs that the baby kept spitting out, making Felicia laugh.

Russo pushed his own half-finished plate of eggs aside as he stared out the window. He knew who was out there – he recognized the cops from the way they got out of the car, looked up at the house, took their time.

It was what police called a Whiskey unit. He knew because he used to work police dispatch, and "Whiskey" was a ten-code for a unit that served warrants. They were coming up the steps, a man and a woman, and he could see the paperwork in the woman's hands.

Russo blotted his mouth with a napkin and stood up from the table.

Felicia sensed something right away. His wife was about as intuitive as anyone he'd ever known. He couldn't get away with shit – not that he wanted to – because Felicia had a nose like a bloodhound. He had to work extra hard to keep secrets and he'd only managed just a few.

There was an edge to her tone. "Honey…?"

"It's alright, Fifi."

He walked past them towards the front door. He smiled and cooed at baby Zoe and tugged on her tiny little jujube toes as he walked past. The baby girl giggled.

The cops knocked. Russo was right there and opened up.

The female officer flashed a smile and held up the piece of paper. "Mr. James Alonzo Russo?"

"Yes."

Russo eyed the big male cop, standing behind the female officer, who was checking everything out – the house, the tiny front yard. Whiskey units often operated like this. Nice, female cop to hand out the bad news; big, heavyweight cop to deal with the fallout.

The female cop, straight-faced now, rattled the paper. "We have a warrant for your arrest."

"Baby? Jimmy?" Felicia was crowding in behind him now, Zoe still on her hip, babbling contentedly, waving around a wooden spoon from the kitchen.

Russo stuck out his arm, keeping them back. "It's alright, Felicia." He hardly ever called her "Felicia" at home. Always Fifi, or honey, or baby. She liked Fifi.

"Can we come in, please, Mr. Russo?"

He held the door so the female cop could pass through. The big cop followed after. He was about the same size as Russo, who was 219 pounds and six foot two. The floorboards of the old neocolonial-style house groaned under their combined weight.

"I'm Deputy Barbieri and this is Deputy Mancuso," the female cop said.

Both cops wore the gray Richmond County Sheriff's Office uniforms. The Sheriff's Office was located right near the NYPD's 120th Precinct in St. George, just a few blocks away.

Russo said nothing, watching as Mancuso snooped around the living room while Barbieri stood with the warrant in her hands.

"Do you know why we're here, Mr. Russo?"

Russo nodded. No point in being coy. "Yeah. The license thing."

"Right, Mr. Russo."

Felicia kept crowding in. "What license thing?" She shifted her focus to Mancuso. "Excuse me, sir? Can I help you?"

Mancuso had wandered into the living room, which overlooked the street with a bay window. The morning light streamed in through the glass.

The bay was just two streets over, hidden from view. Sometimes, though, Russo caught a whiff of the salt air, just like Coney Island. But he'd always liked it here better; it was less crowded than Coney.

Staten Island, his place here with the girls, was home.

Mancuso stopped at a set of shelves and touched a tiny cat figurine. There was all manner of ceramic cats on the shelf – cats cleaning themselves, drinking from tiny milk bowls, or curled up asleep. The big cop raised an eyebrow as he held up one with a ball of yarn at its feet. "This your house, Mr. Russo?"

Felicia pushed past Russo and Barbieri and, holding the baby on her hip, marched into the living room. "This is my grand-parents' home. My grandfather passed away two years ago. My grandma is at St. Joseph's Elder Care."

She held her hand out. Mancuso got the message and placed the figurine in her palm. Baby Zoe made a grab for it but Felicia deftly replaced the cat on the shelf.

The living room was filled with bric-a-brac like the troupe of tiny cats – Felicia's grandmother had been a collector. Russo had swindled away half of the inventory into boxes, mostly when Felicia wasn't looking, but the rest remained, high up so the baby couldn't get at them.

Russo suppressed a smile at his wife's temerity. Here were two Richmond County Deputies in her home, and she wanted them to express good manners and keep their fucking mitts off the cats.

Mancuso dusted his hands and then bent towards the baby. He wore a big grin and said, "Hello there."

Zoe burst out crying. Felicia turned away with her and glared at Russo, demanding an explanation. Barbieri, still holding the arrest warrant, answered.

"Ma'am, your husband was arrested five months ago for aggravated unlicensed driving."

Felicia's eyes widened. "Jimmy... what? Are you kidding me?"

Barbieri went on, "He failed to pay the fine, and a bench warrant was issued for his arrest."

As if on cue, Mancuso took the handcuffs from his belt and held them up for all to see. "We're going to have to take you in, Mr. Russo."

"Take him in?" Felicia's color was blooming. She was getting really upset now. The baby wailed harder, drowning out half of Barbieri's words.

"Very sorry for the inconvenience, ma'am."

"So where will you take him?"

"That depends. We'll take him to the station in St. George but he might have to go to Central Booking in Manhattan."

Mancuso hooked Russo up. Russo didn't resist or act tough. He stood with his back to the big cop and bent his head towards baby Zoe as the handcuffs tightened around his wrists.

He pooched out his lips at Zoe and waggled his eyebrows. She quit fussing and grabbed his mouth, like she always did. Her little pudgy baby hand twisted the heck out of his lips. He made an exaggerated face and said, "Ow! Ow!" and that cracked her right up.

Then he looked at his wife. "Sorry, Fifi."

"Don't call me that." Felicia shifted her hard stare between the two cops. Then she took Zoe and left the room, back into the kitchen. She was getting emotional, Russo knew, and didn't want the police to see it.

Barbieri opened the front door and led Russo out. Mancuso followed, calling, "Have a good day, ma'am."

As they walked down the steps, Russo looked over his shoulder at the kitchen window. He could see the two of them there, and it broke his heart.

The cops read him his rights as they went down the steps, then stuffed him into the back of the cruiser.

He liked this street, St. Mark's Place. It was older, working class, some of the homes abandoned. But it was still a decent neighborhood.

It was better than the row houses, where you could hear your neighbors through the walls. And it wasn't flashy – these weren't oh-look-at-me homes, they were simple, narrow, and charming, even if his needed a coat of paint. He liked the roofs best, that flat top, the angled sides.

Barbieri drove. She pulled the cruiser away from the curb and looked at Russo in the rearview mirror.

"Listen, do you know what you owe?"

He remembered exactly what the judge had said the fine would be – either eight hundred and fifty bucks or a month in jail.

"Yeah, I know what it is."

It was called an AUO – Aggravated Unlicensed Operation. Three years ago he'd been popped for driving while intoxicated. He'd wrecked the car and hadn't been able to afford another one since, but he'd quit drinking.

He just shouldn't have been driving his friend's car, with its stupid taillight out. But it had been an emergency, Jockey had needed his help.

The police had issued him a desk appearance ticket and released him from the police station – it had been the 120th precinct – after he'd spent several hours in jail. He was supposed to come up with the money and show up at the county clerk's office, pay the fine or do the time.

He hadn't.

"You don't seem surprised to see us, Russo. Why didn't you just take the bit? Thirty days in and this would have gone away."

"I would have lost my job."

They rode in silence for a moment. "Listen," Barbieri said. "You want, I'll stop at an ATM for you and you can get out the money. You get out the money, you show up in court with it tonight or tomorrow morning, and boom, you pay it right then and there. They'll probably let you go."

"I don't have it."

Her eyes again in the mirror. "What's that?"

"I don't have the money."

Barbieri traded looks with Mancuso. "Okay. How much you got?"

"I don't have anything."

"Nothing? You have zero dollars in your account?"

"There's seventy-eight dollars in there."

"Christ, how do you get by?"

He spared them his hard luck story. They wouldn't want to hear it anyway. But it was true. There was nothing. He hadn't paid the fine because he didn't have it yet. He'd been trying to raise it but in the meantime there were property taxes to pay. The heat. The electric. They barely had health insurance, so there were the medical costs from having Zoe, whose birth had been complicated.

Then there was the nursing home where Felicia's grandmother lived. Fifi had a big family, but her brothers were scattered, her parents back in Puerto Rico, living on the dole.

Russo shouldered all the expenses on an MTA worker's salary. But working for the subway paid peanuts.

It wasn't like it used to be. Back in his prime, Russo was flush. Those days were over, though, and now he walked the straight and narrow.

But the past wasn't through with him, apparently.

Barbieri seemed disappointed, even worried for him. "Shit, Russo. Now you're going to get locked up for failure to pay. You'll have bail to pay on top of the ticket. You got a good lawyer, at least?"

"I don't have a lawyer."

"Well let's hope your public defender has a few brain cells."

CHAPTER THREE

While Emily was inside trying to get a signal, Brett was still digging. The excitement roiling through him was a mixture of fascination and dread. What if this really was a human? What if it turned into a police investigation? He might have cops all over the property, forensics teams out here for days.

He got the whole second bone, the tibia, exposed. He moved on, slower going now because he was tentative with his thrusts of the shovel. If there were more bones here, he didn't want to crack one in half.

The more he dug, the more he doubted he should even be proceeding. If it turned into a homicide case, or something, they would want qualified people doing what he was doing now.

He was about to quit when a final stab with the shovel hit something with a *clang* – metal on metal.

He knelt down and clawed out some dirt.

He yanked his hand, as if to avoid a snake, and stared.

The box looked like a cookie or candy tin. Something an elderly woman would keep her mints in, just a bit bigger. There was a faded pattern on the lid, flowers and vines twining.

Brett wondered what was taking Emily so long. It had been twenty minutes since she'd gone inside to try to raise a signal and call the police. Maybe she was having no luck.

He reached down and grabbed the box, his heart beating faster. He wanted to have a look at what was in it but worried that he might be tampering with some sort of evidence.

Screw it. This was his property. He'd worked hard to get this house with Emily. He had every right to see what was buried in his backyard – and he was no expert in whether or not these were even human bones. He and Emily were only guessing.

He set the tin down and carefully removed the lid.

Inside was a folded-up piece of paper.

Glancing nervously at the house once more, seeing no sign of Emily, he took the paper out and unfolded it.

Notebook paper, blue lines blurred with moisture, one ragged edge. Like it had been torn from a small, spiral-bound notebook.

In the center of the page, handwritten in black ink, was:

Dr. Rhea Runic 441

A droplet of sweat fell from the top of his nose and struck the paper.

"Shit." He shook it a little in order to dry it out. The sweat drop had struck right in its center, distorting some of the letters.

Brett set the note gently back into the open tin. He grabbed at his pockets, feeling for his phone. He pulled it out and took a picture, then folded up the paper and closed the tin. Finally, he stuffed the tin back into the dirt and stood up.

The anxiety was back, his thoughts swinging between justified-property-owner-within-his-rights and asshole-contaminating-potential-evidence. Worse, he worried that by merely being in proximity to the bones and the note, *he* was the one contaminated. Emily, too. That whatever story lay buried in the ground was only going to bring trouble.

Was that a leg belonging to someone named Dr. Rhea Runic?

He started back for the house just as Emily appeared coming out the back door.

"They asked if it was human bones," Emily called, still a few yards away. Both of them walked funny through the lumpy old overgrown pasture, high-stepping to make their way to each other.

"What did you say?"

"I told them I didn't know. I said it looked human, but I wasn't sure."

"And?"

"They didn't seem overly interested," she said.

They met and Brett suddenly grabbed her and gave her a hug. They kissed and he moved his hands over her. She was surprised, but then responded, kissing him back deeply, locking her arms around his shoulders.

The moment passed and she leaned her head back, searching his eyes. "You stink."

"Sorry."

"Hit the showers, bub."

"Alright."

He started away and she caught his arm. "Hey, I'm just kidding. I like your stink."

He wrapped his arms around her again and she looked into his eyes. "You okay?"

"Yeah. I'm alright. So are they coming or what?"

"It took forever to get a signal. I wasn't going to dial 911 and have the connection go out and have ambulances show up and everything else. So first I looked up the number for the County Sheriff's. They were nice but they said better I call the state police. So I got on with them and then the phone cut out. I called back... long story short, they said they were going to send a trooper out to have a look, and we'd go from there."

He was listening along, thinking it didn't sound that bad, and that maybe the whole thing would just blow over. Or, even if it turned out to be human remains belonging to this Runic person, worrying about cops on the property was nonsense, there was nothing to fear – it might even be interesting to be a part of it.

Maybe there *was* a story here, something he could even end up writing about. It had been years since he'd made an attempt to put pen to paper. Maybe this was just the thing.

But when Emily asked him if he found anything else, he hesitated for a moment.

Then he told her. "I found a little box. Like a candy tin. With a piece of paper in it and a name and number on it."

"Really?" Her eyes got wide, then narrowed. She clutched his arm. "Like a phone number? You're lying."

"Not a phone number. Just a number. 441. I'm serious. Someone named Dr. Rhea Runic."

They both turned and stood abreast, looking at the back fence, the mounds of dirt in the distance. Emily put a hand over her mouth. "Oh my God," she said in a choked voice. "Brett, Jesus, Brett, you think that's who it is?"

"Hey." He took her by the shoulders. "Hey, listen. It's okay. It's going to be okay, alright?"

She stared past him. He wondered if she was thinking about Cleaver, her old dog. Probably not. But her eyes bunched, their rich brown color seemed to darken.

"What… Em. What's the matter?"

"The matter?" She continued to stare, then her eyes cleared. She shook off the pall and gave him a look, furrowing her brow. "I'm just worried this will put off your garden."

He watched her a moment until realizing she was trying to lighten the mood. The bones really had her spooked. Him too, but he decided to play along.

"Hey, well. That's why we're here, right? Live off the land." He put his hand on her abdomen. "To raise whatever kids we have and learn 'em right. Teach them self-reliance. Subsistence living. To hell with human progress."

She cracked a smile.

Seeing that he had her, he moved in for the kill. "We have to prepare for the end of the world. The bodies are piling up."

"Stop it."

She kept grinning a bit, but they were both drawn back to the bones, silently contemplating the possibilities.

"There's going to be reporters and everything," he said. "I'm sorry for whoever this is, you know what I mean? And maybe somebody out there gets some bad news. Or, maybe it's a missing person found and it's good news, or at least closure. But either way, this is gonna turn our lives upside down. And that freaks me out, kinda."

She surprised him with a poke in the ribs. "You can still have your quiet life. And your garden, Mr. Titchmarsh."

"Who?"

"You've never seen him, on the BBC? He's a celebrity gardener."

"*Tit* marsh?"

"Titchmarsh."

She was smiling, though her eyes got that distant look again.

Brett encircled his arm around her waist and they moved towards the house.

The state trooper car, dark blue with a yellow stripe, slowed in the road. It turned into their dirt driveway.

Brett and Emily sat on the porch, her in the old rocker that had come with the house, him on the front steps. He'd been picking at the paint and chasing away hornets, a nervous fire in his stomach.

A female trooper stepped out of the cruiser when it stopped and Brett rose from the steps; Emily stood up behind him, took his hand, and led him towards the trooper.

The trooper slid a nightstick into her belt and smiled at them. Then she ducked back into the cruiser and returned with a wide-brimmed hat. "Morning," she called over, donning the hat.

"Morning," Emily greeted.

The three of them met in the driveway and made introductions. "Trooper Soames" didn't share her first name but seemed relaxed, cordial. She was tall, standing over Brett by a few inches.

Dressed in uniform – chevron patch on the shoulder, black pinstripe down the grey pants – troopers seemed to Brett more like military than police. He didn't think they ate donuts and farted around like the bad stereotype, anyway.

"So, what have we got?" Soames gave them each a bright smile, her eye contact direct.

"It's back here." Brett led them around to the rear of the house over the crisp, freshly mown lawn. He pointed at the back fence, seventy-five yards away.

"Nice property," Soames said as they moved into the higher grass.

"Thanks."

"So you're digging gardens, your wife said? And you hit something with the shovel, and kept digging until you saw bones. Is that right?"

"Yes, ma'am."

The sun was directly overhead, the long grass dried by its rays. The cicadas were buzzing now, that sound of summer Brett had always found a touch eerie, like a chorus of high-pitched rattle-snakes. The sound dispersed as they walked through, always out of arm's reach.

Brett found himself rambling through an explanation as they drew nearer to the hole.

"I kept digging because, I thought, I didn't know what kind of bones it was. The first thing you think isn't human remains. I thought, maybe animal, a deer or something. I've seen a deer skeleton in those woods back there."

"Uh-huh. That's fine. And your property goes into the woods?"

"Yes ma'am." Brett swept an arm. "Seven acres, and it goes into the woods all the way to the interstate on the other side. The woods are a little over half the total property."

"It's really beautiful out here," Soames said. Her banter was light and friendly but her expression grew more intent as they neared the fence. "You two are married?"

Emily spoke up. "Yes, just recently."

"Congratulations. And how long have you lived here?"

"Almost two months," Emily answered. "We'd hoped to get married here, tried to plan it that way, but getting the house took a little longer than we expected."

"Any children?"

"No." Emily glanced at Brett.

"Have you met your neighbors?"

Brett responded. "Across the main road there, that's seventy acres owned by the Price family."

"They have alpacas," Emily added.

"And to the south, our property abuts on the Fitzgerald's. They have four acres. To the north is another family, I forget their name. They have two plots bundled together. About eighteen acres, goes all the way to Hurricane Road. And then, like I said, through our woods is I-87."

Emily gave him a surprised look. He smirked. "I've studied the tax maps."

They reached the site and Trooper Soames slowed her pace. The three of them stood around the edge of the hole, now wide enough to fit a person lying down.

They gazed at the remains, and Soames pulled on a pair of plastic gloves. She squatted for a closer look, saw the tin, and reached for it.

"I touched that," Brett said.

Soames exhumed the box, turned it over in her gloved hands. "You opened it?"

"Yes ma'am. I still… this just kind of happened out of the blue. It's just, you know, I was curious."

"That's alright." Soames pried off the tin lid with a little metallic pop and pulled out the note, saying, "You might need to provide some elimination prints. We'll see."

She studied the note, as he had. Brett and Emily fell silent. Emily found his hand again and gripped it as the cicadas whined in the field and a bumblebee droned past.

Soames folded the note back up and replaced it in the box. She looked off for a moment, thinking. Then she set the box aside. She didn't touch the remains, just seemed to examine them from all sides, moving around the edge of the excavation.

Some of the dirt along the edge crumbled back in.

"We thought it was a leg," Emily said. "Femur there, tibia there."

The moment drew out, making Brett uncomfortable again. He kept reminding himself that he hadn't done anything wrong.

Soames finally removed her gloves and stuffed them in her pocket.

"So, what now?" Emily asked.

"Well," Soames said, looking around at everything, "now I call my supervisor."

"What do you think they'll want to do?"

"Based on my visual assessment – this looks like the bones from a human leg to me – either the supervisor will want to come have a look, or we'll contact the medical examiner right away. We'll talk to the Sheriff's Office, too, see what they say."

Her attention seemed drawn to the tin box again. She towered over it, looking down. "And figure out what that's all about, who that person is."

"Do you recognize the name?" Brett asked.

"Not at all. But maybe it's a missing person. Maybe someone else. We'll see."

She started towards the house and Brett and Emily followed.

Back in the front driveway, Soames rummaged in the cruiser until she found some paperwork and a clipboard. "I only have one of these," she said of the clipboard. "Sorry."

Brett took the paper, a generic form that simply read *Statement* on top and had boxes for name and contact information, plus an area for whatever the witness wanted to write.

Emily used the clipboard and Brett hunched over the porch floorboards.

"Just the basics," Soames said. "This will help me when I talk to my supervisor."

Her gaze lingered on Brett. "There was one case a couple years ago, right when I came on as a trooper, where the homeowner brought the bones they found to the police in a plastic shopping bag. There's no right or wrong way here. But I would let us handle it now – depending on where we want to take it, or the Sheriff's Office – we're probably going to search your property for more remains. And, you know, medical examiners will look at everything, forensics lab will look, and we'll try to determine if we have a crime or a natural death. Investigators will check missing person's reports, cold cases, that sort of thing. I'll be right back, guys. Take your time."

Soames returned to the cruiser, where Brett watched her try to get a cell signal, scowling at her phone as she held it aloft. Then she bent forward, doing something out of view. He focused on the statement and filled out his information, jotting down an account of that morning in simple terms.

When the trooper returned for the paperwork, Brett apologized for the spotty cell service.

Soames waved a hand in the air. "Not a problem. I used my computer. We have our own radio towers that work almost anywhere."

Emily offered Trooper Soames something to drink, but the trooper declined. "Listen, I've got to go, but someone will be along shortly. I'm going to advise you not to do any more digging, don't touch anything else. Okay?"

Brett and Emily agreed. They watched Trooper Soames sink into her vehicle.

She backed out of the dirt driveway, turned into the road, and gave them a wave as she drove off.

"Well, that wasn't so bad," Emily said, watching the cruiser fade into the distance.

Brett was watching it, too. Out in this part of Stock County, visibility was incredible. Stunning and open, like something from Montana. Most places in the Adirondacks, the mountains and woods encroached, and views were obtained by gaining elevation. Brett and Emily had fallen in love with the open expanse – a pricey property they were able to make their own thanks to Emily's family.

It suddenly felt like a fishbowl instead.

"Yeah," he said, "we're going to have more police, medical examiners, reporters. People will read about it and drive out to look…"

"Good. We can have the yard sale you keep talking about."

He ignored her cheeky optimism. "You remember the names of the family in the trust? Who we bought the house from?"

They stood side by side on the porch, still looking off even though the trooper was gone. "Uhm, a couple of them."

"I'll be back."

Brett turned and walked into the house.

Inside was much cooler. The wide plank floors creaked beneath his feet.

He climbed the wide stairs to the second floor, which was warmer, turned down the hall to the small room with the angled ceiling and dormer window overlooking the backyard. It was going to be Emily's office where she would do her market consulting and graphic design work. Right now it was just boxes and a short file cabinet.

Brett slid out the bottom drawer of the cabinet and finger-walked through the files until he got to the mortgage information.

Buying the house had been a lengthy process because the owner wasn't a single entity but rather a group of people in a family trust. The patriarch of that family, Owen Cobb, had passed away, leaving the house and property to his children, some of whom were scattered around the region, others as far flung as Canada and California. There had been eight of them, if memory served. Each negotiation, each request for a seller concession, had to go through all parties before the trust lawyer could okay it.

Brett searched the large file, setting aside the banking information and searching for data on the trustees. They weren't all Cobbs – Owen Cobb had only had two sons, and all but one of his daughters had married, making for three Cobbs and five family members with other surnames.

No one named Dr. Rhea Runic.

"What're you doing?"

He startled, so immersed in what he was doing he hadn't heard Emily approach. He glanced at her, on his knees beside the file cabinet. "Looking for a list of the trustees. That's what you call them, right? Trustees?"

She came into the room and sat down in the swivel chair by the window. It would be her desk chair – once they got her a desk. Right now they had no money for anything extra. Emily was still working, though, usually set up with her MacBook on the bed. Brett was doing road construction during the weekdays, tending to the property in the early mornings and evenings.

"Yes, trustees," Emily said.

He found it. He held up the paper with a smile. "Bingo. All eight names, phone numbers, everything."

"You think the bones have something to do with the previous owner?"

"Well, I mean, that's the first thing, right? We just got this place. Cobb was here for like thirty years or something. He died, it went to his kids, sat here for a while until they ended up selling it. Contentiously."

She looked worried. They seemed to swap positions all the time like this, he thought. When he was gloomy, she was optimistic, and vice versa, like they traded emotions. He wondered if other married couples could attest.

"Ugh," she said. "Could you imagine? Someone in the family murdered someone, or something, then buried them back by the fence?"

"Or, someone else, and the Cobb family never knew about it. The other side of the woods is the interstate. You know, it's a hike, but someone pulls over with a body in the trunk, drags them into the woods…"

"And all the way to the edge of someone's field? You'd think they'd just bury them in the woods somewhere, not by a field, or a house…"

Unless they wanted to relocate where it was buried, he thought. "Remember *Fargo*? Steve Buscemi buries money by a fence."

"Oh, God, that's a movie. But – bones? Someone's leg?"

"Maybe it's not the bones, maybe it's the name and number in the tin meant to be recovered. The bones aren't all that deep, either. Graves go down six feet. This was a third of that."

"Ugh," she repeated and swung her chair around to face out the window.

"Let's Google Rhea Runic." Brett got to his feet. "See what we find."

Emily didn't budge. "Well, you know, the trooper said they'd handle it."

"Aren't you curious?"

"Of course I am. It's crazy. But, you know…" She shrugged and continued gazing out the dormer window and into the field. "Maybe… maybe it's best to leave it alone."

She stood up and crossed the room to him. They stood beneath the peak in the ceiling where both of them could be fully upright.

"Leave it alone?" he asked.

She put her arms around him and they kissed.

Then Emily pulled back. "Just… you know…"

"What?"

"Honey. I know this is really something. But you've got plenty on your plate." She raised her eyebrows. "And you know how you can get."

He felt defensive. "How I can *get*?"

"Babe. You get a little fixated."

He pulled away from her.

"It's okay," she said, reaching for him. "Hey, listen. I'm just saying, you know, we don't know what's going on yet. And it's just… it's a little scary."

"Oh come on. You don't get scared. Upset maybe, grossed out, but I've never seen you scared of anything. You're Italian."

She slapped him playfully on the shoulder. "That's idiotic." She was grinning, but he saw a greater truth in her eyes. She closed the gap between them, put her head against his neck.

"You'd love me more if I cracked the case," he said.

"Stop it." But she joked, "I'd love you more if you were rich."

"See? I knew it."

When she spoke again her voice was soft, their flirty banter over with. "I know what you want. I know what you think about yourself, about me, how we had help getting this place. But you have to know that doesn't matter to me. I believe in you. I married you. You don't have anything to prove."

She stretched and kissed him again.

CHAPTER FOUR

Russo was brought to the Sheriff's Office, where he spent ten grueling hours. He was transferred to NYPD's 120th precinct and twelve more hours drained away. When the bus arrived to take him to Central Booking in Manhattan, it was dawn on Sunday.

The correctional officers hooked him into shackles. The big chain linking the bracelets and ankle cuffs rattled as Russo stepped onto the bus and took his seat.

He watched out the window along with several other prospective inmates as they crossed the long Verrazano-Narrows Bridge and first headed into Brooklyn.

They trucked along through the neighborhoods of Bay Ridge and Sunset Park. Then into the more gentrified areas of Park Slope and Brooklyn Heights, where he caught glimpses of intrepid women pushing enormous strollers in the early morning.

They crossed the Brooklyn Bridge into Manhattan and jostled along with the city traffic until they arrived at Central Booking.

He was hustled inside along with several other inmates. He'd already turned over his wallet and cell phone. A correctional officer in plastic gloves performed a body search, patting him down, checking his mouth for things like hidden razor blades. The officer in charge droned on about how the inmates were to behave like perfect gentlemen while awaiting booking. "You want to get in to see a judge, you don't give us any trouble. Got it?"

The place smelled like urine.

Russo remembered a *Village Voice* article he'd read a ways back about Central Booking, parodying it as a hotel – *Go for the Urine-Scented Everything, Stay Because They Won't Let You Leave*...

Intake took half the day. By three that afternoon he sat in a holding cell with twenty others. Then he was pulled out, finger-printed, photographed, DNA-swabbed, and placed in a different cell. He continued to frog-leap cells through the evening and into the night. At some point he was given a bag lunch with a soggy bologna sandwich, chips, and an apple with rotted spots.

Around six on Monday morning he was called to the back of his cell. There was a row of chairs, each in front of a double pane of glass with a hole in the center, a long narrow room on the other side.

"Okay, Mr. Russo," the lawyer said through the dirty glass. "So I'm Gerald Bloustein; I'm your public defender. I see here you were charged with an AUO, released with a desk appearance ticket. You failed to show up in court. You owe eight hundred and fifty for the fine." He looked up. "Is that all accurate?"

"Yes."

Bloustein dropped his gaze to the file. "Do you have any way to pay this?"

"No."

"My guess is that when you got your AUO, police didn't look too hard at your record. It happens, cops are busy, people slip through the cracks. If they'd looked they probably wouldn't have let you go at that time."

Russo wasn't sure what to say, so he stayed quiet.

Bloustein glanced up again. "You haven't gotten in any other trouble in the past few years?" He lowered his eyes to the file again and continued on before Russo could answer. "I see here you worked briefly as a dispatcher in New Jersey."

"That was a long time ago. Late '90s."

"And now you're working for the MTA, in the subway."

"I doubt it."

"Sorry?"

"I missed both my weekend shifts. No call, no show. They don't like it when you do that for some reason."

Bloustein, apparently devoid of a sense of humor, said, "Uh-huh." His eyes dropped and he flipped a few pages. "You got a bit of a rap sheet. And you did a full year at Rikers from '04 to '05."

The guy wasn't telling Russo anything he didn't already know. Russo couldn't hold it in any longer and leaned forward a little. "I can't do more time. I got a kid."

Bloustein closed the file, slowly, with a grave air. Then he folded his hands over the top of it. "You got lucky in the past, Mr. Russo. You faced some stiff charges. And then you got lucky again when the police didn't give you a real long look. Now," he held up his hands, "I don't know."

This guy was his lawyer? Russo felt the first heat flashes of anger. "I was working on getting my license back, sir. I took the five-hour course. I just ran out of money to put all the paperwork through."

Bloustein's eyes were half-lidded, like he'd heard it all before. "Look, this is what I'm going to do. I'm going to present to the assistant attorney that you've been working hard for..." He opened the file and glanced at something, "... for three years as an MTA worker, as a productive member of society. You've had no other arrests besides the drunk driving charge, and then the aggravated unlicensed." His eyes widened, a glimmer of empathy shining. "You said you have a small child, yes?"

"My daughter."

"That's lovely. Good for you. So, you got picked up on a failure-to-pay warrant, okay? The judge is going to want to make sure you pay this time. Your arraignment for the failure-to-pay is coming up, and he'll set bail."

"Bail? How am I gonna pay bail if I can't pay the fine? I tried to save the money. I was going to pay it as soon as I could."

Bloustein put the file back into the briefcase and closed it with a snap. "Well, I'll ask for a signature bond. Or we can look at a bail bondsman."

A bondsman meant another ten or fifteen percent on top of the bail. It was just adding up what Russo would owe. "I don't know…"

"What could you put up as collateral? Credit cards? Probably you don't have a car."

"No."

"How about your house? You live at…" He checked the file and recited the address.

"It's not mine."

Bloustein glanced up, frowning.

"It's my wife's. Her family home. It's still in her grandma's name, she's over at St. Joe's Elder Care."

"Would she be willing to…?"

Russo waved a hand. "No. What about an R.O.R.?"

Bloustein shook his head. "I'm sorry, I doubt it. The assistant district attorney will lean hard against letting you out on your own recognizance. You pled guilty to a second-degree AUO, bumped up because your blood alcohol level was so high. You had an eight-hundred-fifty-dollar fine, no jail time. But you didn't pay. Chances are, your criminal record won't be overlooked this time."

"So, what?"

"Well, I can see you're a straight-talker, so I'll talk straight. I'm thinking there's about a ninety percent chance you're going to be incarcerated until the fine is paid in full."

"Unless there's no bail."

"I'll do everything I can. You have been working a steady job for the MTA, you haven't been in any major trouble in over a decade, you have a baby daughter. You'd never leave her, you're not a flight risk. Right?"

"Right…"

"Okay then. We'll give it a shot."

Russo was trying to stay calm, but he sensed they were done and felt a trill of panic.

Bloustein readied to leave, then leaned towards the glass again. "I almost forgot. There will also be court fees and a new fine for the consequence of nonpayment of the original fine." He scratched at his nose, examined his fingertips.

"What do you think bail will be?"

"My ballpark estimate would be around five thousand, which is the misdemeanor high-end."

Jesus.

"They call it debtor's prison for a reason," Bloustein said. "Listen, sit tight. Think about any way you can raise bail, plus the original fine and another thousand or so for the nonpayment penalties. Reconsider the bail bondsman idea. Talk to your grandmother-in-law, whatever you need to do."

Russo glanced around the holding cell, getting more riled up. Guys like Bloustein probably didn't understand that coming up with six or seven grand was just about impossible when you had no rich uncle, no nest egg put away for a rainy day, no one to turn to – Russo had left all his friends behind when he'd parted ways with the criminal life. And there was no way he was going to leverage Felicia's ninety-year-old grandmother.

He got himself under control and looked up at the lawyer.

"Thanks for your help."

Bloustein just nodded his head at the guard on his side of the glass, indicating he was finished.

Before walking away he said to Russo, "Should be just a couple hours or so now. I'll see you in there."

The judge seemed grouchy and in a hurry to clear the day's docket. The assistant district attorney was unsympathetic-looking, a slim thirty-year-old in an expensive suit who never once glanced at Russo.

Bail was set for five thousand. In addition to his previous fine and the nonpayment fine, plus court fees, Russo owed eight thousand and twenty-two dollars. It might as well have been a million.

The gavel came down.

Since he couldn't pay bail, he was sent to Rikers Island.

The bus took him back over the Brooklyn Bridge, then crossed the Newtown Creek into Queens and kept going north. The stench of the bus fumes permeated the floorboards, it seemed, rising up into Russo's lungs. He was used to it. He'd lived in the city all his life.

They passed through Woodside next, his old neighborhood. The whole ride to the jail was like a trip back in time – until he saw kids in the distance. They weren't playing baseball, or even spray-painting graffiti. It looked like they were on phones, gathered beneath the red brick buildings, heads bent over their screens.

The bus branched onto the Brooklyn-Queens Expressway and Russo watched one of the COs for a minute, standing by the driver on the other side of the grate, semi-automatic rifle slung over his back.

They exited the Brooklyn-Queens Expressway at Astoria Boulevard, then took a left onto 81st Street, the air brakes hissing.

81st to Hazen, and then they were on the Rikers Island Bridge.

It was one of the biggest jails in the United States – even the world. Neither a state prison nor a federal penitentiary, but a complex of jails, correctional facilities, mental facilities. Politically part of the Bronx, postal-wise part of Queens, a no-man's land notorious for prisoner abuse and neglect.

Russo knew all about it. He'd just never thought he'd be going back. Every mile closer and he felt the knot in his stomach twist tighter.

When the bus pulled up to the main building, Russo listened to the correctional officers. They talked about "bodies" and "packages." Russo knew this meant him and the other fresh prisoners. The last time he'd been there, he'd been in his twenties. Some things had changed – the box had been outlawed. No more solitary. Instead, now, you got fined for your offenses.

More money, Russo thought. He followed the line of inmates into Receiving, their chains clanking, a hot wind blowing the foul stench of the island about. A smell worse than a sewer. He remembered that smell more than anything.

He spread his ass cheeks and coughed, as ordered.

The City of New York had owned Rikers Island since the 1880s. Back in those days, it was used to raise and slaughter pigs. Then it was converted to a partial landfill, full of horse manure and garbage.

The refuse attracted a sizable rat population, which the city had tried to contain by releasing wild dogs. But the dogs ended up attacking and killing some of the pigs. It took poison gas to kill off the rodents.

A nice place.

Then the city had moved humans to Rikers.

Now he was back. He owed over eight grand. There was no way he was going to be able to come up with it. He was going to have to do time after all, the only question was how much.

The COs lined up the new inmates, naked, in the dank, warehouse-like receiving area. The floor was cold. The COs dropped folded jumpsuits at their feet, and Russo wriggled in.

He could be here a year. And if anyone tried to mess with him, and he had to defend himself, he could get prosecuted for a brand new crime, owe more money for the violation, be forced to do more time all over again.

He needed to keep his head down. He needed to figure out how he could get back to Felicia, and the baby.

So far he'd taken it all in his stride, but as the guards stalked along the line of fresh inmates in their new jumpsuits, Russo started to worry.

He was shown to his cell. The door closed and the lock engaged.

His cellmate was sitting on the bottom bunk, partly hidden in the gloom.

The cellmate's foot was tapping, legs moving, like he was anxious.

Russo looked around the small double cell. Toilet, sink, one cabinet in the corner, and the bunk beds. No desk, no chair, nothing on the walls but a tiny mirror and a grimy residue. Like blood. Or feces.

He guessed the space was about ten feet wide by twelve feet long. There was one window, high up, narrow and barred.

He had nothing with him. The clothes he'd been wearing that morning had been taken away. They'd doused him with lye and then sprayed him down along with the other incoming inmates.

In some jails, new prisoners went into a kind of health quarantine for the first couple of days. But not Rikers.

His eyes caught movement and he saw a large cockroach scurry from beneath the bed to the toilet.

Russo's cellmate sprung to life, jumping out from the bunk. The cellmate grabbed the bed post and swung around, bringing his foot down on the cockroach with a *crunch* just before it slipped behind the toilet.

The cellmate took off his shoe. He ran the tap in the sink and rinsed the squashed bug from the sole.

Russo looked the guy over. Covered in tattoos. Wearing inmate shorts and Velcro shoes, no top. His muscles rippled as he rinsed his shoe; he grimaced as he scraped off bits of bug carapace with the faucet. There was a small device clipped to his waistband and a wire snaking up, going to his ears.

Finished washing up, he pulled a neatly folded hand towel from the cabinet. He daubed the shoe with it, almost tenderly, then slipped it back on, unrolled some toilet paper, cleaned up a small smear of goo from the floor and flushed it all down the toilet.

He returned to his bunk and sank back into the gloom.

Russo bent down, carefully, and looked in. He waved a hand in the air and smiled.

The cellmate stared out, eyes shining in the shadows. The muscles in his jaw flexed, like he was grinding his teeth.

Russo stood back up. He didn't want to climb up on his bunk just yet so he sat down on the toilet.

After a little while, the cellmate jerked out his earbuds and jumped out of the bunk again. The guy was a real live wire.

"Alright," he said. "Alright." He looked down and did a little pacing. Russo noticed that one of the tattoos depicted Jesus wearing a crown of thorns, face turned up to heaven.

"Alright, so… fuck. You know? I was very explicit with these motherfuckers, I'm not selling wolf tickets, you hear me?"

Russo thought the guy was addressing him, though he wasn't making eye contact. It had been years since Russo had been on the inside, but he thought "selling wolf tickets" meant talking tough without backing it up. The cellmate was saying he was for real.

The guy kept pacing in tight formation. He clenched his hands. Russo wondered if he was a juicer, the way the veins bulged in his neck, muscles stretched out his shirt.

"I fuckin' told them – and I was just perfectly calm and reasonable – I said, 'I'm an experienced cage fighter. It would be best for everybody in here if I get my own cell. I don't want to hurt nobody.' You know? Simple."

Russo listened to the guy talk for the next fifteen minutes. He went on about professional fights he'd had, how he'd been on a victory streak. He explained that New York State had made cage fighting a legal pro sport right before he got arrested, but he didn't say for what. He finally stopped moving and made eye contact, perhaps searching to see if Russo bought his whole story, his toughness.

Russo had no doubt the dude was a menace in the cage, but that wasn't why he kept his cool, played it nice. He didn't have any desire to pop the guy's bubble if his new cellmate had an inferiority complex.

"I'm Jimmy Russo." He offered his hand.

The kid looked at it like a dog looking at a piece of meat. Then he grabbed Russo's hand in a vice grip and gave it three hard pumps. "Yeah, yeah. Okay. So I'm Nate Reuter."

"Sorry you had to double up."

"Yeah, well, fuck." Nate's anger had evaporated. Now that he was calm, he seemed like he didn't know what to do with himself. He looked around, picked up the hand towel he'd used on his shoe, gave it a violent shake, refolded it, put it away.

Russo asked, "Mind if I go up top, lie down?"

"Nah, man. Have at it." Nate had his back turned, organizing the cabinet. Russo noticed a neat stack of newspapers on the top shelf.

Russo climbed up. The bed shook and creaked.

Nate was watching over his shoulder. "What are you? Fuckin' two-twenty?"

"Yeah, just about."

"You gonna break that fucking bed? Come crashing down on me? I gotta tell you, man, that won't be good."

"I don't plan to."

Russo managed to close his eyes and drift for a little while.

He had another meeting with his public defender coming up, and he went over what he was going to say. He couldn't think of much other than that getting out of here meant everything to him. Maybe the PD would be able to convince the judge to lower the bail, or throw out the driving fine for time served – something. Anything.

When he closed his eyes, all he could picture was Zoe's face. His baby. She felt so far away.

CHAPTER FIVE

Emily walked into the kitchen where Brett was making a snack before dinner. She was holding a pregnancy test in her hand, and barely able to contain her grin.

Brett set everything aside and crossed the kitchen to her.

"Yeah…?"

She bit her lip and rapidly nodded her head. Then she let out a squeal and threw her arms around him.

He hugged her tight and lifted her off her feet. Then suddenly – irrationally, he knew – he worried about smooshing the tiny life inside her.

He set Emily back down.

"Sorry."

"No, it's okay, it's okay." Her eyes sparkled with excitement. "Brett! Baby!"

"Baby…" He felt a grin spread over his face. He knew some prospective fathers acted happy when the pregnancy stick showed positive, but were secretly afraid. Afraid they would have trouble affording it, or that a new baby would finally expose how useless they were as a gender now that insemination had been achieved. But his happiness was genuine.

He knew how capable Emily was. He may have been a screw-up in a lot of ways, but Emily was top notch. She would be an incredible mother.

"Honey, this is fantastic."

"I had a feeling. You know? Sometimes they say you 'just know.' I think I did." Her face glowed. "I got the test – this is one of the better ones that claims it can tell you up to five days from your period, and it's four days from my usual – and… it showed… positive!" She squealed again and gripped him in a hug tight enough to take his breath away.

"Oh my God," she said, withdrawing from the embrace and looking around. She was already thinking about the changes she wanted to make to the house. Emily had begun nesting.

They continued to celebrate. She discussed a healthcare provider she had in mind – an OB/GYN nearby – and a midwifery she was considering that was farther away. They weighed the pros and cons, theorized about birthing interventions and what their birth plan would be. Emily was fully animated, at times talking quietly and contemplatively, then beaming with joy.

Brett's grin faltered when he looked out the kitchen window to the back field, at the people who'd been out there since Saturday morning. The crew had shrunk on Sunday, but now that it was Monday, the forensics group and cops were back in full force. So far they'd uncovered some more bones, taken samples to the lab, and were close, they said, to zeroing in on an age and gender for the person, possibly even a cause of death. A handwriting expert was supposedly studying the note from the tin box and they were checking into the name.

The State Police and Sheriff's Office were both involved. Brett didn't know everything about cops, but he understood that the Sheriff's Office policed the county – theirs was Stock County – and drove vehicles with an old-timey Sheriff's badge embossed on their cars.

The troopers had brought on the state forensic lab to do the scientific work on the bones – he'd even spotted a couple of workers who looked like students. At any given time, there were a few to several people out working. A wide area had been cordoned off, and a large canopy covered the main dig site, flapping in the warm breeze.

The reporters had started showing up on Sunday. Local news channel 6 came first, then the local paper, then the regional paper. By Monday afternoon, press had arrived from as far away as Burlington and Albany.

There was an "Albany 8" news van camped out in front right now, and two people setting up a shot outside the crime scene tape by the back fence. Seeing them was unsettling. Brett guarded his privacy, but what was more, he'd been a journalism major in college and had failed to make a go of it. Their presence was a reminder of something he'd tried to forget.

He wondered if Meg Lister was going to show up at some point. Meg had been his girlfriend at school. Rumor had it she worked for the *Press-Republican* in Plattsburgh.

Forensic technicians, police investigators, possible ex-girlfriends all descending on his private life. And seeing the reporters was a reminder of his own failings as a writer.

But he wondered again if the situation could be parlayed into a fresh start at a career.

Brett pulled away from Emily – their third or fourth hug – and watched as two cops crossed the field towards the house.

"I think we've alerted the natives," he said.

"Oh…" Emily grew pensive.

Ten weeks was Emily's minimum requirement before disclosing a pregnancy to anyone. She'd never had a miscarriage but knew women who had, and telling everyone only to have something go wrong then having to explain it to her family and friends was not a prospect she was willing to endure.

She smoothed out her rumpled shirt and fixed her hair. "Alright. If they ask why we were just shouting like a couple of head-bangers, we'll tell them it was something else. I got a new client, and we're excited."

"Or that I got my erection back after two years of impotence."

She didn't hear the joke and banged out the back door, fast-walking towards the cops.

Brett stood in the doorway, watching. One of the cops was a deputy, dressed in long-sleeved uniform, despite the unflagging sun. The other cop was wearing a suit, gun visible on his hip.

Emily reached the police and greeted them. She gestured to the house. When they looked in, Brett raised his hand in a wave.

The plain-clothes cop waved back, then approached.

Investigator Daniel Morales looked in his forties. His rumpled suit had a stain on the lapel.

"So, these forms are called a DD-5," Morales said.

They'd arranged themselves in the living room.

"Just fill it out as best as you can, and then we'll get into some other things. You mind if I have a look around while you work on these?"

"Of course, please," Emily said.

Brett listened to Morales moving around, the house creaking, doors opening and closing. He was too distracted by it to fill out the form. He whispered to Emily, "Does he *have* to?"

She shushed him, her head bent over the paperwork.

Morales reappeared and took a seat across from them. Like a lot of the house, the living room was populated with antique furniture that had come with the sale. Brett and Emily had gotten rid of a few things, but the living room furniture was nice, and so most of it had stayed.

"You have a beautiful home," Morales said.

"Thank you." Emily smiled.

Through the windows, the sky was lavender in the setting sun. Morales was sitting in the wingback chair, giving Brett a look.

"You work construction?" Morales asked.

Brett realized he was still wearing his bright-yellow Hi-Vis safety shirt, his hands unwashed from the day. "Yeah. Road crew. Working on I-87."

Morales nodded then glanced down at the paperwork in his lap.

"So, we have some information on the bones," he said. "They're from a male, aged forty-five to fifty, about six feet tall."

Brett leaned forward on the couch. "How long have they been in the ground? It takes a while for a body to skeletonize, doesn't it?"

"What they've told me is that six feet down, without a coffin, an unembalmed adult takes eight to twelve years to decompose to a skeleton. But those bones weren't buried as deep. Just about two feet. The closer to the air, the faster the decomp. One month after death and the body starts to become fluid, basically."

Brett and Emily shared a look. He saw his own creeped-out feeling reflected in her eyes.

Morales continued, "And... well, the state forensic doctor could better explain this, but basically, you know, decomp gets affected by other things, too. How the body was left at death – wearing clothes or not – the acidity of the soil, exposure to elements, animal predation. If a body doesn't get enough protection from the elements, it can skeletonize in the span of a year. Maybe two."

Brett felt Emily cringe beside him on the couch. He thought they were thinking along the same lines: the idea that someone had died and was buried on their property a decade ago, that was one thing, but the house had sat unoccupied for three years before it had sold. That the person had been buried more recently was chilling for different reasons.

"And what about the name in the box?" Brett asked. "Is that the person?"

"We weren't able to locate anyone by that name."

Brett was stunned. It wasn't the answer he'd been expecting. "No one? You mean there's no one... Or you mean just in the state?"

Something flickered in Morales's eyes, and for a second his expression was dead serious. But then he relaxed. "There's a couple 'Rhea Runics' in the country, but nowhere near here. It's an unusual name. I talked to each of them. And any deceased 'Rhea Runics' are accounted for, no one missing. What do you know about the previous owner of your home?"

Brett gave Emily another glance. "Uhm, not much." He shared the story of how they got the house, how much of an ordeal it had turned out to be, Emily filling in some of the gaps.

Morales listened but kept fiddling with his tie, taking notes, seeming lost in his own thoughts. He chewed on his pen and gave them a studied look, his gaze switching from Brett to Emily. "The other thing that's a bit of a mystery is that, you know, we've done some pretty extensive digging, and we haven't found the whole skeleton."

"Did you find the head?" Brett asked. "A skull?"

Morales shook his head. "Unfortunately, no. The skull could really help us. You know, if there was any blunt force trauma, it's usually the head. Teeth, you know, dental records are the best. But, nothing. That's why we've been out there so long. Really appreciate you folks being patient."

Brett's head was buzzing with questions, and he had a partial theory. It was the only thing that made any sense.

"So, not the person in the note, and this pretty much rules out a lost hiker, or homeless person, or natural death. Right?"

"Well, cause of death is proving tricky, like I said." Morales crossed his legs. "You know, with bones, you're looking for something like a break, or a bruise. We need more to go on."

Brett thought about the area that had been covered so far outside – the cops had dug up all along the fence, and in a huge semicircle into the field, with his original dig site as the epicenter. There were two small excavator machines out there, and they did most of the work. A search team had ventured into the woods.

"How much has been recovered?" Brett asked.

"The leg, we got an arm, a hip bone, and a foot. That's it."

"And they're kind of scattered around? What's that mean?"

"It could mean different things. It could mean animal predation. It could be pieces of a person that were poorly, or hastily, buried. They're going over the remains carefully at the lab. And they're going to go through DNA testing, see if there's a match to anyone we know. I think we'll dig through tomorrow afternoon, but it looks like this is all we're going to get."

Morales stood and branded his face with a winning smile. "You two have really been great. Thanks." He frowned companionably, adding, "I hope the press haven't been giving you too much grief."

Brett opened his mouth to ask more questions but stopped.

Emily got up with Morales and nodded graciously towards the window. "They're just doing their job."

"Yeah. Well, we have the press conference tomorrow and we'll ask them to be respectful to you folks."

Morales's eyes dropped to Emily's stomach and Brett saw she was holding herself in that protective way again.

She realized it and dropped her hands.

Brett stood up beside her and put his arm around her shoulders.

"Alright." Morales moved towards the door. "That's pretty much it for me, gang." He grasped the doorknob.

"What about the number?" Brett pressed. He felt a light pinch on his arm. Emily was warning him to cool it. "I mean, could the name, the number, mean anything else?"

"We're checking into it."

Morales was just about gone when he turned back around. "Good luck with everything, you two."

He winked and left.

The yellow farmhouse was spacious but the newlyweds tended to gather in the kitchen, even at night.

It was big like the rest of house, but cozy in its simple, rustic way. There was no Tuscan iron chandelier hanging, no granite backsplash above the countertops. Just scratched wood floors (Emily called the marks "character"), faded linoleum, and white cabinetry.

There was, however, a scalloped hood over the gas range, which Brett thought looked a bit ridiculous. The sink was enormous and deep and footed. Beneath it, cleaning supplies were stowed in an old soda crate. Emily was looking there now.

"Those will have to go somewhere. Babies love to get into that sort of thing. The more toxic the better."

Brett sat at the island. The butcher-block top extended out on one side like a lunch counter. The two stools were old and rickety. Sitting at one that squeaked and groaned, he had the newspaper spread out and nursed a beer as Emily roamed.

The outer back door was open, the breeze coming in through the screen, carrying the sounds of crickets, katydids, tree frogs in the woods.

"That was the weirdest thing with Morales," he said, sipping the beer.

Emily kept circling around, taking in all the potential hazards for an exploring baby at least a year and a half away from being an actual problem.

"Lisa's baby was into the trash all the time." She gave the garbage can a wary eye. "We'll need to get one with a lid that latches."

Lisa was Emily's sister in-law, married to Emily's wealthy brother on Long Island. They'd had their first child a year before.

Brett was an only child. The way Emily and Joe barely talked, save once or twice a year during the holidays, he didn't think he was missing much. On the other hand, if it hadn't been for Emily's brother, they wouldn't have been able to afford their dream home.

Emily stopped, looked up at Brett, pulled out of her nesting, it seemed. "What did you say about Morales?"

"I don't know. It's my first time being a guest on *Law and Order*. But, just how he seemed. Like, 'Well, that's all folks.' Kind of goofy or something. Human bones in our field, body parts missing, and it's like business as usual for him."

"How should he have been?"

"Well, it's got to mean something… I don't know. Not good. A person doesn't die and leave bits of their body around. And who buries someone in pieces?"

"You heard what he said. Animal predation…" She trailed off, probably not wanting to follow the thought through to its gruesome end.

Brett imagined it. An animal, maybe coyotes, picking at a body, pulling it apart, dragging hands and feet off into the woods. "Yeah but it was still *buried*. Maybe not grave-deep, but in the ground."

She stared at the dark window over the sink. Brett saw her reflection looking back at her, and she framed her stomach with her hands in a pose. Distractedly, she said, "You don't think that, you know, the wind blew dirt over it, the elements kind of just worked on it, the bones sunk in?"

He took a drink and stared into the bottle. "No. I think murder. I think it's a homicide. You got someone taking *pieces* of a dead person and burying them. And I think that means where they buried them probably matters, right? Don't you?"

When he saw the look on her face he realized he ought to quit. What was the Will Rodgers saying? *Never miss an opportunity to shut up.*

But it was too late. She turned around, giving him her most Pensive Emily look. "Honey. What's going on?"

"What're you talking about? Nothing."

She came a little closer. "You're thinking something. You're bothered."

"Well, I mean. Yeah. Of course."

"You're excited one minute, you're mopey the next – you were just about crawling out of your *skin* when the detective was here. You kept looking out at the reporters. You didn't want to talk to them."

"I don't like the attention."

"It's more than that."

"You're not from here. It's different for you."

She stood right beside him; he could feel her breath in his hair. "You mean you like to hide out. You don't want any of your high-school classmates or your college friends to know what you're doing. Because you think that… I don't know. You don't think you're a success." She put her hand over his. "But, honey, you're doing great. *We're* doing great. Okay? And we'll start another garden."

He didn't say any more about it. They had one more day to deal with the people in the back field and then it was over. Morales would probably let them know how it all turned out.

Maybe.

He spread his hands over the newspaper and read the article on the investigation for the third time.

CHAPTER SIX

Nate Reuter tucked another newspaper into the cabinet. Russo watched from the top bunk. Nate, otherwise a brute, was almost tender in the way he handled getting the paper to fit in with the rest of them, as if it were valuable.

"What's with all the papers?"

Nate didn't turn around but got tight in the shoulders. "I can only keep what's in the cabinet. When it gets full, they take what I got. Fucking ridiculous I can't keep newspapers in my cell. They say it's a fire hazard. Plus, I get them a day late."

"You like to read, huh?"

Nate didn't answer. He shut the cabinet gingerly, his precious possessions neatly stowed.

He'd killed half a dozen more cockroaches in the past twelve hours, a real slaughter. Except when it came to strange newspapers, the kid was a sociopath, coiled and ready to spring at the slightest skitter.

Russo could remember being angry, too. It still happened – like with the lawyer – but he'd learned to diffuse it. He did one of three things to release the pressure when the anger built: he counted backwards from ten.

Most of the time it worked.

When it didn't, he "formed a mental picture," something he'd caught once on a talk show Felicia had on the TV.

The picture he chose was a real place he'd been once with his dad, before Benicio Russo had succumbed to his toxic liver.

Russo didn't even know where it was, but he remembered a field of flowers, and at its edge, a low wall of rocks. Beyond the rocks was another field. One that seemed to go on forever.

Once Zoe had been born, he gained the third and best tactic. The trick to beating his anger was to imagine his daughter, particularly her little toes.

Those toes were unbelievable, the size of Tic Tacs when she was born.

They'd since enlarged to the size of Jujubes, or that candy which used to be popular when he was a kid growing up in Queens – Mike and Ikes. He'd even taken to calling Zoe's feet Mike and Ike, and sometimes called her Ikey-Ikey when he was playing with her, but Felicia had put the kibosh on that. Felicia was a very proactive mother who believed infants needed to be spoken to with adult words so they would grow up smart. "Don't *infantilize* her," Felicia said. That was fine, and Russo agreed, and then he would catch Felicia talking baby babble with Zoe when she thought he wasn't around.

Nate didn't have anywhere for his anger to go. Except for that cabinet, that was his way out, whatever those newspapers signified.

Russo realized Nate was staring at him.

"What's your story anyway?" the kid asked.

"Wrong place at the wrong time."

Nate continued to clock him and pointed a finger. "Don't think I'm stupid, man."

"I don't."

"I see shit. Intuition, know what I'm saying? I know shit."

Russo kept his tongue.

Nate said, "If I was to say you was a hard motherfucker back in the day, would I be lying?"

Still Russo was mute.

"Yeah," Nate said with a crooked smile. "Yeah, that's what I thought."

*

Russo stuck his arms through the slot and felt the cuffs lock home. The door opened and he was brought to the visitation area, shown to a table where Bloustein waited with his narrow face and baggy suit.

The guard removed the cuffs. Russo rubbed his wrists and glanced around at the other inmates. He caught sight of a couple more lawyers, but mostly it looked like family or friends visiting.

Bloustein opened his briefcase on the table and took out a file. He went through it silently. Nothing happened for a full minute.

"Okay, so how are you?"

"I haven't even been able to call my wife yet."

Bloustein's little birdshot eyes lingered on Russo a moment. Then he dropped his gaze to the file. "The District Attorney offered a deal and I think we should take it."

"Take what deal?"

"Plead guilty to all charges – the AUO, the failure to appear, the failure to pay, and serve time."

"How much time?"

"Two years."

"Two *years*?" It was loud enough that the guard looked over and gave Russo the eye.

"It's as good a deal as we're going to get. It gets you out of having to pay."

Two years.

Zoe would be going on four years old. He'd miss all that precious time. And that was if he didn't get into any trouble while inside – he didn't plan to, but sometimes you couldn't avoid it.

He realized something worse. Rikers only held people who were pretrial or had a sentence of a year or less. Two years meant he'd be moved to God-knew-where. Probably somewhere upstate.

Felicia couldn't visit with Zoe unless she borrowed a car. She wouldn't want to bring Zoe anyway, but it would be difficult for her to visit on her own – babysitters were at a premium. She'd never even been outside the five boroughs, except to Puerto Rico. More than that, he knew Felicia was not the type to "visit her man in prison." It just wasn't who she was.

She might leave him. She'd told him more than once she wouldn't put up with anything like this and he'd sworn he was reformed.

"I can't do it."

"You can't do it? I'm telling you your options. You plead guilty, take the hit, you don't have to come up with the money. You plead not guilty, then you have to sit here until trial, which could take months, you piss off the prosecution, and they up the ante. They bring in your past record, they make it about you slipping through the cracks, getting off too lightly, flouting the leniency you were shown. You could end up with more time. I'm just telling you how it is."

"Isn't there a chance you could get me off? Reduce the sentence? I plead guilty and sit here waiting for trial, maybe some time served?"

Bloustein shook his head, his eyeglasses flashing under the fluorescents. "Maybe. But the DA is eager to move these things along – too much of these failure-to-pays crowding the docket."

"I thought you said it would take months…"

"Look, you're here, you've gone through intake. Like I said, the skids are greased. They moved quickly, and this is the deal."

Russo was stunned into silence. He suddenly wanted to reach across the table and grab Bloustein by the neck. Maybe he'd have better luck representing himself. But it had been too long since he'd kept up on the law, the ins and outs. Without some genie in a bottle, some bleeding-heart pro bono lawyer, he was screwed.

Bloustein was watching.

"So? Take the deal?"

"I have to decide right now?"

Bloustein sighed, removed his glasses, and rubbed his nose. "No. Think about it for a couple hours. I'll call you."

"A couple *hours?*"

Bloustein put his glasses back, shoved the papers in his briefcase.

CHAPTER SEVEN

Brett awoke to screams.

Sometimes a murder of crows called at dawn. But the sun wasn't up yet. This wasn't that.

It sounded like human cries. Like a child, shrill and terrified.

He swung his legs out of bed and glanced at Emily, sound asleep. He was the light sleeper; she was gone to the world once she was out.

His footsteps creaked over the old floorboards. The morning chill racked him as he cocked his head, listening for more.

Then it came again, a pealing, high-pitched wail from the back field.

Unable to see anything from the front bedroom, which overlooked the porch and dirt driveway, his imagination filled in the blanks. It was some demon or banshee out there, screaming in the darkness.

There was no gun in the house. Emily didn't like guns. Brett had shot a few but had never owned one. There was a baseball bat behind the door and a large flashlight on the bureau. He grabbed these and went downstairs.

As he descended, the shriek unreeled again, this time a little farther off. He rationalized that it couldn't be a person. It *sounded* human, but someone running around in his back field, wailing in the middle of the night, just didn't make any sense.

He hunched his way through the kitchen, opened the wooden door, and stood before the screen.

The night air blew in, crickets singing. There was one final scream, resonating deeper in the woods.

It could have been an animal. But he didn't know what exactly made that sound.

He waited.

The clock in the kitchen ticked off the seconds.

He'd lain awake with the bat by the bed until dawn, unable to find sleep again.

He took the bat with him now as he walked out of the kitchen into the dewy morning. Everything was muggy and wet, the sky overcast.

Tromping through the back field in boots and long pants, he was soaked around the ankles in seconds. He stopped at the excavation then circled along the edge of the bright orange tape, climbed over the old post-rail fence, and entered the woods.

Spider webs grabbed his face, and he flailed, spitting out the strands. He wasn't any sort of tracker, and only hunted a few times in his life, but he thought he could recognize signs of a struggle if he saw them.

His heart was racing as he moved over the uneven ground. It was even darker in here beneath the canopy of evergreens, maples, and birch. Dark and cool and wet.

And then he saw the blood. Entrails. A profusion of grayish fur in scattered tufts.

It looked like a rabbit had been killed by a predator. It had screamed in the predator's mouth as the larger animal had carried it off, then torn it to shreds.

He'd once seen a fox loping along the tree line, an expression on its face like a grin. But he'd never heard of rabbits screaming like that, though he supposed it was possible. His pulse slowed to a normal rhythm as he contemplated the warring heart of nature.

He left the woods and headed back for the house just as the first of the technicians were showing up for the day.

They waved back at him in the mist, a young man and woman, carrying a cooler. Brett called to them, "You guys want some breakfast?"

"Oh, thank you, no," said the young woman. "We grabbed something before we got here."

"What's in the cooler? Pabst or Genny Cream?"

She laughed but didn't answer. They kept moving towards the site and Brett legged it back to the house.

He stopped and watched everything from the back door. The search team had combed his woods. The total excavated area was probably now twenty yards in diameter, about three yards down at its deepest. The little excavator machines were slick with moisture, sitting unoccupied. They had come on a big truck, leaving deep wheel ruts in the high grass. The truck was due back today.

It was almost over.

Their whole world had been turned upside down because of a couple of bones.

When he finally went back inside, Brett was surprised to find Investigator Morales standing with Emily in their kitchen.

Morales looked at the bat, then Brett, saying, "Life in the North Country, huh? What'd you find?"

"Rabbit, I think. Is everything okay?" He set down the bat beside the door.

Morales placed a file on the kitchen island and gestured while he spoke. "Look, I know you've got to get to work, so I apologize for the last-minute visit."

Brett glanced at the clock. It was seven thirty, and he had to start at eight. While other construction workers arrived as early as six, he drove a soil roller and didn't start until later. The crew was currently working the area's main interstate, 87, which ran from Canada to New York City. The site was only fifteen minutes from his house and he already had his work clothes on. He could spare the time.

Morales opened the file, thicker since Brett had last seen it. "This is just a total moonshot, really." Morales pulled a photo.

Brett came across the room, dimly aware he was tracking mud. Emily stepped beside him.

Morales pointed. "This guy is Nate Reuter. He was a prisoner at Dannemora – you know where that is?"

Brett nodded. Emily said, "Yes."

"Reuter got transferred downstate. He's currently at Rikers Island; they're moving him to minimum security."

"Okay…" Brett took a long look at Reuter's photo. Buzzed hair on the sides, spiky on top. A young guy. Just his shoulders were in the shot, but Brett saw a tattoo twisting up his neck.

"You ever seen this guy?"

Reuter did register familiar, but Brett couldn't place where. Maybe it was just one of those faces. "Don't think so."

Morales set the photo aside and pulled another one from the file. Also a mugshot. This guy was older, even meaner looking, with a scar under his eye, twisting the skin in a funny way. Like a burn more than a cut.

"How about him?"

"No."

Morales continued to hold the photo in the air, pushing it a little towards Emily, who got the hint and said, "No, uh-uh."

Emily was wearing her pensive look, rubbing her lip with the ball of her thumb.

Morales had one last photo, this time of a woman. She had ruddy skin, frizzy hair, her eyes locked in a thousand-yard stare. Hard to tell her age, maybe late thirties.

"And her?"

"No," Brett said, "sorry."

Emily, too, shook her head.

Morales returned the photos to the file. Then he squared his shoulders with them, and Brett felt a strange tension fill the air.

"So, just to confirm, you've never seen any of those people before."

Brett felt defensive. It was like Morales didn't believe them. But Brett figured he hadn't been completely forthcoming. He shifted his weight and said, "That first one. I mean, I think I might've seen that guy before, but I have no idea where."

"Maybe you saw him on TV. You ever watch IFC?"

As soon as Morales said it, Brett knew it was where he'd seen Reuter. "That's the mixed martial arts thing, right?"

Morales nodded. "Cage-fighting, that sort of thing. He was in it for a hot second, and then he went to prison."

"I don't really watch that stuff, but yeah, maybe I saw one of his fights advertised. This was a while ago though. Like, I don't know, couple years. Why did he go to prison?"

Morales hesitated, thinking, then stabbed the file with his finger. "Those three robbed a bank. Well, they robbed a couple banks."

"No shit." Brett was a bit breathless. He glanced at Emily, who looked increasingly uneasy. He moved to her and put an arm around her shoulder.

"And they also ripped off the NCFA," Morales said. "You know what that is?"

"No."

"North Country Fighters Association. They took about thirteen hundred from the NCFA office in Plattsburgh. But their total haul, including the banks, was probably much higher."

"Wow." Brett suddenly felt a touch claustrophobic, even though the kitchen was wide and airy.

"Yeah. And this is coming off a big upset for Reuter – he was heavily favored to win his last fight. So… who knows. Maybe hitting the NCFA was some kind of revenge thing."

Emily asked, "Do these people have something to do with the bones we found? Did you identify the bones?"

Morales sucked in a breath, blew it out slowly. "I'm sorry, I know it's not fair, but I can't say any more at this point. And I don't do robbery cases – that's Investigator Tambor and Investigator Reed, with the State Police."

He kept his eyes on Emily, perhaps seeing how she'd paled at the mention of bank robberies. He added, "There's no need for alarm here. That's not why I'm here, I don't want to worry you folks. Tambor and Reed just asked me, outside chance, you may have seen one of these three people. You haven't," he nodded at Brett, "except on TV. So…" He shrugged and gave them a big, buttery, Investigator Morales smile.

He gathered up his things and looked at Brett. "You need a ride to work or anything? Really sorry to have kept you."

"No, it's okay. I've got the bike."

"The bike?" Morales seemed interested. "What've you got?"

"It's an '89 Savage."

"The LS 650?"

"That's the one."

Morales's grin widened. "Love that bike, man. I've got an Intruder, myself. An 850. I don't care for those big hogs, you know?" He mimed dialing the throttle in the air with his free hand, and made a face like he was wind-blasted by the open road. "Just want something I can cruise on, and the 650 or 850 are perfect." He dropped his hand but kept his grin. "Well, that's it for me. Thank you."

Brett saw the detective to the front door.

Bank robbers?

He watched Morales step off the porch and head towards his car.

CHAPTER EIGHT

"Russo. Phone call. It's your lawyer."

The cell opened and a guard led Russo down through the common area where inmates were playing gin rummy and lifting weights.

A few of them gave Russo the eye as he walked through.

Russo knew how it went. Sooner or later you had to get with a gang. He was mixed-race Latino, so, back during his last stint that had meant either the Latin Kings or Ñeta. He didn't know if the gangs were the same now, if they'd mutated, or what. But the guys eyeballing him were definitely affiliated.

Lone wolves didn't last long in Rikers; they were hunted by the gangs and given the ultimatum to join or be persecuted.

Problem was, being protected by a gang usually meant doing something in return, like smuggling contraband up your ass, or fighting. It was a quick way to get into trouble, too, and add more time, more fines.

"Russo," said Bloustein on the phone. "What's your answer?"

"I'll take the deal."

"You'll plead guilty to all charges?"

"Yes."

"Good. Sit tight. Judge Aiello's got something he calls the 'rocket docket.' Honestly, I think he stole it from a John Grisham book. But I told you, these failure-to-pays are clogging the system and there's been a real push to flush them out."

Russo loved being referred to as waste product. "So, what does that mean? Earlier you talked about two years."

"Yeah, two years."

"How much is bail? Still the same?"

"Same. Five grand. But he tacked on the eight-fifty in fees. Honestly I think the courts are under pressure with all of this fast-tracking. Paying fees lowers the collective blood pressure a little. Why, can you get it?"

Unreal. Maybe Bloustein had multiple clients. Or maybe he just had White Man's Syndrome and couldn't comprehend, let alone remember, that Russo didn't have that kind of money lying around. "No, I don't have it."

"Well, get it if you want out before your sentencing. Hopefully everything stays status quo and two years is the max."

"Hopefully?" Russo gritted his teeth.

Ten, nine, eight…

"Well, you drove when you had no license, and you've had three intoxicated driving offenses in less than ten years. The courts don't like people drinking and endangering the public, especially when they have a rap sheet a mile long."

Flowers and a rock wall. Endless field beyond…

"All that's in my past. And I don't drink anymore."

"Look, this is a plea bargain. You want to make your case, that means a trial. Maybe more time. We went over this."

Baby toes. My little girl.

My Zoe.

"You want me to put you in touch with a bondsman, give me a call. I gotta go."

Russo hung up the phone so hard it made a chime.

Back in the cell, Russo tried to distract himself by asking Nate about his friends and family, following whichever line of questioning seemed to irritate the kid the least.

Nate said he had a daughter who was five. "I was only nineteen when my girlfriend got pregnant. I was at Dannemora before Chastity was born."

Chastity, Russo thought. *Poor kid.* Chastity was a stripper name if he'd ever heard one. But he smiled. "I got a daughter too."

"Yeah? Good for you."

"So, you did time at Dannemora?"

"Yeah. Just came down here couple weeks ago."

Dannemora was in upstate New York, and officially called Clinton Correctional Facility. It was a maximum-security prison. Nate was being transferred to another prison to finish the two years on his sentence. He'd gotten five years for something, but hadn't revealed what just yet, and Russo didn't pry.

The prisons were always shifting inmates around, for one reason or another.

When you first got arrested, you went to county jail. Rikers was different because Rikers was really neither county nor state nor federal. It was its own beast.

For the rest of the U.S., you went to county jail and then got shipped to a receiving center where they processed and evaluated you.

They put you through a series of medical and mental health screenings. They developed a profile for you – how dangerous you were, your crime, social background, education, job skills and work history, health, and criminal record, including prior prison sentences. All this and then they sent you to what they considered "the most appropriate custody classification and prison."

Then, for the most part, they forgot about you.

But after your initial classification, you could, if you minded your Ps and Qs, progress through various custody levels to minimum custody until your eventual release. If Nate was getting transferred to a minimum-security joint, things were looking good for him.

"So what're you doing with the papers?" Russo asked. "Looking at classifieds?"

"Shut the fuck up," Nate said, without any real bite. "Nah, man. I ain't worried about a job."

"No?"

"Nah. When I get out of this motherfucker, I'm all set." He said this, and then he opened the cabinet again and looked in. Like he was checking to see if the newspapers were still there, still neatly stacked.

Seeing it was so, he hooked himself up to his MP3 player and dove onto his bunk.

The bed rocked and squeaked as Nate jammed out to his music, occasionally pounding his chest with a fist.

Russo rolled over and put his hands behind his head. His next visit would be from the girls, and he wanted to rest up. He had to figure out how to tell Felicia he wasn't going to be seeing them for two years. Or more.

At night, the men shouted. They used the cracks between the doors and the floor and yelled so they could hear one another.

Russo remembered being here before, doing a month in the box; what they called the solitary confinement cells over in the Otis Bantum Correctional Center. To pass the time, inmates in segregation played chess by calling out moves in an imagined game. It was quite the mental gymnastics, but even the dumber guys could do it eventually; they had plenty of time to get good.

Now he was in the Eric M. Taylor Center, which housed mostly short-timers and was an angry zoo.

In the morning, he'd go to another building to visit with Felicia and Zoe. But it was getting loud out there, and Russo wasn't sleeping again.

He climbed down from the bunk, careful not to disturb Nate. He could hear the music pumping into Nate's head, the shrieking sounds of heavy metal, and Nate was snoring, his hands protectively over his heart and groin.

Russo went to the door and listened. It was hard to make out any distinct voices in the cacophony, but there was a lot of hooting and catcalling.

Rikers took in over 200 new inmates daily, so it could've just been the initiation of fresh meat. Back in the day, at least, inmates would run bets on who could get a newbie to cry in his cell the first night, just like in that movie with Morgan Freeman and the big tall guy with the baby-face, whatever his name was.

Russo climbed back into bed and put his pillow over his head.

If I was to say you was a hard motherfucker back in the day, would I be lying?

He couldn't take years of this. He'd get out with no job, no wheels, no money, maybe no Felicia or Zoe.

He just couldn't do it.

CHAPTER NINE

Dr. Rhea Runic.

It seemed to come to Brett in his sleep, or, at least, in the borderland of consciousness upon first awakening. He opened his eyes, stared up at the ceiling, and said, "Holy shit."

He swung his legs out of the bed, glanced around for Emily. Her side of the bed was empty.

Dr. Rhea Runic 441.

It was so simple it felt like it had to be some sort of joke. Like an inside joke.

But it was also chilling.

He pulled on jeans and a T-shirt. A lemony-yellow sunshine was already streaming in the bedroom windows, dust drifting in the rays like plankton in the sea. It was going to be a hot one – the forecast said hottest so far that June. He could already feel it burning against the window panes.

As he went downstairs to find Emily, he remembered the anagram games he would play with his mother. They would take their own names and try to arrange as many different words as possible. His personal favorite, and the one he was the most proud of configuring, had been "Blaster Torn."

"Starlet Born" was kind of effeminate, "Rattler Snob" had its merits. But "Blaster Torn" had the mythic, tough-guy connotation a twelve-year-old boy wanted in a code name.

"What are you grinning at?" Emily asked him. She was standing at the stove, smiling bemusedly while scrambling eggs. It was only a quarter past six. Emily was an early riser, always had been, but he normally slept until seven on workdays.

He approached the coffee pot and got himself a cup. "'Bra Rent Slot,'" he said. "And, ah, what was the other one with three words? Uhm… 'Bar Let Snort.'"

"What the hell are you talking about?" But she smiled wider.

He leaned in the doorframe and gazed out at the back field. "So, you're not going to believe this. I mean, maybe it's a coincidence… nah, no way it's a coincidence."

"Brett…"

"Rhea Runic is a weird friggin name, right? I've just been thinking about it and thinking about it. You know, the cops said there's no one by that name around. Or they don't know, they haven't figured it out. I don't know – maybe they have. I mean that guy, Robert Graysmith, the cartoonist who figured out the Zodiac killer's cipher – he was just a guy, you know? Maybe it's not inconceivable that I figure it out."

"*Brett.* You're babbling."

"Rhea Runic is an anagram for Hurricane. The abbreviation for doctor – DR – becomes road – RD. Hurricane Road." He spread his arms like a magician, slopping some coffee on the floor.

Emily scowled, grabbed a dish towel, and sopped it up. From the floor she said, "You mean Hurricane Road, right near here?"

"I would guess. But I have no idea." He bent and took the towel from her, finished cleaning up as she returned to the eggs. "I mean, it could just be some random shit, I don't know, maybe I'm wrong."

He stepped to the sink and washed out the dish towel.

"I was just going over and over the name. I looked up everything I could find on the list of trustees – don't worry, I didn't call anybody. But nothing. So then I Googled. Rhea is a Greek mythological figure, daughter of Gaia and Uranus. Married her own brother, Cronus."

Emily grunted. "Gross."

"And then I looked up 'Runic,' too. There's this thing called the runic alphabet, or runes, which were the letters in a set of related alphabets. Anyway, maybe it put the idea in my head… You know, my family used to do it. Do anagrams."

"I know, you've told me. And you're 'Blaster Man' or whatever. Grab a couple plates."

He laughed and went after plates in the cabinets. "Blaster *Torn*. It was fun. We'd do it on car rides."

He thought about his mother, how she looked from his spot in the back seat. Always with his mother on those long drives to school. She didn't like him taking the bus. Like she was trying to keep him protected after his father moved out.

"Anyway, so… I don't know. There you have it. 'Rhea Runic' reconfigures to 'Hurricane.'"

She plated up the eggs and they ate together for a while. He realized he hadn't given her a good morning kiss and leaned over and planted one on her.

"So you're going to tell the police?" she asked. "Investigator Morales?"

"Yeah, I mean. Yeah. I just thought, first, you know, maybe check it out. See if there's even a 441 Hurricane Road."

She wore an expression suggesting she didn't like the plan.

He touched her hand. "I'll tell him. For sure." He changed the topic. "You make an appointment with the doctor?"

"Yes. For tomorrow at noon."

"I'll come with you."

She gave him another suspicious look. "What about work?"

"I'm not going to miss the first look at our baby."

"You're not going to get a look at anything – it's the size of a pinhead."

"Still. I want to be there."

"How? Callahan isn't going to be upset if you miss work?"

Callahan was the foreman on the road construction job. He was built like a whiskey barrel and had a mouth like a sailor.

"We've got all kinds of problems," Brett said. "Some bigwigs from the state are coming to look at things this week. Work is going to be touch and go. Anyway, it's a weird week. I'll just ask him for the time off."

"What are you going to say?"

"Callahan has four kids and already nine grandkids and he's not sixty yet. He loves kids and family. He'll understand."

Emily's fork clattered against the plate. She looked mortified. "We discussed this. We're not telling anyone until—"

He held his hands up and cut her off. "I know, I know. Callahan will totally get it. I'll just tell him I need a few hours; you have an appointment at the hospital."

She cocked her head and gave him a look which read, unmistakably: you're a complete moron.

"Well, shit, Brett. You don't think Callahan would figure it out? He knows you just got married. I'm sure he knows we've been trying for a baby – I'm sure you've spread that around, 'Oh yeah, gonna knock her up.' Are you kidding? You tell him you need to take me to the hospital, he'll get it."

Emily stood up in a huff, dropped her plate in the sink and hastily ran the tap. There was no doubt he'd messed up. And the whole thing was meant to be a surprise.

She shook her head as she looked out the window over the sink, into the field.

He came up behind her and gently lowered in his plate, shut the water off. He cautiously touched her shoulders. "Okay. I'll just tell him something else."

"Brett, you can't keep anything quiet."

She had him there.

"But that's good, right? I'm transparent."

She clucked her tongue and groaned, then pushed past him and went upstairs. He got some more coffee and hurried up after her.

Work ended at 6 p.m. and Brett hopped on the Savage and gunned the engine.

He drove west from the interstate along the winding country roads, but when he got to the turn towards home, he went another direction.

Hurricane Road twisted up the side of a mountain. The weather had been unseasonably hot, an early start to the summer, but this evening was cooling off, the wind shaking the trees and pushing him around a little on the bike.

He gritted his teeth and leaned into the curves, suddenly thinking about the fact he was going to become a new father. This whole thing with motorcycles and high speeds was probably going to have to go. He imagined himself laying the bike down at seventy miles an hour, his body scraping along the asphalt, flaying the skin from his bones like a cheese grater.

He eased back on the throttle.

He hadn't wanted Emily to see how the idea of letters from Dr. Rhea Runic rearranging to Hurricane Road – a road just ten miles from their house – alarmed him. Transparent he was not. It was as scary as it was intriguing.

He needed to confront that fear.

Perhaps more, he continued to sense opportunity.

He had a baby on the way, and what had he accomplished so far? What would his legacy be? He'd been an average student, middle of the pack. He'd gotten a degree from a state university and done nothing with it. He'd failed at freelance journalism, and the non-fiction book he'd written on the history of North Country murders failed to meet publishing standards.

For six years he'd either bartended or worked construction, withdrawing from the world. And he hadn't been able to afford a house on his own.

What was he going to be in the eyes of his son or daughter? Not that there was anything wrong with bartending or construction work, or even failing at a career, but there was something wrong with just giving up.

Here now was the chance to do something – he was in a unique position to uncover the story behind the bones, the robberies, the address. To face down what he'd really been scared of for years – trying again.

The Savage cruised up the mountain until the road crested. He started down towards Keene, passing a few houses tucked into the woods.

Two visible house numbers so far: 990, and then a little later, 750. He was going in the right direction and continued descending along the serpentine road.

He slowed further as he came along a fresh grouping of houses. Three in a row, and he glimpsed one of the numbers – 525. Getting close now. Odd numbers on the left, even on the right.

He passed a sprawling ranch, bordered by a post-rail fence like his own, horses grazing in the distance, tails swishing.

People who lived on Hurricane Mountain had some money – these places weren't cheap. He knew a little about Keene, which was a small community but with upscale residents. For a lot of people, they were summer homes.

489 was the next number, and the name *Schubert* was wood-burned on a sign staked to the ground. He downshifted and drove slow, chilled from the cool drive along the shaded road. The next number was 455. He didn't understand exactly why, out in the countryside, some numbers got skipped.

The road steepened, plunging down the mountain.

A dirt driveway on the left without a number.

He kept going. He could turn around if necessary.

The next driveway was for 419.

Brett stopped the bike, engine purring.

A big truck came barreling up the hill, blasting past. The vehicle startled and angered him. He shouted at it as it disappeared around the next bend in the road.

He headed back up the mountain, creeping along the road shoulder. This was stupid.

But once he was back at the numberless dirt road, he turned in.

The road split a grove of willow trees, their branches blowing like hair in the wind. The property was gorgeous, tall grass sweeping one way, a field of wildflowers stretching the other.

The dirt driveway went on for a while until he thought it wasn't a driveway at all, but a road going to God-knew-where. Then he saw a house in the distance, surrounded by smaller buildings and an enormous barn.

Brett tensed but kept going, looking out for a sign of a person, a car, something.

In proximity, he saw a rusted tractor parked beside the barn. Everything was overgrown – weeds engulfed the tractor, high as the foot wells, smothering a third of the giant rear tires. The main house was in obvious disrepair, the porch sagging, one of the upstairs windows broken.

Brett stopped the bike, engine idling.

He hit the kill switch and the motor died. He removed his helmet and listened to the wind shushing through the grass.

A horsefly came along and started orbiting his head. He absently batted it away as he dismounted the bike.

Even seeing no one around, he still felt anxious trespassing on someone else's property. Not so much because it was illegal, or that some disgruntled owner might show up with a shotgun, but because it was entering another world without an invitation.

A nervousness squeezed his heart as he neared the porch.

Still no house number, no family signage like *Schubert*. The house was so neglected it looked gray. Much of the white paint had chipped away to expose the sun-cooked wood beneath.

The big barn was in better shape, sort of. At least, it looked better. Unpainted, the knots of the barn-wood had darkened from years of sitting in the sun. The massive front doors were wide open, and Brett stared into the gloom.

A hayloft in the back. Sunlight shone through cracks in the gambrel roof, streaming in dusty, golden shafts of light. Old bridles hung from hooks, saddles were piled in a corner, covered in more dust.

Another building was much smaller, a rusty horseshoe hanging over the closed front door. Probably a foaling shed. Either ranchers took their pregnant mares in there to give birth or they outfitted the foals with horseshoes when they were old enough. Something like that.

He pulled the door ajar. The wind flung it all the way open.

He saw a workbench, tools, and a small area fenced off by two-by-fours, like a pen. Old hay stirred in the wind.

He focused on the descriptions of things, taking mental notes for the prose forming in his mind. Leg bones found in a yard. A mysterious note with a name and number. An abandoned house in the middle of nowhere.

This had to be the place. This horse ranch was connected to those bones. But how?

The final building looked like a tenant house. Two wheel ruts, barely discernible in all the brittle vegetation, led to it. He mustered resolve and followed the path, the evening sun blinkering through the birch trees in the west.

The screen door to the porch creaked in the gusty wind. Witch grass poked up through the floorboards. He opened the door and stepped in.

There were two rooms: a kitchen with a peeling floor, a gloomy main room with a woodstove in the corner, a ratty old couch, coffee table, some books in a pile.

The place smelled musty, rank with mouse shit and mold.

No bedroom – but the couch was the fold-out-bed kind. He crossed over an old braided rug that was probably once colorful, and picked up a paperback book. Still wearing his motorcycle gloves, he looked at the inside cover, hoping for a name.

He found one: *Colby.*

Finally he slid open the single drawer in the table. Found a notepad, a couple pencils rattling around. He took out his phone and flipped to the picture of the note in the tin box. Holding the notebook next to the screen, it was hard to tell if they were the same brand of paper, but they could be.

Now here he was on someone's property, he thought, someone possibly named Colby, and he was in one of their buildings, playing detective.

The excitement ebbed and he hurried out. He'd seen enough.

The day was darkening. Another breeze twisted through, and gnarled clouds rolled over the peak of the mountain, signs of an oncoming storm.

His phone buzzed in his pocket, startling him.

Where are you? What's your hunger factor?

He texted back.

On my way. 7/10.

Feeling foolish, like someone caught playing out a fantasy, he stuck the phone away and looked up.

There was a person standing by the barn, watching him.

CHAPTER TEN

"I got a girl over in Rosie's," Nate said.

They shuffled along in the food line, pushing their trays. The line cook served Russo some rubbery pancakes drizzled with a shiny syrup resembling motor oil.

Nate meant the women's jail, called Rosie Singer's, on the far side of the island near the restricted housing units.

He went on, "You know, we've had some nice visits."

A second line cook dumped a glistening glop of fruit on Russo's tray. Maybe oranges and banana, but hard to tell.

Didn't matter to Russo anyway. "How did you meet? In here?"

"Nah, man. I knew her on the outside."

Russo was already thinking about Felicia and Zoe; now all he wanted to do was plow through his breakfast and will the time to pass. Nate's babble was just background noise.

Someone came up behind them in the line, and Russo gave the inmate a look over his shoulder but said nothing.

Still, he considered the plastic utensils on his tray. It was just an automatic reaction, to look for a weapon in case he needed it. But they didn't keep anything in the cafeteria that was dangerous.

Nate was still going on about his girlfriend inmate. "We talk, though. We hook up meetings with each other, we can get messages around. She's got the smarts, man. She's got it all figured out. And I need that, you know? I need someone to point me in the right direction."

They were almost to the end of the line. The other inmate came closer.

Russo felt his adrenaline kick in.

The inmate grabbed Nate around the neck and dug something into his lower back.

Russo stepped away as the inmate breathed into Nate's ear, "*I gotta a message for ya…*"

Nate gnashed his teeth and flailed in the grip of the attacking inmate, who was taller and heavier. The attacker pulled Nate away from the line and everyone in the cafeteria started hollering.

Russo made fists but felt helpless. If he got involved, it could add time and fines that would put him further away from the girls.

Nate was able to slip out of the half-nelson the guy had put him in. He spun around – Russo saw blood blooming in the fabric of his shirt – and dove into the inmate, throwing him off balance.

They both went down. Russo watched as Nate wrapped himself around the big inmate like a boa. He'd seen guys like this on TV and the web – guys like Royce Gracie, who practiced jiu-jitsu. Nate wasn't just talk. Maybe about some things he acted tough when he wasn't, but it looked like he knew his shit as a ground fighter.

The big inmate was choking, his eyes all white and rolling around, clawing at Nate's forearm, punching blindly. Nate used his legs like a vice and immobilized the inmate. Everybody was shouting – other inmates were running over.

But there was a lot of blood pouring out of Nate. He was starting to lose his strength.

The inmate rolled on top. He stabbed Nate with the shank a second time. Then a third.

To hell with it.

Russo reached down and took the inmate around his ribs, pulled him off Nate, and flung him into a cafeteria table. The inmates there jumped up and moved away.

The attacker shook it off, stood up, ready to come at Russo. Russo stepped protectively in front of Nate and got ready.

The inmate rushed in, jabbing with the shank, but Russo stepped away and the guy went sprawling.

The guards showed up next. Three of them got between Russo and the attacker, swinging their batons to keep the men apart. Two more guards ran into the room. One got behind the attacker and slipped the baton around his neck. The other grabbed Russo.

The guard tripped him and Russo went down.

Face-first on the dirty floor, he kept his mouth shut. He locked eyes with Nate for a second, who was still on the ground.

Nate was pale, not looking good.

Then Nate started screaming.

Russo sat through all the talking and interviews. He didn't see Nate again. It took three hours and he kept repeating his story exactly as events had unfolded. He'd been standing there, getting his pancakes, talking to Nate, and this guy just came out of nowhere, some guy who had a beef with Nate for whatever reason.

He was going to kill Nate, and Russo had tried to stop it.

They led Russo back to his cell.

"What about my visit? I've got a visit scheduled for today."

They slammed the door in his face.

Russo paced the room.

Ten, nine, eight…

Not working.

Flowers. Those white fluffy seeds blowing around in the air…

The image turned red with Nate's blood.

He shifted his thoughts to Zoe, her little baby face, soft skin, pink toes, but now it only made matters worse. What happened in the cafeteria was likely to cost him more time, more money.

Russo pounded the wall. He looked at the bunk, charged it, and ripped the bed frame apart with his bare hands, wrenching metal, tearing fabric.

When he was finished, he backed up until he hit the wall. He slipped down, landed in a heap, and sobbed.

There was a noise at the door, and the shield slid away from the small pass window.

"Paper." The guard shoved a newspaper through. It hit the floor with a lifeless flop. Russo ignored it, feeling sorry for himself.

A few minutes passed and he wiped his nose, snot running down. He got up and cleaned himself in the sink.

He realized his arm was dotted with flecks of Nate's blood, and scrubbed it away. He ran the water over his face, even though it smelled like sulfur. Then he opened the cabinet and used one of Nate's neatly folded towels, blotted himself dry, and hung the towel off the now bent and twisted bunk frame to dry.

He returned to the floor, pulled the paper close. It was yesterday's news.

Russo stared at it, his bad luck temporarily forgotten. It wasn't the *Daily News*, or the *Post*, or even a paper from Westchester or Jersey. It was called the *Press-Republican*, from upstate New York.

He looked over the front page; a headline near the bottom caught his eye:

Police Say Still No Leads in Human Remains Case

After the single paragraph lead, the full article continued on page six.

Seemed like a follow-up story, fairly short.

Russo stood and returned to the cabinet. Above the towels was Nate's limited store of newspapers. Russo pulled out Monday's edition of the *Press-Republican*.

HUMAN REMAINS FOUND AT NEWLYWED'S DREAM HOME

Front page, with a big, full-color picture of a yellow farmhouse and a big field, the kind his father had taken him to as a boy. Another picture within the text showed a young man and woman, arm in arm, an attractive white couple.

Russo started reading.

CHAPTER ELEVEN

Brett didn't move. The person was thirty yards away, hidden in the shadow cast by the barn.

Bank robberies, Brett thought.

Jesus, why had he come here? If there were links between the bones, bank robberies, and maybe some kind of hideout, he'd just walked right into the middle of it.

Criminals who'd had a falling out, maybe. One dead, buried in Brett's field.

One standing beside the barn.

Or, weren't they all in jail? More likely, Brett was just a stupid trespasser and this person was wondering what the hell he was doing here.

The figure walked out of the shadow of the barn and raised a hand in greeting.

Brett waved back.

They drew nearer each other but then the person slowed to a stop. Brett stopped too, still a dozen yards away.

He should've known.

"Hey there," Investigator Morales said.

"Hi," Brett said, struggling for words. He decided honesty was the best route to take. "I'm sorry, I... came here because of the note I found. I just wanted to see. I know I probably shouldn't be here."

Morales moved closer. "I was just going to have a beer – you want one?"

Brett was momentarily stunned. A beer?

He began making excuses, still rambling about why he was here, confessing further his cell pic of the note in the tin box, talking about how he knew it was all stupid, not his place, right up until Morales flapped a hand in the air, beckoning.

"Come on, let's talk."

The thunderheads moved closer. The colorful wildflowers turned gray and the bruised sky rumbled a warning.

"I gotta go," Brett said, "it's gonna rain."

A moment later the first fat, cold drops splattered down. Morales tilted his face upward, smiling and squinting. Then he looked at Brett, as if to say, *Really? You want to ride in this?*

"Alright," Brett said.

They tracked back to Morales's car on the other side of the house.

Maybe he was acting weird, talking about drinking beer, but this was a state police investigator. Morales had been to their house, interviewed them, drank their iced tea.

Still, as Brett sank into the passenger side of the unmarked cruiser, he was nervous. Something they taught you in childhood – at least his mother had taught him – *never get in the car.*

Morales reached over and popped the glovebox. "Paper napkins in there."

They dried themselves off, blotting faces and necks.

Then Morales reached into the footwell by Brett's feet and opened a soft cooler of canned beer. He passed one to Brett and cracked his own.

After the investigator took a long sip, he smacked his lips and said, "Ahhh."

Brett waited for the interrogation. *What are you up to? What do you know? Why would you come here? Do you know what you're getting into? Your wife is pregnant, isn't she? I can tell. You think this is responsible behavior for a father-to-be?*

But Morales just stared out into the storm.

The rain intensified, drumming the roof like falling acorns. Morales activated the wipers, and they both watched as the downpour shifted in curtains, battering the buildings on the ranch.

"So you like that bike, huh?"

The question was so out of context Brett didn't understand for a second. "Yeah," he said.

"Tough going in the bad weather, though."

Brett nodded, took a tentative sip of his beer. Where was this headed? The beer tasted good, salty.

"You play any sports in school?" Morales asked.

"Me? Yeah."

"Let me guess." Morales gave Brett the once-over. "You're a baseball guy."

"Shortstop. Yeah. Most Valuable Player senior year." He didn't know why he said it, he wasn't bragging, but everything felt strange. For a cop car, it looked like an ordinary sedan. Maybe a late model Ford Mercury. Only with a metal grate between the front and back seats. And a light bar in the back, up on the rear deck.

No one tied up and walleyed with terror in the backseat, anyway.

Morales was nodding, smiling. "Yep. Shortstop sounds right. I bet you had a lot of girlfriends."

"Uh, you know. A couple."

"Oh come on." Morales lightly punched Brett in the thigh, and Brett jumped. "Don't be modest. How about your parents. Still together?"

"Divorced."

Morales grunted and seemed to grow less happy.

It was getting more and more uncomfortable. "Investigator Morales, I'm sorry, I know I shouldn't be here…"

"Why? Why shouldn't you be here?"

Brett struggled to respond. "Er, I mean, this is private property. You, ah, you're here, so it's obviously part of the investigation."

"Maybe I was just following you," Morales said, and leaned in with a companionable wink.

Brett considered jumping out. Running.

He'd left his keys in the bike's ignition. It was probably irrational, but his adrenaline was really cranking. Morales was acting funny, and Brett didn't know what to believe.

"You were following me?"

"No, no. I'm just messin' with you. You must've figured it out, huh?"

"What?" Brett played dumb.

"Come on, don't be modest."

Morales crumpled the beer can and tossed it down by Brett's feet. He pulled a fresh one from the soft cooler bag. He took a drink. "Dr. Rhea Runic 441 equals 441 Hurricane Road."

"Do you usually test for anagrams with things like this?"

"You mean all the times we find notes in tin boxes buried next to human leg bones in civilian back yards? No. Not usually. A colleague suggested it. The handwriting expert."

Brett swallowed dryly, unsure of what to say. "Are you the first one to come?"

"Uh-huh. Technically I'm off-duty, so you can stop freaking out over a little beer. It's not my show anymore anyway."

"No? So whose show is—?"

"But you were right. Yeah, you were right, I think. 441 Hurricane Road. I mean, it exists, right? We're sitting here looking at it, aren't we?"

"I don't know. There was no signage."

"Trust me. This is it. 441."

"Okay. Who owns it?"

"Nobody. Well, technically, the state. Before that it was a woman's, named Alma Colby."

"Alma Colby?"

Morales nodded, drinking, looking out. The rain water coursing down between sweeps of the wiper blades painted his face with wriggling shadows.

He set the beer in the cup holder and played with the wedding ring on his finger, rotating it around.

Then he broke out of it and glanced at Brett, letting go of the ring. "Why do you think someone would bury part of a person, just a few bones, in your backyard? And why would they leave that note?"

"I don't know."

"You think someone was meant to find it? Or was it just a message in a bottle, meant for anyone?"

"I'd say… yeah, maybe someone was meant to find it. Someone specific."

Morales snapped his fingers. "Exactly. I think so, too. Someone was intended to find that note." He pointed at Brett. "But probably wasn't supposed to be you."

Morales's behavior certainly remained odd, but at least they were discussing the case. If he wanted information, this was the best place to start. "Whose bones are they?"

"I can't tell you that."

"It's one of the three people from those mugshots, right?"

Morales stayed silent.

The rain continued to beat down, but it was letting off a bit. Brett's phone vibrated and he looked at the message. Morales looked on, too. "That the missus?"

"She's making dinner."

Morales nodded again, a slow, pronounced gesture that gently rocked his whole upper body. "She seems like a good woman."

"Are you… alright, sir?"

"Me? Yeah, man. Don't call me sir. Jesus."

"Okay."

"Look, this human remains case got kicked up to a higher division. Above my pay grade." He seemed to regard the rained-out scene with a look of remorse. Maybe, Brett saw, more than remorse, but a glint of hunger in his eyes.

"Those detectives you mentioned?"

"Well, Tambor and Reed, yeah, they're the state investigators who initially dealt with the robberies. But there's a shadow over them, too." He jerked his head around. "Hey, I wish I had my truck. Could just roll the bike up onto the bed and give you a ride home. I played baseball too, you know that? We got a lot in common, man. I wasn't an MVP or anything, though." He made a face and then gave Brett another slap on the knee.

Brett decided the detective was upset he'd been sidelined. He was drinking, so probably off-duty, but struggling to let go of the case.

"Alright," Morales said. "I gotta go."

"Wait," Brett said. "So who is Alma Colby?"

"Alma Colby is nobody. She's just an old lady who died last year."

"She died?"

"She had no family, and donated the place. This is state land now. The state is supposed to fix it up, offer it to some family in need. It's just been sitting here… you know the government. Everything takes a century. But, like I said, this is out of my hands now. What're you gonna do?"

"Why did you come here then?"

"Boy, you're full of questions."

"Sorry."

"You really want to know?"

"Yeah, I do."

Morales took a long drink of the beer, staring at Brett as he tipped back the can. He burped and said, "It's just… you know, it's an interesting case. The clearance rate for bank robbery is not quite sixty percent nationwide, but Reed and Tambor are closer to eighty percent. They're good. So it's rare for them to have something still hanging."

Morales was evading the question. Still hanging? Did he mean the bones in the backyard? Or something else? He said the human remains case was out of his hands, and that the robbery detectives had a shadow over them. Who cast the shadow? Brett was no law enforcement expert, but he took a guess.

"Doesn't the FBI handle bank robberies?"

"Well, yes. In this case they formed what's called a Major Crimes Task Force with state and local law enforcement. It's the FBI who issues the criminal complaint. Special Agent in Charge on this one was… I think, guy named Roger T. Wilshire. But it's Tambor and Reed who worked the state police end."

Brett said, "Little banks up here in the North Country probably don't carry a lot, right?"

Morales swilled beer and shrugged. "I don't know. Banks give up a couple thousand dollars on average. Most robbers just rob the tellers and don't go for the vault. You know, they're homeless, they're drug addicted, mentally unstable. Lone-wolf types. So that brings down the average. But every once in a while, you get a real crew, like the Fighting Bandits."

"The Fighting Bandits?"

"You got to give them a name at some point. Tambor called them the Fighting Bandits because of their martial arts background. Kim Delahunt was a fighter, too."

"And the third guy?"

"Oberst? Maybe. I don't know."

"And all three of them went to jail."

"Right."

So that seemed to rule out the theory that the remains was one of the bandits, unless there was some fourth member Morales didn't know about, or wasn't telling about.

"Still," Brett said, "a bunch of banks at two, three, even five grand a pop, that's not going to add up to much. You said something about revenge though, back at my house, you said maybe a 'revenge thing'…"

"Yeah, well, what do I know? All I can say is that, you know, the same shit that goes on in boxing goes on in cage-fighting now, too; fight-fixing and all that. I just think it adds extra motivation – you got these three nobodies, they've never robbed a bank before, they're not drug addicts, Reuter was winning fights up until that last one, doing okay, why rob the Association? Maybe because he felt wronged. Maybe he threw his fight, maybe he was coerced, I dunno."

Brett could imagine feeling like that, like the world thought you were a failure, and what it might do to you. "But then why go after the banks? Was the money stolen from the NCFA all the bets collected from the fights? Or was there more, or something?"

"Hey, you want to know more, you should talk to the robbery detectives. I've already said too much."

Brett stared out the windshield. He needed to do some research. He thought he'd avoid the robbery detectives during an open investigation but maybe his ex-girlfriend Meg Lister had some insight.

"All I know," Morales said, sounding a bit sorry for himself, "was I got asked to show you those mugshots. Informally. To do it formally, you come down to the station, there's a witness there, but I was just gathering information, doing as I was told."

He fell silent. The rain had tapered off to a fine mist, and Morales turned the wipers down a notch.

It was time to go. Especially if more police were going to show up any minute because of the note. Brett grabbed the door handle.

"Listen, Mr. Morales, again, I'm sorry if being here is inappropriate or something."

Morales didn't appear to be listening. He was looking into his beer can like the answer to life's mysteries was hidden inside. He shook the can and then drained the rest, tossed it aside. "Alright, so, what are we doing? Am I taking you home? Oh, shit, right, the bike."

"I'll be fine," Brett said. "Thanks."

He was happy just to be free of the car. The space in there had been cloyed with humidity, beer, and Morales's strange vibes.

Brett looked through window at the investigator, glimpsing him between swipes of the wiper blades, and then Morales backed up in the silver Ford Mercury. He turned the car around and drove away.

Brett was soaked. He didn't care. He got on the Savage and fired it up, gave the property one more glance, and then took off.

CHAPTER TWELVE

Russo was staring at the ceiling when the door slot slid open.

"James Russo. Visitor."

He hopped off the bottom bunk, which creaked and rattled. The whole bed was screwed up from his outburst. The guards had eventually found out about it, burst in with their bats out, shoved him against the wall. They'd confiscated everything in the cell – what little there was to confiscate – but not before Russo had read the human remains article in the paper. They'd even taken Nate's collection of hand towels, leaving Russo with just one.

"Is it my wife? I was told I couldn't see her after the—"

"I don't know, inmate."

Russo doubted it. His scheduled time to visit Felicia had come and gone while the guards had renovated the cell. If Felicia had shown, she wouldn't have waited all this time with their fourteen-month-old baby. And she wouldn't be back.

"I need to call my wife," Russo said. "I was supposed to see her."

"Well, you fucked that up, pal."

Russo peered through the slot. "Please. Let me call her."

"Put your arms through. Now."

"Who is the visitor? My lawyer?"

"Inmate. Put your fucking arms through this door or I'm walking away."

Russo did as he was told. It had to be Bloustein there to see him. Maybe Bloustein could convince the guards to let Russo call Felicia.

But it wasn't Bloustein. The lawyer wasn't in the visiting area.

Russo didn't even realize that the female inmate was there for him until a CO sat her down.

She stared across the table, this woman with frizzy hair and a hard face.

"Who are you?" Russo asked.

Her mouth twitched into a sly smile. "How you doing, Russo?"

"How do you know me?" He glanced around, then leaned towards her. "Who *are* you?"

"Nate was impressed by you – you've got some battle scars. That's what he said. He likes you."

Russo pieced it together. "You're from Rosie's... you're Nate's girl?"

She grimaced. "His *girl*? Sure, yeah, okay. That Nate, he lives in his own little bubble. You notice that? Or is it just me?"

Russo was taken aback by the whole thing, his brain running to catch up. Inmates visiting one another inside was irregular – this woman must've had some pull with a CO who bent the rules. While there were certainly a few guards who tried to make jail a bit nicer, there were more inmates who knew how to game the system.

He didn't say anything about Nate. He just looked at her, waiting. He guessed her age, about thirty-five. She was white, with maybe a little "black Irish" in her, Russo's uncle would have said, back when people said things like that.

She ran her finger across the table, making playful little swirls. "You ever heard of something called 'mutually assured destruction?'"

Russo was liking this less and less. "I'm gonna ask you one last time, who are you, then I'm outta here..."

"I'm Kim. Okay? Kim Delahunt. Now that we've settled that ultra-important business, let's cut to it. You read the latest paper? The upstate paper?"

"What paper?"

"The one Nate has delivered to his cell every day. The *Press-Republican*. Along with a few others, you know, for appearances."

"Okay. Yeah. I read it."

"See that article about the human remains?"

"What the fuck is this about?"

"What is this *about*? This is about you getting out of here, Russo. Oh, look at you. That put a wrench right into your grinding gears, didn't it? I can smell the smoke. What if I told you, Russo, I could raise your bail money? I could get you out of here," she snapped her fingers, "just like that?"

She let the proposition hang in the air a moment.

"Nate said it was five large, right? Five big ones and you go home. Home to 1773 St. Mark's on Staten Island. Home to your wife, Felicia, and that adorable little baby girl. Have I got your attention, Russo? Or do you want to keep fucking around like a tough guy?"

Russo's mouth worked, but no sound came out. He gripped the table, his teeth on edge, and whispered, "What did you say about my family?"

She wrinkled her nose at him and glanced away. "Okay. Alright. Well, maybe it's just not the right time." She turned her head back, slowly. Her eyes were hard. "Maybe you want to fuck around in here a few more weeks, months, years, see if you get in any more trouble."

She acted like she was going to leave.

Russo knew he was taking bait – could practically taste the bullshit in his mouth – but he patted the air with his hands, trying to calm her down. Again he looked at the CO, the one who'd brought Kim into the visiting center.

The CO was looking everyone over, seemingly disinterested in Russo and Kim in particular. Definitely servicing the inmate somehow – Kim had things wired.

"Alright," Russo said. "I'm listening."

"You talk to your wife today?"

"No."

"Right. Because of what happened at jug-up. You really stepped in there, from what I heard."

"What about my wife?" He wanted to keep Felicia as far away from this as possible. But he thought he saw where it was heading. It grinded his gut, made him want to vomit.

"Well, you should talk to her. Hear what she has to say."

"If anyone goes anywhere near my family…"

She raised her eyebrows and stared. "Nate said you was a cool customer. But maybe that's just for show, huh? Maybe you're just an angry motherfucker like every other motherfucker in here."

A guard – the other one, who had brought Russo in – called over. "Hey. Tone it down."

Kim raised her hand and demurred.

"I'm cool," Russo said to Kim, imagining himself leaping across the table and taking off her head.

Flowers in a nice field and Zoe laughing…

Kim lowered her hand. "Good, that's what I wanted to hear. That's what I believe, too, Russo. I know someone who can handle their business when I see them. Nate does too. Someone who can follow through. And you'll want to follow through – remember what I said about mutually assured destruction?"

"What am I supposed to do?" He felt heavy, ill, but he had to admit – the thought of getting out of here, under any circumstances, was appealing. Maybe it was a con – *probably* it was a con, and he just didn't see the angle yet, but what if it was real?

"The article you read," Kim said, "that happened upstate. And I don't mean Westchester. I mean, way the fuck upstate. God's Country. Redneck central. They call it the Adirondacks. You ever heard of that before?"

"Yeah I think so."

Kim nodded as if this was all fine and good. "I have something up there. Something that I need to get back. You're going to go get it for me." She paused, perhaps for effect, or for him to let it settle in a bit.

Drugs or money, probably. It wasn't her grandmother's old sewing machine, that was for sure.

Kim leaned in, her eyes narrowing to points. "This is the one and only time you're going to meet me, Russo. I had to pull a lot of strings to make this happen. And you know, by pulling strings I mean…" She pantomimed giving a blowjob. "A one-time opportunity. You need to decide, right now."

It seemed like when he wasn't suffering through intake procedures, bus rides, and holding cells, he was forced to make sudden decisions. A hurry-up-and-wait kind of world.

"As a bonus," Kim said, "I can throw in a nice phone call to your wife. Make sure you get to talk to her today instead of having to wait the twenty-four hours."

"For real?"

"Yeah."

"Why?"

"Why does anyone do anything? It's in my interest. Just like helping you. You decide what you're going to do, let me know, and I'll tell you how to do it. Like I said, talk it over with your wife."

"But why me?"

Kim leaned back a little, their eyes connected. "Let me worry about that."

"When can I call my wife? Right now?"

"Soon as you walk out of here. Your CO will take you right to the phone. I'm really good at what I do." She pressed her tongue into her cheek and winked.

In the end, the thought of talking to Felicia, hearing his wife's voice, was what did it.

*

"Jimmy?"

She sounded scared. Usually Felicia didn't get scared – when the cops were at their house hooking him up, she'd been concerned, even pissed, but not scared.

"What's the matter, baby? What is it?" Russo tried to stay calm. There were several other inmates making their calls from the phone bank, and one glanced over, like he could smell trouble.

Russo turned his back to the inmate as Felicia continued, "Jimmy, someone's been here."

Son of a bitch. No. "What do you mean someone's been there? At the house?"

"Yes, Jimmy, at the house."

Russo could hear little Zoe start crying in the background. Zoe cried, all babies cried, but Zoe was real chill. She'd come into the world with this kind of placid expression on her face – Russo had been there, propping up his wife on the hospital bed, and Zoe had come out, and she'd been just like a little Buddha or something, blinking up at them.

There were tears suddenly sheeting his vision. What the hell had he gotten his girls into?

"Hold on, Jimmy…"

He heard the phone clatter, and then the muffled sound of his wife shushing the baby. But Zoe was inconsolable.

He waited, twisting the phone line, glancing over his shoulder. More inmates were watching him, even the CO standing in the corner seemed to eavesdrop. Russo hunched his shoulders and tried to close his body over the phone booth, like he could protect his family this way.

Ten, nine, eight…

Finally Felicia came back on, and Zoe was still crying, closer, because Felicia was probably holding her. "I tried to put her down for a nap. She's not having it."

"What's wrong with her? Who's there, babe? What are you talking about?" His voice was an urgent whisper.

"Jimmy, there's a guy."

Zoe was really wailing now. Russo could barely hear his wife. "A guy? You said a guy?"

"He's been outside all day, off and on. Walks with a limp."

"What? Babe, I can hardly understand what…"

"He's wearing this black coat. He's there, he leaves, he comes back. He stares up at the house. I would go out there, but—"

"No," Russo said, his volume rising. Screw the rest of them if they heard. "Don't talk to him, don't look at him."

This had to be what Kim Delahunt was inferring – some guy, working with her, on the outside. Russo and Felicia lived in an okay neighborhood, with its share of weirdos, a few drunks who talked to themselves as they staggered home from the bar, but this was different.

"Stay inside the house," Russo said. Then he blurted, "Call the cops. Call County – talk to that woman, Barbieri."

The baby kept howling, and Felicia set the phone down again. Russo didn't know if Felicia had heard what he said about the cops. A few seconds later, Zoe stopped crying. Then Felicia came back on.

"What did you do? Knock her out?" Russo had calmed a little, trying humor.

"I'm giving her a bottle."

"Honey," Russo said, taking a breath, "this guy, is he outside now?"

"No. He left, I don't know, about fifteen minutes ago. Then I started to put Zoe down."

"Did you hear me about the cops? Call the cops."

"I already did. They told me they'd send someone around – that was over an hour ago. Where were you today?"

Russo closed his eyes and ran a hand over his face. He tried to ease the tension developing in his neck by rolling his shoulders back, standing up straighter. "I'm really sorry, babe, about that. Stuff out of my control. My cellmate got into it with someone in the cafeteria and I was standing there. I had to talk to the… listen, I'm sorry."

She didn't say anything. Russo pictured Felicia and Zoe sitting in the kitchen at the table, beside the old landline phone they'd kept from when her grandparents lived in the place. Zoe sucking down a bottle of milk.

After a moment, he resumed the low voice and said, "Tell me again about this guy."

"He's fucking weird, is what. Black jeans and jean jacket. Acts like he has a bad leg. I don't know what else to say."

"How tall?"

"Uhm, maybe six feet. Skinny."

"And the cops haven't come yet."

"No."

"Alright. You've got the door locked, I'm sure. Listen, I want you to call Jockey."

"Jockey? Hell no."

"Babe, listen to me—"

"I don't want his big ass up in here, knocking everything over, raiding the fridge. He'll eat everything in sight. And isn't he the one who got us in all this trouble in the first place? I knew I shouldn't let you go out that night. You don't think I know what you're doing, but I do. Yeah, we met a little later in life, Jimmy, and I know you've got a past…"

Russo wanted to argue, but waited.

"Shit," Felicia said. "I'm going to have to go back to work. I don't have a problem with going back to work, but who am I going to get for Zoe? That woman, Theresa, she's still all filled up with kids. And forget that other place. Dirty floors, runny-nosed kids watching TV all day, nuh-uh. No way."

They'd already had many talks about Felicia going back to work, but Russo hadn't wanted it. He wouldn't stop her, he just preferred Felicia stay home with the baby. At least for another few months or so. Zoe was a dynamite kid, walking for months already, a quick study. But she was only going to be a baby once. They wanted more kids, but not until their finances changed.

"I don't care what Jock eats," Russo said. "Let him eat the fucking furniture."

"Don't curse at me, James…"

"I'm not cursing *at* you, I'm just cursing. He—"

"Fine. I'll call him. Does he even know? Does he even know what his dumb ass caused having you drive his car that night? That's what you did, isn't it, Jimmy? He was having some stupid problem and you went and bailed him out. Now look at you."

"No," Russo said softly. "He doesn't know."

His real name was Horatio, but they'd called him Jockey since he was a kid. At ten years old his meteoric growth had outstripped his supply of clothes, and his parents sent him to school in high-water pants so small and tight that the other kids said they looked like the clothes of a horse jockey.

To his credit, Jockey embraced the nickname as a point of pride, which shut everybody up.

He was loyal, and the guy could bench something like two-eighty. He worked as a janitor for an elementary school on Staten Island. But he hadn't always.

"Call him. Have him swing by, have a look. If this guy shows up again, Jockey will talk to him, see what's up. I'll call you back as soon as I can. Listen, Feef, I'm gonna get out of here."

"Alright," she said, sounding resigned and distant. Tired, too. Between the baby and her locked-up husband…

"I mean it, Fifi."

"You're getting out?"

"Yeah."

"Just like that?"

"I'll explain later."

A silence developed and he listened to the clicking sound on the line as the jail recorded the conversation.

"I love you," he said.

The baby started fussing again, and at the same time the CO came up behind Russo and told him his time was up.

"Feef? I gotta go."

More crying, and if she said something, he didn't hear. He tried waiting, but the CO was looming and Russo was already in hot water. He hung up the phone, feeling like complete shit.

CHAPTER THIRTEEN

Where the new bridge was going in, there was a crumbling chasm and workers had laid out a massive plastic sheet over one side of the scree to prevent erosion.

Brett watched as men with suits and hard hats stood around on the far side, either hustling about or huddled in pockets of serious conversation. Callahan was among them, looking stressed. There were problems with the project and things were tense.

Traffic was reduced to one lane and 45 miles per hour northbound and south. It had taken weeks just to redirect the highway – Brett had been one of the workers to roll the crossover road. There had been setbacks, some big rainstorms, but lately it had been the heat everyone was contending with. Heat and rumors of being temporarily shut down by the state.

Sitting in his soil roller, Brett ate lunch and flipped through his phone. The bank robberies had taken place three and a half years before and there was a glut of articles, most of them around that time, with a few flimsy follow-ups.

He found much of what Morales said confirmed – the press had dubbed Nate Reuter, Kim Delahunt, and Jerry Oberst "The Fighting Bandits." After ripping off the NCFA coffers for a paltry $1,338 in cash, the Fighting Bandits had knocked over two banks on the same day, the first in Plattsburgh, the second in Lake Placid.

A week later, the crew hit two more banks, again in the same day. These were in Glens Falls and Lake George, a ways south of Plattsburgh and Lake Placid. Then a final bank takeover in Albany.

Police had quickly linked the bank robberies to the NCFA heist and had been out in full force to capture the bandits. The FBI had sunk its teeth in too, forming the joint task force with the state police and several County Sheriff's Offices that Morales had mentioned. But it was the actions of a brazen, off-duty cop during the Albany heist which brought them down.

The crew was hit with a slew of charges, but none considered "aggravated," since no one had been armed for any of the takeovers.

The results of their court cases were harder to find. But it seemed that Oberst got the stiffest sentence, since he had priors and was considered the "mastermind." He'd been one of Reuter's trainers, and the police opined that after Reuter had lost a title bout fight, Oberst felt slighted.

Oberst had then convinced Reuter they needed to rip off the NCFA. Kim Delahunt joined them in the effort. But with such a meager haul and a taste for theft, the bandits had moved on to the banks.

Brett wanted to know how much it had all added up to, but the papers weren't reporting any amounts besides the NCFA heist.

"Bank robbery cases the media picks up on distort the reality of the situation," Investigator Reed was quoted in the paper as saying. "Movies and TV make it seem like there's this big payday waiting. But there's not. That's what we believe pushed the Fighting Bandits to keep going. It becomes like an addiction – you can never get enough."

Brett scanned one article after another, hunting for a total amount, but there was nothing.

A worker yelled from the ground, "Larson! Lunch is over! Callahan wants to talk to all of us."

Callahan scuffed his way over, kicking up construction dust in the dry morning.

"That's all she wrote." He was red-faced and sweating. "Transportation Board has got to review the specs. No more work today, tomorrow is a no-go, too. Maybe Monday we come back, fuck if I know."

The retinue of suit-wearing men in hard hats was still milling around, glancing in Brett's direction. Callahan looked like he was going to have a heart attack by the end of the day, the way he was going. Maybe it was best he caught a break.

"Get out of here," Callahan said to the crew. He seemed to sag as if his bones could no longer support his weight.

Brett jumped on the bike and didn't look back. Instead of taking the usual route home, he bulleted south on the interstate until he came to roughly the spot he thought abutted on his property. He pulled off onto the shoulder and dismounted the bike, imagining someone entering the woods from this spot, never to return. To wind up with pieces of themselves scattered in his backyard in a shallow grave.

The cars blew past as he moved closer to the edge of the woods. He checked his phone for an internet signal and searched for the *Press-Republican*. Meg was currently working there as assistant to the features editor.

For a moment he just held his phone, looking at her number. Then he made the call.

"Brett?" She sounded tentative. "How are you?"

"Good, Meg."

"Yeah? Oh my God, you're like a total celebrity now." She laughed, the same way he remembered her laughing years ago, with a brittle tension. "And your wife is *beautiful*. So happy for you. What are you up to these days?"

"Working for Fleece Brothers. Doing construction."

"Oh… wow. Okay. Cool."

"Actually working on a big job right now, on 87."

"Ohh," she said, "so that's *you* guys messing with my commute…" She was growing more playful, relaxed. "I hear there's a little trouble there?"

"Yeah, that's us."

"Hard to picture you on a road crew." She fell silent.

Brett felt a tightening in his chest, wondering if this had been a mistake. "Listen, reason I'm calling is, I'm curious about something. It happened a few years ago – do you remember the Fighting Bandits?"

"I think so. I mean, I think that was before I was working here."

"Oh, okay."

"But what do you want to know? Maybe I can help… Wait – is there some connection between those robberies and the remains on your property?"

She was quick.

He winced, thinking he was possibly in the wrong, giving a reporter ideas about something during an open investigation. "No," he lied, "I don't think so."

"Oh." She sounded disappointed.

"But, you know, I might, uhm…"

"Brett, are you thinking of writing a story on this? Like a freelance piece?"

"Yeah, maybe." He exhaled. "Or maybe a book." He stared into the woods, feeling mixed emotions. The last time he'd seriously tried writing, it had interfered with his personal life. It had, in a way, ended their relationship. She had to be thinking it, too.

"Brett, that's great. Good for you."

"Yeah?" A relief. Maybe he'd dodged a bullet, and the past was in the past. "You think you could help me out?"

"Totally, of course. What can I do?"

"Just a few questions. Do you have time?"

"Absolutely. I could go through the archives and see what we've got on the… What were they called?"

"The Fighting Bandits." Brett straightened up and focused. "So, one thing I'd like to know is, I mean, I went through the *Press-Republican* articles, all the articles I could find, and really nowhere does it talk about their total haul. How much they got."

"Oh, yeah, no. One thing I can tell you is you're not going to see that."

"Is it illegal or something to disclose that? Maybe it puts other banks in danger if people find out how much is kept in a vault, or whatever?"

"Well, it's not *illegal*, per se. Most of the time it's not reported because it's not a very big amount. You know, we're in the business of sensational headlines, and a five-hundred-dollar robbery is not very sensational."

"I thought maybe case law established that publishing the amount of stolen money could open the publisher up to civil damages."

"Listen to you." She sounded pleased, then grew serious. "Well yeah, there could be some concern about that, a bank suing a paper because they emboldened some would-be robbers, but case law can't make something illegal. It would be a pretty clear First Amendment violation to block newspapers from publishing the amount of money stolen from a bank. You know, what it could be is a lot of things. Like, the bank didn't want it reported. Or, maybe the police asked for it to be suppressed. I mean they can't, legally, enforce that – it would be unconstitutional. But maybe they had an arrangement or something with the banks, and asked the banks not to disclose it to the press. Maybe you just need to ask the cops how much they recovered."

Or maybe they didn't recover all of it, he thought, feeling a thrill.

"Listen, thanks so much." He headed back to the motorcycle.

"Sure. Hey, why don't we get together? Maybe I can help you with this book. I mean, I don't want to be presumptuous. Jesus, that just totally came out wrong. And now I'm babbling. Help…"

"No, stop. It's cool. Yeah, let me, ah – let me just keep mulling this over, get my bearings on it. I'll call you again, okay? We can meet up, you know. Catch up…"

"Alright, sure. Great."

"It was good to talk to you."

"You too, Brett."

"I'll be in touch, alright?"

He hung up, put his phone away, and draped himself over the bike. Maybe he should just let the whole thing go. Here he was, worried from the moment he'd found the bones that this thing could upend his life, and now he was sniffing around, calling a newspaper for information, getting involved with an old girlfriend.

He got going on the bike and drove home fast, as if he could out-race the sense of guilt.

CHAPTER FOURTEEN

Russo hated feeling anxious and was generally unaccustomed to it. But this was brutal. He had no one to talk to, no way to know what was happening on the outside. He'd heard nothing about how Nate was doing, either. He couldn't eat, couldn't sleep. Another night had passed listening to echoing voices, the clanking, the dripping, the footsteps of the guards as they checked cells.

He kept going around and around about what to do.

He paced his cell, did some push-ups, paced some more until he'd exhausted himself.

He lay down in the bunk, breathing hard, turning it all over in his mind.

This odd guy, Felicia had said. Limping around outside. Dressed in black. Looking up at the house.

Russo hoped she'd called Jockey. Maybe the cops had finally responded to her call, too.

Only now he felt torn about getting the cops involved.

On the one hand, Kim Delahunt's offer sounded like a fantasy. Like something an inmate cooked up to amuse themselves, or a con. If so, then the cops were the way to go.

Because, why him? If this woman needed something picked up, why not hire some thug on the outside? Why go to all this trouble?

Leverage, he figured. Hiring someone on the outside was a huge variable, probably tough to control. With Russo, Delahunt had something to hang over his head. Whatever she was after was worth it to her to pay Russo's bail and blow a few prison guards.

So, on the other hand, if it was a real offer, maybe he needed to keep a lid on it. If the cops hadn't shown up at the house yet, it might be for the best. Getting police further involved might only piss Delahunt off, and put Felicia and Zoe in more danger.

Plus, he'd already told Felicia he was getting out. It had just come out of him in a rush, wanting to soothe her, to protect her and the baby. So for now, he needed to play ball.

Someone rapped on the door, startling him.

Russo ambled over as the slot slid open.

"Newspaper." The inmate who delivered things slipped it through and Russo took it, glancing at the headlines. Nothing about the human remains story.

"Delahunt wants your answer."

The paper-deliverer was still in the corridor. Russo bent and peered through the slot. It was now or never.

"Tell her I'll do it."

"Check the sports section."

The slot slammed closed inches from his nose. Russo scooped up the paper and sat down on the toilet. He hunted for the sports section and opened it up. A single sheet of paper slipped out and wafted to the floor.

He grabbed it. Four sentences in scratchy handwriting:

My associate will bond you out in the morning.
Take Trailways bus from Port Authority to Lake Placid.
Your contact will meet you there and give you further instructions.
Rip this note and flush it.

Russo reread the note several times, then obeyed the last instructions. As he watched the shreds swirling down the drain, he thought what Delahunt wanted him to retrieve was probably drugs.

But whatever it was, it wouldn't be good, and could only bring more trouble.

Saying yes had been the right thing, whether Delahunt was legit or not. Now all he had to do was get bailed out, go home, and put a stop to it. Delahunt was small time, it seemed. She wasn't omniscient, and she was hard-up for help. He would put an end to it at home, call the cops if he absolutely had to.

He felt a little better, like he'd made a decision at last.

Just for safe measure, he did some more push-ups. If nothing else, spending time in the joint was getting him back into shape.

CHAPTER FIFTEEN

After dinner, Emily had a "honey-do" list for Brett. "You can start with the mousetraps," she said. "One more mouse jumps out and scares me, I'm going to pop this baby out prematurely."

Brett was eager to get to work on the book, but he happily obliged. Emily was the furthest thing from "high maintenance" and asked very little of him in the way of domestic chores. If there was something she needed, it was a legitimate issue. And he'd been listening to the mice in the walls night after night, fantasizing about catching one and flaying it alive while its cousins looked on in terror.

The previous owners had left behind various things with the sale of the house, including some gardening tools, some old Christmas decorations, ant bait, and some mousetraps. Brett headed down into the basement, trying to remember where he'd put the traps when he'd cleaned up down there the last time.

He didn't love the basement. As far as basements went, this one was on the unappealing end of the spectrum. Emily had ventured down a couple times, but it freaked her out and she generally avoided it.

The four windows were high, small, and covered in cobwebs. If you purchased a home with a sloped lot, you might get a nice basement walkout, but the farmhouse they'd bought only had the standard cellar doors, made from heavy-gauge steel which had probably once been fire-engine red. Now the doors were a rusty brown, more cobwebs festooned in the precast space beneath them.

The ground was uneven, the concrete cracked in several places due to hydrostatic pressure and the settling of the house over years. The boiler in the corner was in relatively good shape, and only a few years old, whereas everything else in the damp space was ancient. It was a place, Brett thought, where Indiana Jones might find a lost artifact. And all he wanted to find were the mousetraps.

He eventually located them high on the shelves, which were against the back wall beside the cellar door. He pulled out a plastic bag containing several mousetraps clattering together.

He spent a few minutes cleaning the rust off with a wire brush, then gave up on the idea and decided to buy new ones after work the next day. These old things wouldn't kill a mouse. If the traps even sprung, they'd probably disintegrate into dust.

He joined Emily back upstairs and they finished the dishes together, then streamed *The Americans* on Netflix. Emily fell asleep in the middle of an episode after mumbling how the first trimester of a pregnancy made a lot of women tired. Brett helped her to bed after the show. He felt restless and went into Emily's small office.

She'd been organizing, and the space was really coming together. He sat down at her computer.

The cops had connected the human remains to the Fighting Bandits even though Morales said the remains hadn't yet been identified. As unwieldy as the detective had acted, Brett believed him. He knew, at least, without a skull and teeth, it would be hard to make an identification. And DNA testing and matching took a long time.

That left Dr. Rhea Runic, or, really, the Hurricane Road address, to link the bones with the bandits. And now there was the possibility of unrecovered heist money.

He brought up a Google map of the Hurricane property and looked at all the places surrounding it. What he needed wouldn't be on the internet. He needed to see the deed history of the house, but he doubted someone could just waltz into the county offices and ask to see a property's entire history. Could they?

What little he could find online was that the property had been donated and was lined up to be renovated, though it was unclear when work would begin.

He searched for Alma Colby next, found her obituary in the online version of the local paper.

So far, everything Morales had said was checking out.

There was a knock on the downstairs door, giving him a start. It came again, soft but audible. A second later, his phone buzzed on the table.

He started down the stairs, stopped, went back into the bedroom, and grabbed the baseball bat.

Moving with a bit more assurance, he descended to the front door, checking the silhouette against the drape. It looked like a woman.

Meg was standing on the porch. His old college girlfriend was smiling, holding her phone with her thumb hovering over the screen.

She glanced at the bat as he stepped out.

"Oh shit – are you…?" She backed up, unafraid but alarmed. She was holding a stack of newspapers, and kept jerking her eyes towards the windows. "I'm sorry, oh, man. I knew it was too late."

He closed the door and set the bat against the wall. "No, no. It's okay. What's going on?"

"Did I wake your wife?" Still glancing at the house as if she expected to see Emily looming in the windows like Norman Bates in *Psycho*. "That's why I called you, I shouldn't have knocked…"

"It's okay. Sorry to scare you. Come on, sit down."

They took to the porch steps and she balanced the stack of papers on her knees. "I brought you these. I know you can find them online but I thought it, you know, sometimes it's better to just hold something in your hands."

She looked pretty much like he remembered her. Meg had always been self-conscious about her weight, which you could only understand if you knew her mother and two sisters. They had perpetually been on some diet, obsessing over everything that passed their lips, and yet not a single one of them had carried a detectable ounce of fat.

Regardless, Meg tended to prefer black clothing, as if it would hide the extra pounds which existed solely in her mind. Her hair was light blonde, pulled back in a clip, spilling down around her ears and neck. She wore Blundstone boots, a pair of designer jeans. She looked like a hip reporter. He was happy she was doing so well.

He took a newspaper off the stack. There was a picture of the Glens Falls Sun & Trust bank on the front page, and the headline read:

FIGHTING BANDITS HIT GLENS FALLS

He skimmed the article for a second, just the usual where and when, and then turned to Meg.

She was watching him with a little grin. "You look good, Brett. This is a nice place."

"Thank you. And thanks for bringing these…"

"Yeah, of course."

He glanced at her car in the driveway, a silver Subaru Impreza. "You just on your way home from work?"

"Yeah. Sometimes I don't get out of there until late. And, you know, I stuck around to pull these papers together for you."

"It's really great. You live close by?"

"I live in Essex."

"Oh, so you're pretty close."

"Yeah, pretty close. It's just a little out of the way. I'm right near the water – I can see the ferry coming and going."

"Awesome, Meg." It was awkward sitting so close to her. He hadn't seen her in years. He could still remember her speech about why she was breaking up with him. How, in her words, he seemed to sabotage his own potential.

He took a breath, trying to shake the memory. "Hey, you know, I wonder – is one of these articles about the off-duty cop who got in a tussle with the bank robbers?"

Her eyes lingered on him for a second, but then she shuffled through the stack. "Yup. I think so…"

He waited while she searched, but she couldn't come up with it. There were about fifteen papers. More than he had found on the web, for sure. "It's alright," he said. "I'll look through them."

"So, you're really doing this, huh? Writing a book?"

He shrugged, and felt the blood flush his skin. "Yeah. I guess it depends on where it all goes, though."

"I think it's great. Can I see where you found the bones?"

He gave her a look. He'd expected maybe she would say something about their past, perhaps to clear the air, but she was more interested in the story.

"I'm sorry," she said, stepping away. "I know it's so late. Maybe I should go…"

Brett glanced down at his sock feet. "No, hold on a second. We'll go take a look."

He found his boots inside, listening for sounds of Emily upstairs. The guilt was back, weighing on him, but Emily had conceded to his writing the book and that's all this was – research.

He took Meg out into the back field, using a flashlight to light their way. The fireflies were out, winking on and off, and the crickets were singing. They tromped through the grass and goldenrod until they got to the edge of the excavation.

"Holy shit," Meg said. She walked around the edge, pointed towards the center. "You found them somewhere in there, right?

I mean, I've seen the pictures and read the reports, but this is... wow. Are they going to fill all this back in? They're done, right?"

Her voice was loud, excited, and he gave the house a glance over his shoulder. The upstairs light was still off.

"Yeah, they're done. Basically. They asked if they could keep it like this for a few more days, then they'll fill it back in. They took a lot of pictures, soil samples, everything. But they didn't find any more bones after that first day. Just a foot, most of an arm – no fingers, though – and a hip bone. Whadyoucallit, a pelvis."

"Right, right. Wow. What a thing, huh? I bet you guys were just like, *what* is going on, right?"

"Yeah, it's been strange. Having all the cops here, the reporters, getting asked all the questions. You almost feel like you did something wrong."

She gave him another one of her looks, eyes sparkling in the moonlight. "Yeah. Shit. Look at me; I've got you all the way out here. I'm gonna get out of your hair."

They started back, Meg walking faster ahead of him. She said over her shoulder, "I'd like to meet your wife sometime. Emily, right?"

"Yeah. Emily." He caught up to her. "So this off-duty guy... like I said, I'll take a look. You remember anything?"

"Uhm, I remember he pulled his gun. It was their last robbery, I think. It was the one in Albany."

"So he was a city cop? Or county? Or what? I guess I'll see."

"Yeah I can't remember. I was just an intern. I mean this was, what? Three years ago? Three and a half?"

"About that," he said, not really remembering. When all this was happening, he and Emily had been in a brand new relationship together, that time when the rest of the world pretty much fades from existence.

He considered that since the bank robbers had been unarmed, the penalties could've been lighter. As long as no one got seriously hurt.

Wondering about when the Fighting Bandits might get out of jail, he walked Meg to her car and she nodded at the stack of papers left on the porch. "Let me know if you need anything else, okay?"

"Thanks again, Meg. Really nice of you."

"I want a big fat credit in your book." She winked and got behind the wheel.

He raised his hand in the sweep of her headlights as she backed out and pulled away. Then he gathered up the papers and returned inside, feeling an odd mixture of relief and dissatisfaction.

He stayed on the main floor, kicking off his boots and going through the papers at the kitchen island. He pored over the articles. At one point he tiptoed back upstairs for a notebook and pen. Then he kept going, and halfway through the stack he came across the article in the *Star-Tribune* on the Albany bank robbery.

The headline read:

HERO DEPUTY INTERRUPTS BANK HEIST

His name was Gentry Parker and he was a Sheriff's Deputy with Rensselaer County. Parker was smiling brightly in the inset picture, in his fifties, with wavy salt-and-pepper hair, uniform pressed, and decorations spangling.

The first half of the article laid out the specifics of the robbery, more where and when, and then the second half got into Parker's involvement.

Parker had sensed an opportunity to intervene when two of the three bank robbers were arguing near one of the tellers.

Brett was impressed. He imagined the gumption it took to try and stop people crazy enough to attempt a bank robbery. Even though they weren't carrying weapons, unarmed gangs could be more dangerous, according to the research he'd done. They were most likely to inflict injuries to victims during the commission of their crime compared to other types of robbers, alone or in groups. But they were the *least* likely of all types of bank robberies to fail in their efforts. Parker had upended that second statistic.

Brett wanted to talk to him.

There was definitely a story here. He could feel the current of it, like electricity hidden in the walls. This thing was humming.

He put the papers back together after making a few notes. Unfortunately it was too late to call the Rensselaer County Sheriff's Department – it was past midnight. It would be unprofessional.

He left the kitchen, hitting the light switch.

As he climbed the stairs in the darkness, the glow of the unfurling story dimmed.

By the time he was removing his shoes in the bedroom, he felt worried again.

He felt dread.

He stood looking at his wife, their child growing within her.

He tried to name his fear.

Missing money, that was part of it. Bewildering cops like Morales, drinking beer, staring out at that rain-grayed ranch like a guy left behind on the sidelines of life. Getting involved with old girlfriends like Meg.

Maybe they were signs.

He slipped beneath the covers.

He was starting a new family. He was a newlywed and a homeowner. There was a lot on the line.

He needed to talk it all over with his wife.

CHAPTER SIXTEEN

Russo was out.

Or, almost.

He was in out-processing, getting his things back.

From there he was sent to the bullpen to wait for the bus. He dug through the bag of his returned possessions and his hand closed around his cell phone. He moved to the wall away from other people and started keying in his home number, then stopped.

Felicia was as sharp as they came. Even from the landline, she'd know the difference between a call from his cellular and a call from the jail. He moved to one of the pay phones in the bullpen and dialed out.

"I know who the guy is," Russo said to Felicia. "In the black jeans. He's a bail bondsman." It was mostly the truth.

"A bail bondsman?"

There was something so wrong with this, lying to his wife – but at the same time, he could taste freedom.

"Yes, Feef. A bail bondsman. Like a bank loan, only for the bail."

"I *know* what a bondsman is, Jimmy, you don't have to mansplain it to me. You hired him?"

"Yeah. I hired him." He'd promised himself he would never lie to Felicia. But was there another way?

"I don't understand… why didn't you just tell me you hired him before?"

"Did the cops come?"

"Twice. He wasn't here… He disappeared before they came."

"Was it Barbieri?"

"Who?" Felicia sounded agitated.

"The female cop who hooked me up."

"No, it wasn't her, Jimmy. I didn't invite them in for coconut pudding. Two cops got out of a police car, came up and knocked and I gave them a description, told them what time he'd come around. The second time I just saw the police car drive by. They didn't stop."

So the cops had been there. There would be a report. But the bail had gone through, so Delahunt hadn't pulled out. No need to get the police further involved, he could take care of it on his own from here.

"What about Jockey?"

"Oh, Jockey is here. Yeah, he's upstairs sleeping in the baby's room."

"Did he talk to the guy?"

"Jockey said he was coming over last night after work. Okay? He gets here at ten o'clock, smelling like a distillery. He's been sleeping it off all morning. Great friends you got, Jimmy."

Russo didn't care – it was actually good news. He was in the clear. "The guy was hanging out because he was soliciting," Russo explained. He was surprised how easily the lie came, like he'd never stopped pulling it over on Felicia. "When I asked in here about him, they said, 'Check the American Bail Coalition.' So I did, and that's where I found him."

"What?" She was banging around in the kitchen, Zoe babbling in the background, probably in her high chair. "The guy *hangs outside* my house – that's his way of getting business? Why didn't he just come to the jail? Or knock on our door?"

"I know, he's kind of a weirdo. I'm sorry about all of this, honey." Russo shut his eyes, hoping she would just let it go. Too many more questions and either he would cave or she would smell something rotten. She probably already did, but she was as eager for his release as he was. He hoped, anyway.

"Well, alright." She sounded exasperated, but convinced.

Russo opened his eyes. *Thank you, God.* The next part, though, would be even harder. Even if he planned to go right home and blow off this deal with Delahunt, he wanted to be smart about it. If he had to change his mind for any reason, he'd need a buffer zone. Felicia couldn't expect his return right away.

"So when will he post your bail? When will you get out?"

There she was with the question, right on cue.

"It might take a couple of days. Process the paperwork, get in to see the judge. I gotta wait on my lawyer to get here, too, so we can get it all set up." In truth, it hadn't taken long at all. Kim Delahunt's associate had posted cash bail directly to the jail, the quickest way to be released.

If he ended up home straight away, he'd modify his story.

And he planned to. He imagined himself cozy in bed with his two precious girls that night.

"What did you put up as collateral?"

Russo felt punched in the gut, even hunched over. Damnit. This is what happened when you married a smart Puerto Rican girl who'd grown up with four brothers.

Felicia went on, "We don't have a car. You don't have any other assets... Russo, did you use the *house*?"

"No, I didn't use the house, Feef. Jesus. Don't worry what I put up. I've got my own means, okay?"

"Mmhmm." She wasn't buying it, but she let it go. Her voice softened and she said, "Alright, baby. We'll see you when you get out. You'll understand I'm not taking the ferry and the bus all the way back out there again, right?"

"I know... I know. Okay. I gotta go."

"Okay, Jimmy, be safe... So we're not going to see this weirdo again, are we?"

"No," Russo said, hoping it was true.

"Okay..." Felicia moved the phone from her mouth and Russo heard her shout, "Jockey! Get up! Time to get out of my house!"

He hung up. That part was over. He still felt like crap for all the deceit, but he was on his way home. One way or another, he was going to get back to his girls. Nothing would stand in his way.

Freedom never tasted so good – even the stink of the place didn't seem as bad as he walked to the bus.

No shackles on him, back in his clothes from five mornings ago. The sun was just rising above the ocean as the bus carried him over the Hazen Street Bridge into Queens. In Queens he'd pick up the subway. Rikers didn't offer transportation from the prison direct to Staten Island, he needed to take the ferry from Whitehall Street in lower Manhattan to St. George.

Queens Plaza was a huge network of roads, elevated trains, park walkways, and swathes of green landscaping. The airbrakes hissed and the bus let Russo out.

Everything was wonderful. The birds tweeting and flitting amid the pin oaks, the people moving through the park, chatting, bicyclists zipping by with puffy backpacks, the rattle of the subway as it rolled into the elevated station.

Russo jogged up the stairs with extra energy and found the platform for the M train.

A sign hanging above the tracks read: *8 Ave Local via 53 St to World Trade Center. Late nights on opposite track.*

It had been years since he'd been at Queens Plaza. He was surprised to see "World Trade Center" still written in as the destination for late nights on the E train. The last time he'd been here, the twin towers had actually been standing.

The subway came blasting through in a warm rush, pulling along the ammonia-stink of brakes. When the doors opened, Russo boarded and sat down next to a pair of skinny, bearded hipsters. As the subway rolled towards the tunnel, he eavesdropped on their conversation.

They were covering topics like "creative culture" and "remix-ing" and he lost interest. He glanced across the car at a black man sitting alone. Russo recognized the guy from the plaza; he'd been standing close as the subway had rolled in. The man caught Russo looking and stared back just as the subway plunged into the dark tunnel and headed beneath the river.

The lights flickered as the subway blasted through the tunnel. When the man stood up, he moved in strobe-like pictures, then sat down beside Russo.

They rocketed out of the tunnel.

"Feels good to be out, huh?"

"Say what?" Russo was on guard. "Do I know you?"

He saw signs for *53rd Street* blasting by.

The guy took something out of his pocket. "Nice to get your shit back. I been inside, too." He held up the phone, studying it. Russo's good feelings started to drain away. He debated just getting away from the man sitting next to him. Guy said he was an ex-con. It was like prison was following Russo, and he wanted to shake it loose.

"There's always that first call," the guy said. "Who's it gonna be?" His lips split in a toothy grin.

Russo felt something tingling at the base of his neck. The subway chattered along, an express, next stop Port Authority.

"Maybe we'll call my buddy in St. George."

The guy turned and faced Russo. Russo saw a shaved slice in one of his raised eyebrows.

The guy said, "I'll tell him everything be good. You're on your way. Adirondack Trailways bus at nine fifteen, you on it, no need to hurt the women."

At their mention, Russo felt a flash of anger. He glanced around. The hipster couple had gotten up and were standing by the doors.

Russo grabbed the guy by his shirt and leaned in close. "You don't touch them."

"No," said the ex-con, barring his teeth. "I don't. *He* does. Richard. And Richard is one twisted fuck. You gotta get on that bus, Russo. You don't, or you call the cops, or you do something to me... It won't be good."

The subway rolled to a stop.

Russo got off. He threw a look back and saw the man step off, too.

Port Authority was a mob scene. Russo hadn't been here recently either. Working for the MTA for the past couple years, they'd moved him around a bit, but he'd yet to work a really crowded hub like this.

He climbed out of the bowels of the station to higher sublevels then walked two blocks underground to get to the bus station. His legs felt rubbery, his stomach cold.

The ex-con followed him the whole way, hanging back.

Russo stopped along the way at an ATM and checked his bank balance. It was his own private account; Felicia didn't have any access. He'd been telling the truth when he'd told Barbieri that he only had seventy-eight dollars, but he shared a joint account with Felicia as well. Last he'd looked there'd been three hundred dollars in it. She would have gone through most of that by now, but she should have enough left until he got back.

He withdrew sixty dollars from his personal account, the most he could get since the ATM only dispensed twenties. He hoped it would be enough for the bus ticket.

Fuck. He was doing this. He no longer had a choice – they were going to hurt Felicia and Zoe if he didn't do what they said. He'd been fooling himself that he could just renege on the deal.

He got to the Trailways kiosk and grabbed a fare and schedule brochure. The schedule showed that the bus left at nine fifteen like the inmate said. It was now eight forty-five.

The bus ticket to Lake Placid cost seventy-seven dollars. He didn't have another dime on him. Just the three twenties from the ATM and an empty, growling stomach.

He looked around for the ex-con. Didn't see him. How did they expect him to follow through if he couldn't even afford a ticket?

He stepped out of line and called Jockey. It was a weekday but it was early and Jockey wouldn't be at work yet. He hoped.

Jockey didn't answer, but a recording of his sleepy voice said, "Yo, I ain't here. Do your thing."

Russo huddled against the wall and left a message. "Jock. It's me. I need a favor, man. You got to call me back right away. Urgent, bro."

He hung up and looked around again. There were a dozen people in line. More were sitting against the walls, some standing in the big floor-to-ceiling windows, looking at the bus fleet outside. One of the buses was backing out of its spot, getting ready to take on passengers. His bus.

Russo swallowed his pride. He hustled around and solicited each passenger who looked at least remotely approachable. "Hi, so sorry to bother you, I'm trying to get to my daughter, and I'm seventeen dollars short..." He went on like this for ten minutes, feeling embarrassed but pushing it down inside, thinking of Zoe.

He'd raised a total of eight dollars when his phone rang. He moved to the wall again, feeling the eyes on him. He'd asked half the people around him for money by now. The doors opened and the bus driver called for people to form a queue.

Russo answered. "Jockey?"

"Jimbo? They let you keep your phone in there?"

"No. I'm out."

"You're out? You're *out*, bro? That's fantastic."

"Didn't Felicia tell you? You were there when I broke the news to her. I got bonded out. You don't remember?"

"Oh shit, oh yeah. Yeah, I guess I knew that."

Russo squeezed his eyes shut for a moment. Jockey was such an ox. He opened his eyes and gazed at the crowd lining up. He needed nine more dollars. Just nine fucking bucks away from getting this thing done. Did he need to get Jockey involved? Jockey would forget what he was doing and stop at a Dunkin Donuts before he even got here. And he worked on Staten Island – it could take him an hour to make the trip.

Russo was on his own.

"Hey I just wanted to say, you know, keep an eye on Felicia and the baby. Okay? Before work, after work – hell, call her during work. I'm out, but it's going to take me a while to get home. Felicia knows this. Okay?"

"Yeah, of course, Jimmy. I got you."

"Did you see that guy she was talking about?"

"Hey, Jimmy, why don't I just come pick you up? Get you home faster, bro."

Russo rested his head against the wall, thinking fast. Inmates had two release options, basically. Russo had opted for the early morning release. The other option was to wait in the bullpen – anywhere from twelve to thirty-six hours, depending on how many other inmates were getting out – and then take a bus to Canal Street, in Manhattan. He told Jockey he was going the Canal Street route.

"No way out of it, bro, I just gotta wait." Years of honesty and now the lies were piling up.

"Alright, man."

"Jock, did you see that guy? The skinny guy with the limp?"

"Yeah, I saw him."

Russo popped open his eyes. "You *did*?"

"Yeah, man. I seen him and he got onto a bicycle and he rode off."

"He got onto a *bicycle*?"

Boarding passengers were really looking now, and Russo realized his volume was too high and toned it down. People were slowly streaming out the doors to the garage. A Trailways worker was loading bags into the bins.

The idea that this guy, Richard, who wore black jeans and a jacket, also rode a bicycle, it was just bizarre. Russo didn't know whether to be relieved or even more worried for how bizarre it was. He started questioning the whole thing again. Maybe Delahunt was just real small time. Maybe she was mental, and playing some weird game. The whole thing could be a wild goose chase, cooked up by Delahunt and Nate because of some upstate story about human remains. All he had to do was go home right now. If this nutjob on a bicycle showed up, so what? Russo would run him off. Find out his deal first, then scare the living shit out of him.

Someone was getting close to Russo as he stood beside the wall.

Jockey kept talking in his ear. "Yeah, I told you, I got your back. I went by already this morning. I seen the guy there, coming out of the house."

"Coming out of *the house*?" Russo's voice was a pale whisper, but his veins were twisting.

The person getting close said, "Hey, hey buddy."

Russo spun around and saw a man dressed in a suit and tie, holding out a twenty dollar bill. He had a kind look on his face, a touch of nervousness in his eyes. He pushed the twenty at Russo. "To help you get to your daughter."

Russo took the bill, temporarily speechless. The man smiled and moved to the line and Russo finally said, "Thank you."

The guy raised a hand as he stepped to the back of the queue.

"What?" Jockey was saying, "Thank me for what?"

And then Russo saw the ex-con from the subway near the back of the bus station, watching Russo. He held up his phone and wiggled it.

He had to take the ex-con's threat seriously.

"Just keep an eye on them," Russo said, pulling his gaze away. "All day. Call in sick. You hear me? But don't let Felicia know you're there, Jockey. Don't go inside looking for snacks. Hit up Umberto's on the corner if you get hungry. I'll see you when I get there."

Russo hung up before Jockey could protest. Jockey would do what Russo said, and they could keep in touch by phone.

Keeping his eye on the ex-con watching him, Russo moved towards the ticket counter. It was ten after nine. He was one of the last to buy a ticket, and he had eleven bucks to spare. He jogged to the concession stand and bought a coffee in a Styrofoam cup and an enormous fritter. The coffee tasted like saltwater, but he didn't care.

He handed the bus driver his ticket and the driver smiled. Russo stepped outside into the heat and stink, and climbed onto the bus. He took one last look and saw the inmate watching him from behind the floor-to-ceiling windows.

Russo stuck up his middle finger. The guy grinned.

Then Russo took his seat. It was happening.

CHAPTER SEVENTEEN

Brett forgot about everything once Emily came walking out of the bathroom and turned over the pee cup to the nurse, who smiled and left with it. Two minutes later the gynecologist came in, said, "Congratulations, you're pregnant," and Emily and Brett were hugging and grinning all over again.

"This is wonderful news," the gynecologist said. She had voluminous brown hair and a mole on her upper lip. "Very promising, but we're really early on, so let's take good care, and come back at eight weeks, we'll have a peek with the ultrasound, alright?"

They left the hospital, drove through Lake Placid, then stopped and bought baby tomato and other vegetable plants at a place in Keene. Emily bought a pair of cloth gardening gloves – they only had size large left – and grabbed several packets of seeds. Maybe they would get lucky with a late summer, from lingering warm temps into October, and even November, and harvest the zucchini and squash and carrots. Emily had always loved the idea of gardening, but now that she was pregnant, Brett thought she was excited for it in a different way. She'd be drinking spirulina smoothies, too, and putting headphones against her belly to play classical music for the baby before long.

They decided to make one more stop, slowing as they neared the unmarked dirt driveway on Hurricane Road.

He brought the Prius to a halt and stared down the road bisecting the shimmering willow trees.

There was a vehicle parked in the distance, a black SUV, just before the turn where the road disappeared from sight.

"There could be unrecovered money stashed here," Brett said, eyeballing the distant vehicle. He didn't see Morales's silver Mercury anywhere. Maybe they were FBI.

"What?!" Emily blanched. "You're kidding me."

He told her all about the night Morales had surprised him. Their discussion about the Fighting Bandits, the suggestion that there was more to the story than what the press had reported. And he relayed Meg's visit from the night before, the lack of reporting on stolen money recovered.

"Meg Lister? Why do I know that name?"

"Because I told you about her. We dated in college."

"*That* Meg?" Emily's face bloomed with color, her forehead creased with a scowl.

He was already waving his hand in the air. "It's nothing. That's nothing…"

"Nothing? This is the girl that broke your heart, right? You're telling me there's no part of this that has to do with impressing her?"

Emily stared out the window.

"She's a source," he said. "That's all. This doesn't have anything to do with her. Just getting information."

"Alright," Emily was a bit breathless. "I want to go home."

They drove away, up the windy mountain road. Brett's trepidation grew. "I'll let it go. It's not worth it."

"No," Emily said. "That's not what I'm saying." She softened. "Listen, I'll be honest, okay, I don't love this."

"Em—"

"But, *but*, okay, I see how it affects you. Alright? I haven't seen you this… I don't know, excited, this flame lit inside you, since I don't even know when. Yeah, you're excited about the garden, but this is different. I know what it means to you." She touched his arm, and he gave her a glance as he drove.

"Thank you, baby. Just please know that… that Meg is not…"

"I know."

"I felt… I was in shitty shape back then, you know? I was drinking a lot, not going anywhere. I don't blame her for leaving."

Morales leapt to mind, particularly how he'd been twisting the wedding ring on his finger. Brett wondered if he'd been having women troubles of his own, on top of everything else.

He told Emily about it, the beers, the odd chumminess, the way the investigator seemed preoccupied.

"Sounds like he's frustrated the case has passed him by," Emily said after a moment.

"Yeah that's what I thought, too."

They fell silent.

Close to home, he said, "I'll do whatever you want. If you want me to let this all go, I will."

"No," she said again, but with more determination this time. "You shouldn't give up. Maybe you could talk to the off-duty cop, or the robbery detectives, right? Like Morales suggested."

"The robbery detectives might be a little harder to get at."

"Okay, well, try them later on then. Talk to the off-duty cop first. Or whatever you think. But just be careful, okay? I have to take care of myself, but you do, too. Alright?"

He took her hand in his. He lifted it and gave her knuckles a kiss, grateful the tension had passed.

"We need a baby name we can get good anagrams out of," Brett said. "That's important."

She thought about it. "Blaster Torn. It's a good solid name."

"Starlet if it's a girl, though."

"Agreed."

Their yellow farmhouse appeared down the road.

"We're so corny," she said.

"We totally are."

*

Emily put on a sunhat and the oversized gloves, and went out into the backyard with a small shovel. Brett watched her for a moment – she had a wheelbarrow carrying the baby plants and she set about digging spots for them in the secondary garden he'd plowed after the cops had torn up his original.

He felt an unexpected rush of love for her. Not just because she condoned his work, but for how level-headed she was. Italians were supposed to be hot-blooded and temperamental, but Emily was a rock. Sure, she had her flare-ups, but they were nominal. The way she'd responded to his reunion with Meg hadn't been bad at all.

He set himself up to work in the dining room. The spare bedroom above was going to become the baby's room, and there was no other convenient space. They didn't really need a dining room anyway – they mostly ate in the kitchen.

He'd also had the landline reconnected so they could stop screwing around trying to get cell coverage in odd corners of the upstairs.

After booting up his aging Sony laptop, Brett did a little surfing and bookmarked all the articles on "hero cop" Gentry Parker. Most of them were the same, quoting the original article from the Albany *Star-Tribune*. One provided a bit more background information on Parker: he was unmarried, no kids, and had been a cop in New York City before transferring near Albany.

Brett still didn't know precisely where to start. He was tempted to just jot down the lines already in his head, beginning the piece with his discovery in the back field while digging his garden. But something he remembered from writing in the past was how stubborn the words became once they were on the page. He needed more first.

Morales had told them about the three bank robbers. He hadn't left any photos behind, but all three Fighting Bandits were online.

Reuter was an impressive fighter. He'd gone 11 and 0 until he was defeated in a final match, which had upset expectations. Brett found several fights on YouTube and watched the twenty-two-year-old drop kick, wrestle, punch, and choke his way to victory.

It was a brutal sport, but there was a strange artistry to it. Reuter employed sophisticated-sounding moves like the "D'Arce choke," "arm bar," and the "inverted kimura." Just about every match went to the ground. That's where it seemed to be won – on the ground. After coming on like a wild animal, Reuter would get this serene look on his face. Then, like a boa, he would wrap around his opponent until his opponent "tapped out" by slapping the canvas, or Reuter.

When it was over, Reuter would spring to his feet and walk off stage without any fanfare, as if looking for his next victim. He was a machine, seemingly unstoppable until the unexpected loss of his final bout.

One article showed Reuter's mugshot – the same one Morales had shown Brett and Emily – alongside the mugshots of Kim Delahunt and Jerry Oberst. It was one of only a few articles that showed all of the Fighting Bandits together.

Brett turned his attention to Delahunt. Not as many fights online, but from what he found, she was as tenacious as Nate Reuter. He hunched over the table and flipped back through the articles to find the report of Kim Delahunt's sentencing. It took some time, but he found out she'd been sent to SCI Cold Brook, a medium-security state prison not far from where he lived. As he dug for more information on Cold Brook, an interesting article popped up, a scathing exposé on corruption within the penitentiary.

The article described how guards were accused of having sexual relations with some of the female inmates, in return for favors the guards would then grant the inmates.

There was no mention of Delahunt in the article about the Cold Brook scandal, though, and no guards had been named. But he found a link to a *New York Times* piece expanding on the scandal. It involved multiple prisons, part of a lawsuit filed by several female inmate plaintiffs.

The inmates were identified as "Jane Jones" numbers one through six. The guards were referred to only as "Officer A," "Officer B," and so on.

The lawsuit alleged that sexual abuse was "rampant and persistent in New York State prisons" and more detailed allegations cited forcible intercourse, verbal threats, harassment, and voyeurism.

Brett's palms started to sweat. He left the table and wandered into the dark kitchen, pulled a beer from the fridge, and cracked it open. He drank half in one go, swiped his mouth with the back of his hand and returned to the dining room.

He found more articles on the sexual misconduct story, some of them commenting on how not all instances of sexual relations were nonconsensual, but that sometimes female inmates used their sexuality to entice the guards, sleep with them, and then use the encounters either to string them along for favors or to blackmail them into doing those favors. The article called it "honey-trapping."

Brett noticed that this article – which came from a blog, and not a newspaper – had a string of reader comments after it, and the preponderance of those were angry backlash.

"How dare you victim-shame – you are disgusting!" read one.

"Sexist, ignorant garbage!" read another.

Brett closed it all down. The last thing he cared to do was engage in debate about prison sex – but he couldn't stop wondering if Kim Delahunt was involved. There was a good chance of it, since female inmates made up such a low portion of the state prison population – around four percent. And that was for the whole state. If there were 800 inmates at Cold Brook, that meant around 30 females.

What if she'd stashed the money from the Fighting Bandits' heists, and what if she'd told one of the guards? Maybe she'd cut one of the guards in to help assure her good behavior status, to aid in an early release. Or something.

Tomorrow was Saturday. He considered checking out Cold Brook prison, just driving past to have a look.

But if Delahunt was involved in the lawsuit, they would've likely transferred her to another prison. And he wouldn't know where.

His time would be better spent talking to Sergeant Gentry Parker.

He called the Rensselaer County Sheriff's Office.

"No," the deputy said, "we don't have a Sergeant Parker here."

Brett was momentarily speechless. He hadn't anticipated this. He mentally formed words that didn't come.

"Ah, okay, I'm sorry. I was under the impression he was with Rensselaer County…"

"He was. Parker is retired."

Brett was relieved. "Oh. Okay. Well, I'm researching a book on the Fighting Bandits. I'd like to speak to him about his role in the final robbery, if at all possible."

"Uh-huh." The deputy sounded unimpressed. "I'm not at liberty to give out his personal information."

"I understand…" His brain-mouth connection was faltering again. "Can I just ask you, uhm, is there anyone there I could talk to about the Fighting Bandits? Do you have a spokesperson, media relations, something like that?"

"Who did you say you were with again?" The deputy sounded skeptical. "Which paper?"

"I'm not with a paper. I'm doing research for my book."

"What did you say your name was?"

Brett felt a twinge of fear but knuckled under. "Brett Larson."

"Okay, Mr. Larson, let me tell you what. You've heard of a phone book, yeah? Parker has lived in the same place in Troy for thirty years. Gentry A. Parker. Got it?"

"Got it, thank you, sir."

"Don't mention me in the book."

The deputy hung up.

So Parker lived in Troy, a city in Rensselaer County notorious for its mean streets. It was about two hours away, a straight shot down the interstate.

He opened the internet browser on the Sony and brought up the white pages.

The porch door squawked and banged shut as Emily came inside. Brett heard her run the tap in the kitchen sink. He left the computer and walked into the room.

She was washing her hands. "Any luck?"

"Parker lives in Troy."

"He's a cop with the Troy Police?"

Brett shook his head. "He was a deputy sergeant with Rensselaer County. He's retired. Do we still have that old road atlas?"

"Yeah, I think so. In the living room. On the top shelf, there's a pile of maps."

He found what she was talking about, pulled down the big road atlas. It was battered and timeworn; a big stain in the middle of the front cover.

He flipped to New York as he brought it into the dining room and laid it out on the table. Google maps were one thing, but it was nice to have a physical map, too.

He grabbed a highlighter pen from a drawer in the kitchen, then went through his notes on the robberies, starting with the NCFA headquarters, which was in Plattsburgh.

The Fighting Bandits had robbed the headquarters. Then a day later hit two banks in rapid succession, one in Plattsburgh, the other in Lake Placid. He used the highlighter to draw a line, moving southwest from Plattsburgh to Placid. The next banks were in Lake George, then Glens Falls. This time a straight, southerly route.

The Fighting Bandits had been apprehended in Albany, thanks to the hero cop, Parker, who had slowed them up enough for police units to respond. He finished drawing the line down to Albany.

He returned to the computer and opened Google, plugged in the name of the bank, got a closer look.

It was just outside Albany's city limits. When first apprehended, the robbers would've been taken to Rensselaer County jail. The jail was run by the same Sheriff's Office where Parker had worked.

Emily stood in the dining room doorway, still cleaning her hands, getting the garden soil from under her nails. "What's up?"

"I don't know. I think I've got where the bank robbers were first taken to jail. I don't know where they went from there, though, but they wouldn't have stayed in County for too long. When they got sentenced, anyway, they would've gone to state prison. Maybe federal, because they were bank robberies, I don't know. But I bet Gentry Parker does."

He glanced over his shoulder at her. She was looking at his research, spread out across the dining room table.

"This could be pretty big," he said. "I think I'm gonna do it. Tomorrow morning, I'll ride down to Troy and talk to Parker." He felt like his heart was going to beat out of his chest.

CHAPTER EIGHTEEN

The bus stopped in Albany, and the man who'd given Russo twenty bucks disembarked. Once they got rolling again, they left the city behind. Russo glimpsed rolling pastures, old barns, and slices of pristine lakes surrounded by log cabins. It was like traveling back to a simpler time.

That long-ago trip with his father must've been up here, somewhere. A deep field and that short wall of rocks, going on forever in both directions. The more he thought about it, the more he realized it was one of his last memories of his father.

He leaned his head against the glass and caught a few winks. He'd barely been sleeping in jail and the snooze was just what the doctor ordered.

When he awoke, the bus was driving into Lake Placid, a small town that, according to the big sign on the way in, had twice hosted the winter Olympics. They passed a horse showground and a small airport.

In the heart of the village, the bus pulled beneath the overhang of a big building with a row of international flags blowing in the wind. It was a sports complex with ice rinks inside. More signs declared it the place where the Americans beat the Soviet Union in the 1980 hockey game.

Russo disembarked. The air was much cooler than in the city, and smelled fresh. No stink of car exhaust, urine, no garbage piled in the streets. He doubted they had rats or roaches here. The people walking by were white, slim, athletically dressed.

Except for one guy, who caught Russo's eye.

He wore hiking boots, cargo shorts, and a blue work-shirt, sleeves rolled. He was about the same size as Russo and carried a tension in his shoulders which, along with his military buzz cut, marked him as a cop. Or, possibly, a prison guard. He made eye contact with Russo, then turned and walked away.

Russo followed.

The man climbed into an enormous truck and the engine roared to life.

Russo waited, feeling totally out of place, standing in front of some shop with Olympic memorabilia dressing the window. A framed photo showed the US hockey team in victorious celebration. The caption read: "*The Miracle on Ice.*"

The guy stuck his hand out of the truck and wiggled his fingers. Russo approached, trying to look casual, and then got in the passenger side.

The big man flipped on his blinker and pulled into traffic. He didn't say a word as they drove through the village, then made a right-hand turn at a tiny post office.

Russo saw a lake; its surface a near-perfect mirror reflecting the royal blue sky.

After a couple more turns, the guy turned his head, gave Russo a look.

Russo was wearing his work clothes, a simple pair of navy Dickies and a white button-down shirt, wrinkled, that had seen better days. There was an MTA patch over the breast pocket.

"There's a bag in the back," the guy said. "You look about my size."

Russo hesitated. The guy just kept driving, watching the road. They'd left the little village behind and were driving through an evergreen forest.

Russo pulled the bag onto his lap and went through it. He found some kind of slippery athletic top, thick work pants, a pair of weird socks. Like wool, but not.

"Boots are behind you."

He'd just had his hard-soled shoes buffed the previous week. Even though no one ever saw his feet while he sold subway tickets from a pillbox booth, it was an old habit to wear sharp-looking footwear.

The boots were brown hiking lace-ups, scuffed but in good condition.

"You want me to change in the truck?"

"No. We're almost there."

Russo was patient as the guy piloted the big truck over a bumpy road, twisting through more forest. He noticed a river curving close to the road, then it disappeared out of sight as they crested a hill.

"Am I gonna get your name?"

The guy gave him a hard look. Russo pegged him as a CO, no doubt about it now – the look in the guy's eyes was the one a lot of guards gave inmates and ex-cons. "You can call me Shelly." He turned his face back to the road.

In the console was a tin of chewing tobacco, some receipts, loose change, and an old-looking cell phone. Russo's phone was outdated, too, but he thought this one looked more like a prepaid. The kind you bought minutes for.

Shelly slowed the truck and turned onto a dirt road. They ground over uneven terrain until they arrived at a small log cabin.

Russo didn't know much about mountain architecture, but this place looked like something out of *Jeremiah Johnson*. An open front porch, a stone chimney sticking out of the roof, piles of wood around, a detached snow plow resting in some high grass.

Shelly stopped the truck and killed the engine. He got out and walked inside. Russo followed.

Before Russo got to the front door, Shelly reappeared, holding a shotgun. "Whoa, whoa. Hold up. Get changed on the porch."

Russo started to undress, staring at the shotgun. Before long he noticed the bugs – hard to see at first, just tiny little black things, biting the shit out of his exposed flesh.

Shelly watched him closely, his lips bending into a crooked smile.

"Black flies."

Russo hurried into the clothes he'd been given. They didn't exactly fit like his own clothes, but they were close. He pulled on the shirt, wondering about the fabric. It was like something a runner might wear, he thought. He laced up the boots and stood, feeling ridiculous.

"People dress like this up here? That's the point, right?"

Shelly just gave him a look, the smile gone. He was chewing something and he spat out dark spit.

"There's food in there. In the cabinet. And I'm gonna need your phone. You can get it back after you're finished. There's no cell service out here anyway."

Shelly held out his hand.

Russo was loath to turn the phone over. It was his lifeline to the girls. But he did it.

"I'll be back in the morning," Shelly said. "Six a.m. sharp." He stuck the phone in his pocket and stepped off the porch.

In the morning?

Russo couldn't take it anymore. He followed Shelly to the truck.

Shelly spun around, aggressive.

Russo held up his hands in a gesture of peace. "Wait a minute. I'm staying here *tonight*?" He shook his head. "I can't do that. Whatever I'm supposed to do, whatever you need me to pick up, whatever this is, I gotta do it now."

Shelly wrapped both hands around the shotgun like he meant to use it. Russo got the sense Shelly resented the hell out of being the one to pick Russo up, give him clothes, bring him out here, like a babysitter. But he calmed down and looked at his watch.

"This is how it is. We don't have time today. It's already quarter to five."

"I don't care, I gotta get back. That bus takes all fucking day and there's only one that leaves early in the morning. Seven a.m."

Shelly glared. "This is the deal."

They were just a couple yards apart. Russo glanced back at the house, then around at the trees. Giant pines and tall spruces and other trees he couldn't name, forming an enclosure. There was a hazy mountain peak in the distance.

He had no idea where he was. Shelly said phone service was non-existent. It didn't matter much because Shelly had taken his phone. He had his watch, his wallet, and the clothes Shelly had given him. That was it.

"You *really* want me to stay here for the night. In your cabin."

Shelly's face darkened. "Who says it's my cabin?" He took a step forward and jabbed a finger at Russo. "You better stop asking questions, and start listening. You talked to Kim, right?"

"Yeah…?"

"She gave you the terms."

She didn't say anything about spending a night in the middle of the woods.

Russo heard something snap through the brush and it made his heart leap. He looked into the dark trees and Shelly glanced there, too. But Shelly acted more curious than alarmed.

Probably some kind of animal, Russo thought.

Shelly finished walking to the truck, opened the door, dropped the shotgun inside. "There's some books. In the back, on the bottom shelf by the TV that doesn't work." He stepped up into the rig and fired up the engine.

The last thing Russo saw was that ugly face behind the glass, smoky with the sky's reflection, and then Shelly got the truck turned around, crashing through the underbrush, and drove away.

Russo listened until the sound of the engine faded completely, and slapped at his neck as something bit him.

He stood there a minute, thinking about the dirt road on the way in. It couldn't have been more than a mile. He could easily walk back out to the main road – there was still plenty of daylight left – and stick out his thumb. Hitchhike back into town…

And then what? He had no money. He could find a place to sleep, maybe, but he didn't even have the fare for the return bus the next day. Felicia had the card for the joint account he'd left with her when the cops picked him up. She wouldn't be worried about him yet. He could see this thing through, and even if he got on the road and made his way back home to her later than he'd planned, it could still work.

Besides, if the ex-con from the subway had been in touch with the man in black, Shelly was probably in touch with him, too. They were all obviously working together. There was no way out.

He scratched at more bug bites and then walked back to the cabin.

The inside was dark, cool, and smelled like a musty closet. He spent a few minutes checking everything out – the toilet had a pull-chain flush, the kitchen sink was so shallow you could barely get two dishes in there, the stove propane, just two griddles on the range. No refrigerator. Probably no electricity.

He found a chair in the main room and sat down in the gloom. The chair puffed up dust and more mildew smell, making him sneeze.

Son of a bitch.

Russo tried the TV. It was small, battery-powered. When it didn't work he opened a compartment and found batteries crusted with corrosion.

He turned to the bookshelf Shelly had mentioned and a few paperbacks. He browsed them and found one called *The Outsiders*. It looked short. He read the first page without comprehending.

It was too hard to take his mind off of things. What was he here to get? What did it have to do with the article about human remains, if anything? But he grabbed another one, sitting cross-legged on the hard cabin floor like a preschooler.

The other book looked like it could've been for a preschooler, in fact. It was titled *The First Crow*.

The cover showed a crow flying, at least it looked like a crow, but rainbow-colored. Desperately needing a distraction, he read the story.

In primordial times, during a long, harsh winter, a group of birds got together and found "The Great One," a brilliantly plumaged bird with a lengthy wingspan and the most beautiful singing voice in all the land.

They asked the Great One for help, to ease the suffering of the endless winter.

The Great One flew to a mountain where a fire was burning. It took a burning stick in its beak and flew back to the others.

But along the way, Russo learned, the fire grew hotter and covered the bird in thick, black soot.

When the bird returned, the others barely recognized it. It promised them that it was their beloved Great One. When it tried to prove this by singing, all that came out was a scathing "Caw."

The fire had done irreversible damage, turning the sonorous bird into a modern crow. But the land was saved because the fire spread. It melted the ice and brought warmth and light to all.

Russo set the book aside. He thought about it for a moment, then realized he needed to move his bowels. He found the tiny bathroom and closed the door. No need to close it, of course, but the privacy was just too good to pass up.

Something fluttered against the window, startling him. A huge bug was bouncing against the screen, intruding on his sanctuary.

When he was finished, Russo slammed the window shut.

There was no way he was going to find sleep tonight. It wasn't even seven o'clock yet. He was free but still locked up. And he was being drawn into some criminal activity which involved at least two inmates, possibly a prison guard, and this mystery man Richard and his bicycle.

Maybe he should've done what his public defender had suggested, pled guilty, done a little time, worked off the fine as best as he could.

He'd worried Felicia would leave him. Afraid he was drifting back into the "old life," a bad influence on the baby, a lousy provider. It was her grandparents' house they lived in – she could easily have kicked him out.

Because of his fear of abandonment, he'd put her in danger.

Hey, maybe after your father dies when you're seven, and your mother leaves you at thirteen, you worry people can't be trusted to stick around.

The pop psychology didn't make him feel any better. They had him in a vice, using his wife and daughter to get him to jump through their hoops. Maybe it would be best to just see it through.

Or, maybe there was a way out.

He thought about the prepaid phone he'd seen in Shelly's truck. It made sense – if Shelly was in law enforcement he'd know that if he ever got caught, his phone records could be subpoenaed and incriminate him. Prepaids were stealthier.

Shelly was keeping in touch with Richard, just the way the ex-con had been. "They have to be talking somehow," Russo said into the empty space.

He formed an idea.

CHAPTER NINETEEN

Sergeant Gentry Parker lived in a white house with peeling paint in a run-down neighborhood.

Brett had never been to Troy, but what little he'd seen of it so far was troubling. Abandoned homes, empty lots with busted chain-link fences, grubby-looking plazas with fast food shops and delis, a barber shop with the striped barber's pole unmoving.

Parker's street was residential, a block over from a commercial strip. Brett parked the Savage, removed his helmet, and crossed the street to a white picket fence about to tip over.

He attempted to push open the gate, but the bottom part scraped to a halt against the walkway. He had to shimmy through.

There was a neighbor, two houses down, grilling some meat, smoke billowing up. Who grilled this early on a Saturday morning? The neighbor was bare-chested, covered in tattoos. He gave Brett a hawkish look.

Brett climbed rickety steps to a porch and a windowless door. He knocked and waited, a fresh load of adrenaline twisting through him, skin crawling.

He wasn't a detective, he wasn't a reporter. He was a journalism flunky and failed writer turned construction worker here on a crazy whim – he could maybe write a book about the human remains found in his backyard. And now he was going to question an ex-cop.

There was shuffling on the other side of the door. It opened a crack, caught by a short chain, and a man with a ragged beard and hollow eyes peered out. He looked behind Brett first, then at him. "Who are you?"

"Brett Larson, sir. Are you Sergeant Gentry Parker?"

"Retired. How did you find me?"

"I looked you up, sir."

A dog barked from inside the house. There came the click of claws on hard floor. Parker's face disappeared for a moment and he ordered the dog to sit. Then his eyes popped back into view, half-lidded and bloodshot. "You a reporter?"

"No sir."

"Then what are you doing here?"

Brett cleared his throat. That dog sounded huge, and mean. Parker was no joke, either. "I'm Brett Larson."

"You said that…"

"I live up in the Adirondacks. Near Lake Placid. I found bones on my property. Maybe you read about it?"

Brett could sense the man calculating. The dog barked again and Parker yelled at it, irritable, before saying, "No. So – what? What're you doing here?"

"I was hoping maybe we could talk. I'm actually… I'm writing a book about finding the bones, and everything that's happened since then."

"Good for you," Parker said flatly. "Please tell me what it has to do with me."

Brett was careful. Parker looked like a guy who was down on his luck. Maybe he'd been doing well at one point – he'd been a hero after all – but things had changed. Brett decided to run with the truth and see how far it would take him. "The police have somehow connected the remains to the Fighting Bandits."

Parker didn't say anything, and it felt weird, standing here on the guy's porch as the seconds drained away.

Brett looked over at the neighbor's yard. The neighbor had wandered away from his grill and was up against the fence, unabashedly staring over as he sucked down a can of beer.

The chain rattled and Parker opened the door. Maybe it was the humidity, the heat, but did people around here wear any clothes? Parker was standing there in a pair of boxer shorts, nothing else, his considerable belly hanging over his waistline.

"Come on in. I got nosy neighbors."

Brett glanced at the guy grilling, still watching. *No shit.*

Parker held the door with one hand and gripped the collar of his dog with another. The pooch was straining like hell to either tackle or take a bite out of Brett. Or both.

But Brett liked dogs, and as soon as Parker closed the door, Brett held his hands out, nice and easy, and Parker let the dog give him a series of slobbery licks. It was a Rottweiler, short-haired, brown and black in wriggly patterns, wagging its nubby tail.

"Let me put on some pants." Parker pulled the dog off Brett. "This is Sandy. She's alright, she's friendly. Unless you fuck with her. Sit down, Sandy."

Sandy sat, panting, tongue flapping, razor-sharp teeth glinting as she made a doggy smile.

Parker left the room, headed towards the back of the house. His voice boomed back, "So you found those bones, huh?"

"Yes, sir." Brett looked around. The curtains were drawn over the windows, the room was hot and gloomy and smelled like dog breath and old nicotine. A fan chattered as it spun listlessly, barely displacing the haze.

An elegant grandfather clock in the center of the room with a long gold pendulum, the one piece of stately furniture. Otherwise, a chintzy coffee table was cluttered with newspapers and pizza boxes, sagging shelves barely supported books that tipped together like old drunks, and the striped couch had dog-chewed armrests spurting foam.

Parker reappeared, dressed in pants, pulling on a T-shirt that read *Joe's Crab Shack*.

Even the TV set was old; an actual cathode-tube deal, or whatever they were called, sitting on the floor encased in a wooden box. There was a tennis game playing, the sound turned down.

Parker glanced at the TV and said, "That's the old set. I've got my flat-screen upstairs. I don't want any of these punks looking in the windows and seeing my sixty-two inch in the living room. Lot of drug addicts in this neighborhood, always hard up for cash, something to pawn."

Brett thought about the desperation it would take to actually rob the house of a retired police officer with one of the most vicious breeds of dog known to man, but he kept quiet.

Sandy got to all fours and circled around Parker, looking up. Parker patted her head and then folded his arms, giving Brett a long look-over.

"So they linked the remains to the Fighting Bandits."

"Yes, sir. That's how I found out about you. I read about what you did."

Parker seemed unfazed by the mention of his heroism, more interested in something else. "How did they link the bones to the bandits?"

"I don't know, sir."

"Huh. But you know they did."

"I was shown mugshots."

"They took you down to the station?"

"No. At my house."

"Huh."

"There's a state police investigator who says the case is with their robbery division. And it could be the FBI following up on a note found with the remains."

"A note."

"Yes, sir. With an address on it. Well, sort of."

"Sort of?"

"It was a scrambled note. An anagram."

Something flashed in Parker's eyes. Brett felt momentarily silly – the fact of the anagram pitched things into conspiracy theory territory.

But Parker reacted like it was perfectly plausible. "And they're looking for the unrecovered heist money at that address."

"I think so. They haven't been able to tell me much. I've only really spoken with the one investigator."

"Who is he?" Parker had this look like his gears were really turning.

"Uhm, his name is Daniel Morales."

"Morales… Hmm…" Then his eyes cleared. "So you're here, what? You got a private ticket?"

"What's that, sir?"

"Stop calling me sir. A private ticket… your license to be a P.I."

"Oh, no. I'm not a P.I. I'm ah… I'm writing a book about it."

"Uh-huh. A book?"

"Yes. And I was hoping to talk to you about that day in the bank."

Parker fell silent a moment, standing motionless in the dimly lit room as he evaluated Brett's words.

"Well, I really don't want to be part of any book. Sorry."

He moved as if to open the door to let Brett out, and Sandy leapt to his heels. She seemed to sense the change in the air and gave Brett a nasty eye.

"I think something is going on," Brett said quickly. "Something the police aren't saying."

Parker was close enough that Brett could smell the beer on his breath. A low growl escaped Sandy's throat and Brett felt his testicles shrink, trying to bury themselves up in his pelvis.

"I'm not interested." Parker leaned past Brett and turned the knob, pulled the door open.

Brett had to step out the way of its arc.

"The parts recovered are bones from the leg and hip, part of an arm," he blurted. "And, I'm not an expert, but DNA tests can take a while, and they have to match the sample they take to something in a database, right?"

Parker just looked at him. Sandy was so close Brett thought she could take a piece out of his leg with a quick snap of her jaw.

"I just..." Brett felt something give way inside himself. "I just have to know. It's my property, my family. I uncovered these bones, and the cops are acting strange. Morales found me at the address, poking around, and we got in his car. He was drinking." Brett's eyes darted to the beer cans overflowing out of a box beside the couch. "Maybe there's money on the property."

"You don't want to get involved with any money." Parker's voice was cold as ice.

"No, I don't."

"You shouldn't be involved in any of this. You don't know what you're getting into. What do you think, you're going to write a book and it's going to solve all your problems? Make you a celebrity? Being a celebrity sucks, trust me."

"No." Brett realized it was the truth. "I think... I'm thirty years old, and I got a baby on the way, and my life isn't all that much. I just want to *do* something."

"Well with a baby you've got all the more reason to protect yourself," Parker said. He nodded at the open door.

"Please..." Brett knew things could get worse any second. This guy could snap him in half, let his dog clean the meat from his bones.

"Goddammit..." Parker suddenly lunged towards Brett, and there was no time for him to get out of the way.

CHAPTER TWENTY

Russo woke to the sound of a truck pulling up outside. He'd slept in his clothes on top of the blankets even though the night had gotten fairly cold. Colder, anyway, than home was this time of year. When he got out of the bed his muscles felt stiff.

Shelly came barging in with a plastic shopping bag. He barely spared Russo a glance and then went about things in the kitchen.

He turned on the tiny gas range and rummaged around in the plastic bag, pulling out a dozen eggs, and some milk and bread. His truck keys were hanging from a carabiner attached to his belt.

Russo slowly drifted closer, stretching out his neck, his arms. He wasn't groggy despite the fitful rest – he felt alert, and, more importantly, he felt resolved.

"Shelly…"

The big man, dressed in a flannel hunter's shirt, blue jeans, and boots the size of small cars kept his back turned. "Can't start the day on an empty stomach." He pulled a frying pan from a box full of dishes.

"I'm not going to do it."

Shelly kept about his business, taking a stick of butter from the bag, opening one end of it and smearing it around in the pan. The butter started to fry, and the aroma filled the dank cabin.

"You ought to think about that."

"I have." Russo dared to get a little closer. "Yesterday you were worried about the time. You had me dress in these clothes. It sounds like I'm supposed to pick something up from a business, maybe even a bank. You obviously don't want to do it. Like you want to keep your face off the cameras. Or you're hiding from something or someone else."

Shelly cracked an egg on the edge of the pan, then another, then two more. When he was done, he slowly turned around and leaned against the counter. He stuck his hand down into the pocket of his jeans and pulled out the prepaid phone. He pressed a button and held it screen-out for Russo to have a look.

"Recognize anybody?"

Russo leaned in and stared at the small picture. It was a selfie, of all things, with some man Russo had never seen before, gaunt and ugly, smiling a horrible smile in front of Felicia and the baby.

They were in Russo's kitchen.

The man was wearing a black jean jacket. He was standing right beside Russo's wife, his arm around the baby...

Russo grabbed the phone. He charged into Shelly, got him in a bear hug and twisted him away from the counter. Russo grabbed up the frying pan, hot with sizzling butter and raw eggs, and threw it.

Shelly ducked and the pan clanged across the floor.

Then Shelly came for Russo.

Russo was ready. He drove forward like a train, hitting Shelly's face with tight punches, three in a row, right-left-right. Shelly's head snapped back with each blow and then he went down, dropping to one knee, planting his palm to keep from falling over, holding his other hand in the air in an attempt to ward off more attack.

Russo slapped the hand out of the way and hit Shelly again, this time taking the man all the way down to the ground.

His knuckles throbbing, his mind blank, Russo jumped on top of Shelly and clawed at his waist. Detaching the keys from the man's belt was a struggle but he managed to snap them free as Shelly moaned and recovered.

Russo ran out of the cabin to Shelly's massive truck and flung open the driver's side door.

The plan was simple: pretend to be Shelly and text the ugly man in black some new instructions – the deal was off. Let the woman and baby girl go. Russo even knew his name – *Richard* – probably a mistake for the ex-con from the subway to have told him. Russo would make use of it.

But, what if there were code words? He had no way of knowing how familiar they all were. Richard might sense something amiss.

Standing on the running board beside the driver's seat, Russo searched the contacts on the phone. There were only three, and no names, just numbers. One number was a 917, typically a New York City cell phone. Russo selected it and scrolled through the messages. They were all the same, each originating from Shelly, one every hour.

OK

OK

OK

It would take five hours to drive home in Shelly's truck. Russo already thought of how he would dispose of the vehicle back in the city. And if he texted once an hour like Shelly had been doing, he might make it.

On the other hand, Shelly could walk out of here, find another phone, and alert Richard.

Russo spied the shotgun in the back of the truck. At the sight of it, he tasted metal in his mouth and his fingers tingled. Maybe all he needed to do was tie Shelly up, though. He just needed those five unfettered hours.

Or, better yet, there was an even simpler solution.

He grabbed the gun, stepped down, and walked back to the cabin.

Shelly was just getting to his feet, wiping the blood from his mouth with his sleeve. He looked at Russo with pure animal rage in his eyes, then looked at the gun Russo was leveling at him.

"You're going to call him." Russo held the phone out. "You're going to call this guy and you're going to tell him the whole thing is off. It's over, it was a mistake."

Shelly's eye was twitching, turning red. His lower deck of teeth was swimming in blood, visible when he spoke. "You fucking stubborn convict." He started coming, walking across the room towards Russo without a care in the world.

Russo dropped the phone, grabbed the gun barrel, and pulled the trigger.

The trigger went *click*.

The next thing he knew, Shelly snatched the shotgun out of Russo's hands. Russo made a half-hearted move for it but was too stunned to really do anything.

Shelly flipped the gun around and rammed the butt-end into Russo's nose.

Russo dropped like a rock.

CHAPTER TWENTY-ONE

Parker yanked Brett inside and closed the door.

"Goddammit," he repeated. "Alright."

Sandy was barking at her master's abrupt movements, sensing violence in the air. Once Brett was inside, his pulse jacked, scalp tingling, Parker grabbed the dog and petted her. "Easy, we're alright. This guy won't take no for an answer. Alright, girl." After glaring at Brett a moment longer, Sandy settled and padded off into the room, curled up on the couch where she kept her watch from a distance.

"Listen," Parker snapped. "Okay. You got three main ways to ID a body when DNA is not an option. Alright?" He moved to the couch and sat down beside his dog. Brett stayed by the door, feeling both relieved and strangely immobile. "You've got dental," Parker said, "you've got surgical implants, you've got skeletal injury or disease… Jesus, have a seat. You'll make her more nervous just standing there by the door."

He pointed to a chair beside the couch and Brett crossed to it, Sandy tracking him as she sat beside Parker. He could feel the springs of the old chair pressing into his ass as he settled in.

"There was a case a few years ago where we found the skeleton of this guy," Parker went on, "and we could see the skull was healing, rib fractures were healing, some other stuff. We looked up incident reports and found one where the injuries sustained in this domestic violence case were consistent. We consulted with the family, found out it was this guy whose wife had clobbered him with an iron."

"She killed him?" Brett took a notepad and pen from his bag. He did it gingerly, trying to be subtle, not wanting Parker to think too much about it and change his mind.

"No, no. That was the past. He'd wandered out into the woods one night to get away from her, died from exposure, wasn't found until the next spring by a couple of hikers. Anyway, to get a DNA match, you've got to have a sample already that will match the victim, or you get family, you know, from a missing person, you'd get the family swabbed out and sampled or use their hair, and so on. Then you can establish a match."

"That's what I thought." Brett was glad to find Parker knowledgeable about the remains identification process, and his heart was slotting back into a normal rhythm. "Do you get DNA samples from all criminals who go to jail?"

"Well, that's a big la-de-da issue. Some people refuse to give samples, but the Supreme Court pretty much cleared the way."

Brett scribbled a quick note, then glanced at Parker, who gave the pad a look but didn't object. Still, Brett asked him, "Do you mind?"

"I don't want my name in any of this."

Brett hoped Parker would change his tune over time, but conceded for now. "Of course. Whatever you want. So, the Supreme Court?"

Parker looked up at the ceiling. "Yeah, this was two-thousand-thirteen, I think. Supreme Court said it was okay for police to take DNA samples from people arrested for serious crimes. They're really trying to expand the national database that will match new suspects to evidence from old crime scenes."

"Like the one in my backyard."

Parker shrugged. He scratched Sandy around the ears. She was still panting, clocking Brett like she hadn't quite made up her mind. Then she dropped her head to her paws and looked away, as if watching the tennis playing out silently on the TV.

Brett made a couple of notes, wanting to further research the story on mandatory DNA collection from inmates who'd committed "serious crimes" – whatever that meant. Probably felonies, like bank robbery. From what Morales said and what Brett had corroborated on his own, a lot of bank robberies went unsolved – forty percent in New York. Having a bank of DNA samples to draw on could come in handy when it came to all those pesky unsolved cases rolling around, tarnishing a detective's clearance rate.

"So they could've swabbed out those three when they were processed in," Parker said, meaning the Fighting Bandits. "There could've been a match, something else found at the scene. Were there clothing items, other trace evidence?"

Brett realized he hadn't thought of it before – the tin box. Maybe the bones hadn't been forensically identified, but they could've found all sorts of things relating to the box and its note – fingerprints or DNA. "Yes, there was the box that contained the note I told you about."

"The anagram."

"Right. Does that, ah, does that mean anything to you?"

Parker seemed to tense a bit, and Brett hoped he hadn't just hit a landmine. Parker's eyes seemed to shrink to black flints of coal. "I'm not going to speculate on that. All I can say is that the Bandits aren't the only ones interested in recovering that money."

Sandy's ears pricked up and she lifted her head.

"Okay," Brett said, feeling the pressure rise. "Who else might be interested?"

"The people who it belonged to."

"You mean the banks?"

Parker frowned. "No, I don't mean the damn *banks*."

"The NCFA? They only had, like, thirteen hundred stolen..."

Parker took a deep breath. "I mean whoever deposited the money in the first place."

"Oh, okay, I see…"

Brett felt a bit underprepared. He hadn't considered that the money belonged to anyone in particular, let alone someone who'd be agitated enough to try and get it back. "Isn't money like that insured by the bank? And this is multiple banks, so, I mean…"

"Even if it's insured – which it isn't always, especially if it's being laundered – there's still the principle of the thing."

"Laundered?" Brett felt his stomach twist. "What exactly are we talking about?"

"Look," Parker said, his eyes growing cold, "this is what I'll say to you, and this is *all* I'm going to say, and like I told you, I don't want my name in any of this, you understand? Whoever's money that is, they're probably the same people who buried that person in your backyard. And they're the worst kind of people. You get me? Alright?"

Brett opened his mouth to ask more, but that gleam in Parker's eyes dissuaded him. He decided to switch topics to Parker's role in the final robbery.

"Can you tell me about that day in the Albany bank? How did it happen? What was it like?"

Parker seemed to relax a little. Or maybe it was resignation. "I was off-duty at the time. It was in the middle of my two-week vacation."

"So you didn't arrest them, right?"

"Correct. I didn't arrest them or process them in."

Brett chose his words carefully. "But you resumed active duty while they were still in county jail?"

"I did." Parker seemed to be waiting for Brett to make an accusation.

"How long were they in the jail?"

"They all pled guilty to the banks and the NCFA heist. They all took deals. It was a few months to sort it all out. I don't know the exact length of their stay."

Brett wondered if it were true. These were high-profile inmates and Parker had been intimately involved in their capture. There was more than a good chance he knew the exact duration of each of their stays. But he let it go.

He flipped back a few pages in his pad to previously taken notes. "And then Delahunt went to SCI Cold Brook, Reuter and Oberst to Dannemora. Do you know why they were split up?"

"I'm not a judge. Probably something to do with Delahunt being a woman, and how many women COs they got at Cold Brook." He raised an eyebrow and said, "Of course, now you've got this deal with the lawsuit, these women inmates suing for sexual misconduct and all that."

Brett felt a jolt. "Yeah. Right, I read about that. And I saw one article, sort of presenting a counterpoint, I guess, that sometimes a female inmate uses sexual encounters in her favor."

"It happens. They can run up a real juice card."

"What does that mean?"

"They can find ways to influence the guards."

Brett decided it was time to cut to the chase. "Sergeant Parker, do you think the bandits stashed their money somewhere, and do you think any of them, Delahunt, maybe, are trying to recover it? And that maybe they're trying to get to it before these other people – the original owner of the deposited money who you don't want to mention – are able to get their hands on it?"

Parker just sat for a moment, stroking Sandy's fur. The dog was clocking Brett again, her head erect. Then Parker eased up a little, groped around on the coffee table and pulled a cigarette out of a battered pack. He lit up and squinted against the smoke.

"Their big score was in Lake Placid. They hit the bank right after a deposit, and it was the only bank where they took the vault. All the banks after that, they got a couple grand, maybe. My thought is that they were going to double-back for the money after Albany."

"But you stopped them."

"Yeah, I slowed them down, and the troopers and Troy PD got there. The three of them surrendered pretty easy. They weren't armed."

"How did you do it?"

Parker sighed, settled back into his chair. It was like he had a type of storytelling fatigue. But he launched into it after a moment.

"What they did was, they came in and the two of them got in a line, like they were ordinary customers, like they were a couple. I didn't think they were. She was much older, kinda ugly, he was this young guy, all muscles and tattoos. Totally had my alarm bells ringing. They tried though, they had the look – you know, hats and sunglasses. And the woman's hair was bleached." Parker tapped some ash into an overflowing tray. The smoke formed a growing lenticular cloud in the room.

"Most people hadn't heard about this crew yet – they hit the banks in close succession – but I'd heard about it from some guys in robbery division. Anyway, they were note-passers. Nobody knew what was happening, but I was close, I saw the note, saw the teller's reactions. But then the two of them started arguing about something. They suddenly ordered all of us to the ground. I went down, and I didn't see anybody carrying. Not around the waist, not the ankle, so… I got up. I got up and told them to leave. That's when the guy came at me, and we fought."

Brett imagined Parker and Nate Reuter after all he'd seen of Reuter's cage fights.

"How did *that* go?"

"Guy was like a human Rottweiler." Parker petted the dog. "No offense, Sandy."

Sandy ignored him.

"He was the strongest son of a bitch I ever wrestled. I don't know how long we went at it – just a few minutes. But it was long enough. He got me in some kind of a choke hold, had my arm back like this…"

Parker demonstrated and Brett said, "Arm bar, I think."

"By the time I managed to pull my piece, there were sirens, and the two of them ran out. I never fired a shot. Anyway, they were stopped before they got into Oberst's car. Oberst took off. They found him at a diner the next day, just sitting there, eating his soup."

"No shit."

Parker stubbed out the cigarette and stared off. "So you know, I get all this 'hero cop' in the papers. But then some of the other customers that day, they talk to the press, too. And after a while, it just sorta comes out that the hero cop got his ass kicked just long enough for other cops to respond. A human punching bag, why didn't I pull my piece sooner, all that crap." He gave Brett a level look. "Like I said, the fame ain't all it's cracked up to be."

He looked away at the TV and stroked Sandy's head. It felt like an awkward moment. Parker hadn't really answered Brett's question about the bandits still trying to recover their money, either. But then Parker broke the silence.

"Sometimes, you know, I wonder."

"What?"

"About Oberst. About how he's just there, the next day, la-de-da in the diner. I wonder if Oberst just wanted to get caught."

Brett was dumbstruck. "Why would he want to get caught?"

Parker shrugged. "I mean the feds had a case on the bandits, and they made recommendations to the DA during the prosecution, but ultimately it remained mostly a state case for a few reasons – the robbers never crossed state lines, they also hit the NCFA, it was an unarmed robbery, and they got peanuts from most of the banks. But Oberst still had the big haul from that second bank they hit. What do you do? You stay running from the police the rest of your life? There's a five-year statute of limitations, but that's a long time to hide and not get caught. And if you stay on the run, stay in hiding, it eventually goes fully federal, so then you've definitely got the FBI hunting you." Parker sat up straighter, looking animated. "*Or*, you take the hit, go down for a few years, plan to come back and get the money."

Brett thought about it. "Wouldn't investigators really lean on him, though? Dangle-a-deal type of thing – if he told them where their money was, he'd get a lighter sentence? What was his sentence? What were all their sentences?"

"Delahunt got ten years. But with good behavior – and that juice card I bet she was playin' – it could easily have been knocked down to five by now. Maybe even less if she's part of this thing at Cold Brook. Reuter had no record, got less time. He was being processed out last I heard; went to Rikers on his way to six final months in a minimum-security facility. Oberst? I don't know... Maybe he's the body in your backyard."

Brett opened his mouth to respond to the comment about Oberst, but Sandy started to growl. She was staring at the door, her ears folded back, muscles tensed.

Sandy bolted from the couch, barking. Parker went after her saying, "What's going on, girl? What's going on?" He pushed aside the curtain and peered out.

While Parker and the dog were occupied, Brett's mind was buzzing. What Parker said made some sense – if you were going to rob banks, and you did it unarmed, and you managed to scare up a good bit of cash and hide it away, why not throw yourself on the mercy of the courts? They'd all pled guilty, two of them got relatively light sentences, and even then they only served half the time.

The questions remained: Was Oberst really the one in the ground? Had his DNA matched the bones, or been found on the note, and the cops weren't saying? The anagram was a coded message. Someone was meant to decipher it and recover the stash. Maybe Oberst had died with a note meant to tell the others where the money was, but why? Who killed him? These "other people"

Parker was talking about, most likely. If so, why hadn't they taken the note? Or had they been the ones to leave it for some reason?

Parker flung the door open and yelled at someone out on the street. "Hey, get out of here!" He had to restrain Sandy. The pooch was pulling against her collar, ready to pounce. "I see you again over here, I'm gonna let the dog loose on you!"

Sandy kept barking and Brett rose, came cautiously closer, to see what it was all about. He could just see over Parker's shoulder down to the sidewalk. There were three kids standing there, eleven or twelve years old, two boys and a girl. They aimed squirt guns over the lopsided fence and shot water onto the unkempt lawn. Then they cackled like it was the funniest thing in the world and ran away.

"Get out of here, you little…!" Parker shouted after them.

He spun around and saw Brett standing there. "Where the hell has the respect gone?" His face was bright red, sweat glistening. He seemed to remember the conversation, and his jowls drooped. He shouldered past Brett, still holding the dog by the collar, and said, "You too. Interview over."

CHAPTER TWENTY-TWO

"You think I'm gonna leave a loaded gun lying around anywhere near you, you dumb fuck?"

Shelly's voice drifted around like it was in front of Russo, behind him, to the side of him. Russo's head was spinning, the ceiling rotating when he opened his eyes. It was like the fluid in his inner ear was all messed up, and it took a few seconds for things to calm down.

The shotgun wasn't loaded.

He was getting rusty. It had been too long since he knew how to live this kind of life.

There was blood splattered down the front of his shirt, drying. His nose felt broken and there was more blood on his fingertips when he touched it.

"You're not going into any fucking bank." Shelly was at the sink, washing his hands, then applying a cloth to the corner of his mouth. He tongued the spot where his lip was split, scowling. His eye was really swelling. Russo was glad.

He slowly rose to his feet. Shelly cut him a sidelong look but didn't make a move. Russo tried to get his balance, gripping the kitchen counter for support. He shook off the lingering dizziness and squared his shoulders with Shelly.

Shelly threw aside the rag, which landed next to the gun resting on the counter. He took a step towards Russo. "Don't you try that again – you hear me?"

"What," Russo said, the last of his patience draining like the blood from his nose, "do you want me to do?"

Shelly cocked his head, like it was the first reasonable thing he'd heard all day. "I want you to do what you're told. We're going to get into my truck. We're going to drive somewhere – it's not far – a nice drive in the countryside, you'll love it. There was a problem, but now it's solved. You're going to go and get me what I tell you to get, where I tell you to get it."

Shelly leaned against the counter and looked out the window. Russo wasn't sure what he meant about a "problem," but assumed Shelly meant him, trying to escape.

"You're right," Shelly said. "It's money. This whole thing… this thing got fucked up, and now we have to fix it. But it's an easy fix. We're just trying to minimize collateral damage, and that's why we wanted to do it before five p.m. Because he was at work."

"Who was at work?"

"Don't worry about it. There's no one there today. We're clear."

"Listen, why do you need me? Why not one of these two other guys you're working with? Why not you?"

Shelly simmered. "You don't worry about me. You hear me? That's none of your fuckin business. And these other two? What color was the guy with you on the subway, at the train station? Huh? You see any blacks in this white bread community? He'd stick out like a sore thumb. And the one with your family, he rides a fuckin bicycle. He's a psycho. And he's with your precious wife and daughter, so dummy up."

Russo felt the fear and rage return at the mention of Richard, imagining what this "psycho" might do to his girls. He rolled his head around, trying to loosen the unforgiving tension in his neck, then glanced at the clock in the main room – it was getting late, going on eleven in the morning.

"Alright, for fuck's sake. Let's go."

*

They drove back along the lake Russo had seen the day before, this time on the opposite side of it. Shelly was taking them along the outskirts of the Olympic village Russo had arrived at. They passed the welcoming sign as they headed out. Russo saw two giant structures scraping the sky. Despite himself, he asked what they were.

"Ski jumps," Shelly said with a detectable note of pride.

They were both pretty banged up, Russo thought. Shelly had washed up and let Russo do the same, but Shelly's eye was turning black. Russo had a wad of toilet paper stuffed up one side of his nose. He took it out now that the blood had congealed.

The village faded behind them, the country road dipped and curved through more forest, with breaks in the trees opening on views of rugged mountains. They passed alongside two narrow lakes surrounded by cliffs. Russo had never seen anything like it. People were actually up there on the cliffs, hanging by ropes.

For fun.

They drove down a massive decline that must've gone on for five miles, like they were leaving the high peaks behind, and Russo's ears were popping. They entered a small town called Keene and made a turn. Russo saw a sign marking it Hurricane Road.

Shelly seemed to be in no hurry, and kept checking the time on the dashboard like he was waiting for just the right moment. It was late morning – Russo wondered what that moment could be. Something about a guy working, Shelly had said back at the cabin. He obviously was trying to avoid someone. Maybe the couple from the newspaper article.

The road shot upward and they seemed to be climbing into yet more mountains. Russo closed his eyes and tried to picture his daughter.

To his dismay, her face was hard to conjure.

Her sweet laugh was far away.

CHAPTER TWENTY-THREE

Brett found a diner in Troy and ordered a coffee and a late breakfast. He laid out the notes from Parker and a binder he'd loaded with newspaper clippings.

He looked over the materials with pride. For the first time since the whole thing began, he felt real confidence. He was doing it. He'd just come from interviewing an ex-cop who'd played a significant role in the story of the Fighting Bandits. Parker had turned reclusive, hounded by the media, his vaunted status as a hero carrying a dark side – to some, his efforts had been more laughable than laudable. He was a broken man hiding out in a derelict neighborhood. And Brett had gotten gold from him.

He called Emily first and shared the news.

"I think you should tell Morales," she said.

"Tell him what, exactly?"

"Everything. Just all this stuff you've found out – that woman bank robber accused of having relations with the CO. I mean, we're thinking the same thing, right? The theory that someone stashed the money, left a note to find it, and maybe they're getting help from some Cold Brook prison guard."

Brett was silent for a moment, knowing she was right. At least, a chance to talk to Morales again – to see what was happening at the Hurricane Road property, if anything – was a good idea.

And he kept his tongue about the others Parker had mentioned, to save her the concern.

"You feeling alright?" he asked her.

"Yeah. I'm good. Got some work done this morning with this new account, and I'm getting ready for yoga."

"Good. How's the baby? Walking and talking yet?"

"Ha. No. Going to need to spend a little more time baking in the oven. Patience, honey."

"Alright."

"Love you."

"You too."

"Hey," she said before he hung up. "Did you check the mousetraps this morning before you ran off, Gonzo?"

He laughed at her reference to Hunter S. Thompson. "No. I'm sorry. Mouse hunter became story hunter."

"Alright…"

"I'll do it when I get home."

"They'll start to stink."

"Well, they're in the basement, babe, I mean…"

"I'll do it."

"Alright. Bye."

He called Morales next and left a message. He thought it through carefully beforehand, and had decided to play it cool, just mentioning that he was available if Morales needed anything, and that he hoped the detective was well. Morales would nose it out that Brett had something interesting to discuss, Brett was sure.

He started writing longhand, just like the old days. He opened with his discovery of the bones, and wrote a little about meeting with Morales and the cop's odd behavior before he stopped. He needed to find out where the rubber met the road when it came to libel. He didn't want to get the investigator in any trouble, but he wanted to tell an honest story. The tale was still unfolding, though; the truth pending.

By the time he'd finished eating, he'd gotten a few hundred more words into recounting his experience with Parker. The writing felt good though, incredibly good – it felt great – even if his hand was beginning to ache.

But piecing this whole thing together, best as he could, there was still the glaring gap between the bank bandits and his backyard.

How the cops had linked the body or the tin to the Fighting Bandits could only be DNA evidence. They were tight-lipped about it – at least, Morales had been – perhaps because it was sensitive, relating to an ongoing investigation.

Regardless of whose DNA matched the bones or the tin, even if it was Oberst, why had he been buried in an old cow pasture once owned by the Cobb family?

It was either random or purposeful.

After Owen Cobb had died, the Cobb family formed a trust and sat on the place for three years. Brett flipped through his binder to the page of trustees. He had the original list generated during the purchase of the house, and then his own, which branched out into extended family, whatever he'd been able to find searching public records.

Remembering the protracted process of buying the house, there was always one of the siblings who seemed to drag their feet. The family was far-flung, and Brett and Emily's realtor would excuse the delays due to the distances, the coordination of the family. They all needed to get together and agree to everything. Brett had gotten frustrated – Emily, too, even more so – wondering aloud how it could be difficult to get six people on the same page in their day and age of emails and FaceTime.

"Like herding cats," the realtor had explained. "That's what it's like."

Fair enough, Brett and Emily had thought. But it had lingered, particularly the sense that one of the family members didn't want to sell, like an ambivalent juror holding up the verdict. All the other siblings seemed to want out from under the property – it required some measure of maintenance, and moreover, it wasn't liquid while it sat there unoccupied and unsold.

The realtor had finally admitted about the one sibling. It was just gossip, really – the realtor had heard from someone who knew the family trust's lawyer that Susan Resnick, the eldest daughter, was a holdout. She didn't want to let the place go.

Brett and Emily had tried to be understanding.

He took out the deed on the property, and then the information he had on Susan. It was basic stuff, just her date of birth, spouse, two children and one grandchild. There was an address – Palo Alto, California. But it was the date of birth he studied. Compared to the original purchase of the property by Owen Cobb, Susan would've already been seventeen years old. Hardly the sibling to have the most nostalgia for the property when she'd likely only lived there a year. Of course, maybe his thinking was flawed – not all kids left home at age eighteen, especially not fifty years ago when women had far fewer opportunities.

But then he checked another date – her marriage was three years after the purchase of the house.

He paired the documents, checked the dates again. Susan Cobb had married John Resnick when she was twenty. That certainly fit the era. And it confirmed, in all likelihood, she'd lived at the Cobb farm for a relatively short time. So why had she been the one to cling to the property? There could've been a number of reasons – maybe she was the most sentimental of the bunch, and that was all. He just didn't know.

In the end, though, everyone had finally come together and they'd purchased the house. Emily's brother had provided them with the down payment and closing costs, something Brett still struggled to come to terms with.

He paid for his meal, packed up his things, and left the diner, the thrill of writing gone and his heart now heavy.

CHAPTER TWENTY-FOUR

Russo tried to keep track of where they were. If another opportunity came to get the truck from Shelly, he'd have to know how to get the hell out of the countryside.

They'd left Hurricane Road and turned onto a new route called 9N. He thought he could backtrack to Lake Placid if need be, but they kept getting further away. Then they took a few more turns in a small town with a courthouse and tiny grocery store.

His hopes of driving his way out of the region were at an all-time low as they slowed near a yellow farmhouse.

The place sat alone, nothing around it but gorgeous meadows. There was a single car in the driveway, a lima-bean-green Prius. One of those hybrid deals. Shelly continued to slow, rubbernecking the scene. Russo saw something crazy out back – a dirt spot in the earth surrounded by crime scene tape. Like a frigging alien landing site.

Or an enormous hole that had been filled back in.

Then it all came together for him.

This was real. It involved the people here and the bones they'd found after all.

But Shelly hit the gas and left the farmhouse behind, throwing Russo back into confusion. They drove until they came to an interstate, and Russo recognized where they were at last. The interstate was I-87, a major artery connecting Montreal, Canada, to Albany, to New York City. This was the road the bus had driven north on the day before. This was his way back home.

Shelly headed south, in the direction of New York, but slowed after just a couple miles. He was scrutinizing the road shoulder, and the treeline beyond. Then he pulled over.

"Alright." Shelly checked his mirrors, perhaps hoping no police were around. He handed Russo a pair of bolt cutters. "This is what you're going to do."

CHAPTER TWENTY-FIVE

Before leaving Troy, Brett gave Meg a call at the *Press-Republican*.

She seemed happy to hear from him. "I was worried, you know, I shouldn't have just dropped by your house…"

"Oh, it's fine, no problem."

"So, how are you? What do you need?"

"You told me the banks don't report how much was taken, but I'm curious about the Lake Placid bank. It's just an idea, but where I live is closest to that bank."

"Well you're kinda near Plattsburgh, too."

"Yeah, you're right. I mean, Placid is thirty minutes. But, yeah. Equidistant."

He wanted to honor Parker's request to be kept out of things as long as Parker wished it.

Meg was already clicking away at keys. "Okay well let's try Placid first. Alright… There are four banks in Lake Placid. Let me see…"

He paced the quiet city street near his motorcycle while she continued to click away.

"Okay, they hit Center Bank. Yeah, it's a fairly small bank. There are eight branches in the North Country. Main office is in Saratoga. So where does that leave us?"

"Well, what else can you find out?"

"I can give you the basics, banking hours, maybe the names of the tellers…"

"Yeah that would be great. But what I want to know is how much money was stolen there, and what the difference was with that bank. The bandits didn't hit the Plattsburgh vault – the first bank they robbed – and my understanding is they didn't hit any other vaults afterward. I guess vaults are notoriously hard to get into. But I have it on good authority that they hit the Placid vault."

"Okay, I see where you're going. Yeah, I'll do some digging."

"Thanks, Meg."

"No problem."

He mounted the bike and prepared to leave. The quiet city street got louder when someone laid on a horn.

Meg asked, "Hey, so where are you, anyway?"

"I'm just out doing some research. I took the bike down to Albany, checking out one of the banks that was hit." It wasn't a total lie – he was going to visit the bank next, have a look at the site where Gentry Parker, aged 58, had tousled with Nate Reuter, twenty-two-year-old mixed martial artist known for decimating his opponents.

She practically squealed with delight. "Listen to you! Private-investigator-true-crime-writer on a motorcycle!"

"Yeah…" He thanked her again, hung up, and cranked the engine to life. As he cruised towards Albany, he felt the dread starting to creep back. Unarmed bank robberies and the thrill of unrecovered money were one thing; Parker's remarks about angry "other people" trying to get *back* that laundered money – that was something else.

CHAPTER TWENTY-SIX

Russo saw the woman coming towards the woods and dropped instinctively into a crouch, trying to make himself as small as possible.

As she drew nearer, Russo got a better look. About thirty years old, dark hair, maybe five foot six, a runner's athletic build. The kind of hipster that had taken over Brooklyn, Russo thought. Now they were infiltrating the countryside.

But she was more familiar than that.

She was the woman from the newspaper article, one half of the attractive white couple.

And she froze for a moment, looking in, almost right at the spot where Russo was hidden. It was like she'd heard Russo and was listening for more. Then she tossed something she was carrying and turned away.

She was wearing white and blue gardening gloves.

Emily Larson. That was her name.

Russo watched her walk off towards the house, then stop again, and start fiddling around on the ground. Looked like a garden there, or something.

She was supposed to be leaving, according to Shelly, on her way to an appointment. Either she wasn't going, or she was taking her sweet time.

She finally moved off from the garden and back into the house.

Russo waited, patient. The meadow between him and the house was similar to the one from his childhood memory, but not quite as pretty.

Of course, the giant dirt spot by the trees didn't lend to its beauty.

The Prius was so quiet he never heard the engine turn over. He just caught a glimpse of it slipping away on the road, then it disappeared beneath a rolling hill.

Emily Larson was gone.

He emerged from the woods and neared the huge dirt patch, the kind you'd leave big old footprints in, so he kept to the grass. He watched the house as he approached, then stopped. She'd left those gardening gloves sitting there beside a pile of pulled weeds. Russo picked them up and tried them on. Tight, but they just fit.

At the east side of the house were metal doors that led to the basement. The chain wrapped around the handle was a joke – he didn't need the bolt cutters he was carrying. It was a dummy chain, not even locked.

He set the bolt cutters down, slid out the chain with a loud rattle, and tossed it aside. He opened the doors – they gave off a rusty squeal like they hadn't been opened in years – and went down the concrete steps.

The basement was pitch black. The other thing Shelly had provided was a small flashlight and Russo clicked it on. He found a string dangling from a light bulb a moment later and pulled it.

Funky-looking basement. Uneven floor, cobwebs everywhere, old tools and junk scattered in the shadows. Typical of a hipster couple in an old farmhouse, he thought. The Larsons didn't take care of what was beneath them, only what they could see.

He realized he was trying not to like them. The fact that he was in someone's home, looking for stashed money stolen from a bank was playing havoc with his conscience. Not because he cared about money that was probably federally insured – and, as far as he was concerned, perfectly earned by bandits who'd managed to upset the grim bank robbery statistics and actually score a decent haul – but because he was supposed to be past all this. Felicia would lose her mind if she knew what he was doing. And the people who lived here, they hadn't done anything wrong. He was just glad they were gone.

Shelly had described shelving against a back wall. Russo saw them; four shelves split into cubicles, and drew closer. There were things etched into the woodwork – he read a couple of names – *Peter, George, Susan, Kasey* – each scratched in, as if by a nail, and each naming one of the cubicles. Probably done by some family who'd lived here previously, for the kids to store their ice skates and baseball mitts.

Not anymore. There was a pile of magazines in "Peter's" cubby – *National Geographic* and *Boy's Life* – the edges curled, the covers water-stained. But besides the copious black curds of mice shit, the rest were empty. He shined the flashlight into the cubicle marked *Susan*.

The shelves had no back panel. Behind them was the foundation wall.

This was it. Russo got a grip on the shelves and slid the whole unit to one side. He grunted as he pushed. Dust plumed up and made him sneeze. He moved the shelves until they stopped at the corner of the basement, then picked up his flashlight and played the beam along the foundation. It took a few moments running his hand over the wall, but he found the edge of a thin board, painted to look like cinderblocks. The board was stuck, perhaps from mildew, but he popped it loose.

Behind it was a small door, just four feet high. Russo opened it to reveal a room. He'd heard about places like this – certain houses of a Cold War vintage had been built with bomb shelters. The space was creepy as hell, smaller than his jail cell at Rikers, pitch dark. He didn't relish going in there, but he had to – the beam of his light landed on four heavy-duty garbage bags sitting on the ground.

Russo held his breath, grimaced, and squeezed into the room. He grabbed the first bag and tried lifting it up. Heavy, but not too bad. He quickly hustled it out into the main basement and went after the others.

He dropped the last bag onto the ground. He'd made a bit of a mess and could see his shoeprint in a patina of mortar dust on the floor. Glancing around, he found a brush and a dust pan hanging on the side of a rickety-looking workbench. Good enough. He closed the door, grateful to banish the room from sight. He slid the painted panel back, then wrenched the shelves into their original position. A couple whisks of the broom and everything was good as new, his footprint vanished. He dumped the grit in the dust pan out in a trash bin next to the workbench and replaced the tools.

Then he halted at the sound of some subtle noise outside, like tires rolling over dirt.

A car door slammed shut. He'd left the basement doors gaping and the sound drifted right in. Then there were footsteps above him. Someone was here.

CHAPTER TWENTY-SEVEN

Brett was walking towards the Albany First Choice Bank when Meg called him back.

"Brett, listen – Oberst is missing."

"The third bank robber? He went missing from prison?"

"No. He got out after eighteen months. But then I found a report that the police were looking for him after that. He's been missing a while."

Brett continued moving towards the bank, slower now.

"And that's not all." Meg took a breath. "So, I think Nate Reuter was dating a woman named Heather Resnick, a teller at Center Bank."

Brett stopped walking altogether. "Resnick?"

"Yeah. I checked her out – she's Susan Resnick's daughter…"

"Susan Resnick was originally a Cobb. From my house. Jesus, Meg, from my house?"

"Yeah, hold on, it gets even crazier. Oberst turned state's evidence, so he dealt for an early release, and I would imagine he went into protective custody."

"Like witness relocation?"

"Maybe. But then there's this missing person's report on him. So it could be just a mix-up, maybe that local and state cops didn't know he was in witness relocation. On the other hand, you know, someone could have got to him."

She paused, letting it sink in.

"Like, killed him? Buried him in my backyard?" Brett pawed at his face, glancing up at the gray stone of the bank, but growing less concerned about his book, and more about his wife, his life.

"Or pieces of him." Meg said quietly.

Brett turned away from the bank. "He turned state's evidence? Why? You mean to give up the other robbers or something? But they were already caught."

He heard her typing. He could also hear people in the background and remembered she was at work, taking time to help him out like this.

"Well, I'm digging as deep as I can, and it looks like Oberst might've been tied to organized crime. Or maybe he had some information… I don't know."

"What sort of organized crime?" Brett felt a chill despite the warm day, remembering again Parker's comments about other people involved. Bad people. "What've you got that's solid?"

"Listen to you, you sound like you're on a TV show." The flirtatiousness was there, but hollow. Meg sounded worried, too.

"This is what I can tell you," she said. "When you make a large deposit at a bank, the bank requires you to fill out a CTR. That's a cash transaction report. It's, you know, about anti-money-laundering and the Patriot Act, blah-blah. But if you *don't* file a CTR, I mean, if you refuse, or there's anything strange, then you get an SAR report filed against you. That's a suspicious activity report. Statistically you're likely to get away with it if it's a one-time deposit, but then insurance might not cover it. That's why these organizations use banks all over, to spread it out…"

He was listening, watching the people coming and going from the bank. He wanted to understand what she was talking about, and how she'd come across this information about an SAR, but he was more concerned by the Cobb connection. The previous owners had ties to the bank robbers?

If it was pieces of Oberst's body he'd dug up in the field, the cops had surely known. Then they'd kept it quiet not only because there'd been missing heist money but because of an ongoing investigation involving organized crime.

Dr. Rhea Runic…

A security guard stepped out the front doors of the bank. It could have been Brett's imagination, but it looked like the guard was watching him.

Dr. Rhea Runic 441. Just an anagram, right? Someone having fun. It had given Brett a false sense of levity, that the whole thing was just a game. That he could write a book about it, reboot a career.

But someone had killed Jerry Oberst and buried him at the Cobb family's home. He was sure of it.

But why? Why there? Did it have to do with Heather Resnick?

"Brett?" Meg sounded far away.

The guard was definitely watching him, hands on his duty belt, gun on his hip. Brett thought he might look suspicious, frozen there on the sidewalk, holding a phone to his ear, staring at the bank.

What if the note had been a deception? Not something designed to convey where the money was, but a trick to divert law enforcement to where it *wasn't*?

Brett turned and jogged across the street. He timed it poorly and a car jammed on its brakes, blaring the horn, almost hitting him.

"Hello?" Meg asked, "You still there?"

"Yeah, I'm still here."

"Why would anyone kill someone at your house?" She was thinking the same things he was.

"It's only been my house for a couple months. Before that it sat unoccupied, for like three years."

He swung his leg over the seat of the motorcycle, stabbed the small key in the ignition.

An empty house in the country. A young woman intent on not selling it – Heather Resnick, a bank teller who had dated the cage-fighter-turned-bank-robber, Nate Reuter.

It wasn't addiction that drove the Fighting Bandits. They'd been looking for something specific. They knew to look at the Lake Placid bank because Resnick worked there, spotted the SAR report, and told one of them.

But the bandits had robbed three more banks after Lake Placid. If the mob money had been spread out and they were looking for more, they'd never found any. Parker had slowed Reuter and Delahunt, leading to their capture. Oberst had practically given himself up.

That clinched it. Placid was the only big score, like Parker said. The bank was thirty minutes from where Brett lived. The note from the tin could have been a trick – if the mobsters had killed Oberst, they might have planted it with his remains.

Then where was the actual money? Maybe they'd already recovered it and were long gone.

But if not, then…

His thoughts trailed off, his heart starting to race, his palms greasing with sweat.

Across the street, the security guard came down the steps, talking on a radio, staring at Brett.

"Meg, I'll call you back." He stuck the phone away, revved the engine, and shot out into traffic.

CHAPTER TWENTY-EIGHT

Russo listened as someone walked from one end of the house to the other.

Footsteps not too heavy, didn't sound like boots – it had to be her.

The woman. Emily.

Her soft pounding faded away. As if she'd trotted up to the second floor.

Russo stared out the open cellar door at the square patch of blue sky. He looked down at the money. Shelly was down the road about a quarter mile, pulled off onto the shoulder. The plan was for Shelly to come to the house at precisely twelve thirty. Russo would simply walk up out of the basement with the bags, then carry them to Shelly's truck out on the road, and away they would go.

Shelly hadn't wanted to set foot inside the house. Russo got the impression he was paranoid. He'd taken all these extra precautions, getting Russo up here a day ahead of time, giving him new clothes, leaving him out at the cabin – he was checking to make sure Russo wasn't followed, or working with anyone else. Paranoid, but if he was a prison guard, he had good reason. Any trace evidence he left behind at the scene – a hair, a booger, anything at all – and Shelly's ass would be grass.

It was twelve twenty-two, according to Russo's watch. He'd gotten half the bags free and had about eight minutes left before Shelly showed up.

Russo started to feel angry. He felt taken advantage of. Compared to Jockey, okay, Russo was Albert Einstein. But maybe he wasn't the sharpest tack in the bunch otherwise. They'd leveraged him by threatening his wife and daughter. He still had the mental picture of the freaky-looking man and his girls in the background. Russo thought about taking Shelly and bashing his head in, then driving the truck full of money straight home.

But Shelly was in constant contact with the man in black. He was sending Richard messages every hour. If Richard didn't get the OK, for any reason, he was going to have his way with Russo's wife and daughter.

The pounding resumed, growing louder, someone descending the stairs. Then the telltale bang of the front door. Russo waited for the sound of the car driving away. Probably the woman forgot her purse or something and she was leaving again. He edged closer to the open cellar door. He heard the car door slam shut.

Good. Bye-bye, lady.

But no quiet engine, no pebbles ground beneath tires. Instead, after a few moments, Russo tensed and jumped away from the cellar door – someone was walking round the house.

He leaned against the concrete wall, keeping still.

"Jesus, Brett…"

The steel doors gave their wrenching squall as Emily closed up the basement. She must've thought her husband had left them open.

The sound of the chain dragging over the doors was incredibly loud, like Russo was in a metal tomb.

He waited and listened as the crunch of footsteps faded back to the front of the house again. A fat bead of sweat rolled down the side of his face and he swiped it away.

His DNA was in the basement. Like Shelly, he was in the system, too. Christ, he'd just been swabbed a few days ago. If forensics came in here for any reason and swept the place with all their lights and potions, he'd be gone for a lot longer than a couple years.

He mentally racked up all the charges he'd get so far – breaking and entering, criminal trespassing, and, oh yeah, possession of however the fuck much money this was.

Stolen money, no doubt. The newspaper articles hadn't mentioned it, just the unidentified remains found in the backyard, but that wasn't surprising. Newspapers didn't know anything.

But the worst of it all would be losing Felicia, not getting to see Zoe grow up. Not being there for them.

From the frying pan, into the fire, his father had been fond of saying.

What in the hell was the woman doing out there? Then Russo heard the front door open, more clomping across the floor. A few moments later, water running. She was in the kitchen. It didn't sound like she was going anywhere.

Her footfalls faded up the stairs again.

He looked at the cellar doors. Maybe she'd just dummy-locked them like before, hooking the padlock through links in the chain but not squeezing the shackle into the locking bar. People did that when they'd lost the key but still wanted to keep up the appearance of security. Most of the time it worked.

He'd check to see, but the doors were so damned loud, if he tried to open them and they gave off that metal squeal, he might alarm the wife. He didn't know where she was. She'd gone upstairs, but she could just be using the commode. Maybe that was why she'd come home – to use her own bathroom. Or she was here for good.

He was trapped.

It was almost twelve thirty. Russo had thought it all through and decided he could get the rest of the money out while waiting for the woman to leave. If she ever did.

If Shelly came and saw Emily's Prius, he'd just drive right past the house. Who knew how long he would wait to circle back. Russo could only hope that the son of a bitch would still send Richard the all clear at one o'clock.

Enraged, he looked down at the bags. What the fuck was this all about? Whose money was it?

Still wearing the gardening gloves, he knelt down and opened one.

He'd never seen that kind of cash before, not like this. All fifties and hundreds, tight bundles, wrapped in plastic.

He'd heard from some bank robbers he'd met along the way that the marked bills – the ones that got you nailed when you tried to spend them – were usually twenties, and he didn't see any.

He looked through the other bags and found the same. Fifties and hundreds. No bundles of twenties, which was where banks typically hid the dye packs, the kind that exploded after a countdown or certain distance from the bank, dousing the robbers in red or blue ink. So either this was drug money or smart robbers who'd demanded higher denominations. He remembered thinking how sharp Kim Delahunt was. Had she and Nate Reuter knocked over a few banks? Or maybe one big one?

The fifties and hundreds could account for it being vault money, too. Banks didn't always have a lot in the vault, but when they did, it was typically when a smaller branch had a cash accumulation awaiting transfer via armored car.

Like someone knew when a large deposit had been made.

An inside job.

He closed up the bags, the faces of dead presidents disappearing. He stood and looked at the set of stairs leading to an interior door. He hadn't heard much movement since the woman had gone up the stairs a second time.

He checked his watch. Twelve twenty-eight. Even if he managed to get all four heavy bags up the stairs, he still had to get to the front door without being heard, and there was every chance Shelly wouldn't stop with the Prius in the driveway.

Russo didn't know what to do.

The only choice, really, was to risk being seen. Shelly wouldn't take that chance, but maybe Russo could convince the woman to drive her car around back or something. He didn't want to hurt anyone, especially some lady he'd never met and had no idea what was going on, but he had to think of his own girls. Emily could wind up staying home for the rest of the day. Just waiting it out to see what happened as time stretched on, no telling what moves Shelly was going to make… no. It wouldn't fly.

He tried the steel doors first. He got beneath them and pushed on one. The door groaned open a smidge and stopped, caught by the chain. He applied a little more pressure but the chain held taut. It could be just the shackle caught in the links, but he was already making too much noise. He let the door settle back and sat in the cramped space, listening.

When he was sure Emily wasn't alerted, he crossed the basement and crept to the top of the stairs to the interior door. He tried the handle to make sure the door was open. The knob turned freely.

He left the door ajar, went back down, and retrieved the bags. He grunted up the stairs with the four of them and then pushed the door open and stepped into the kitchen. He'd barely gotten a few steps when he heard footsteps pound down the stairs, and he froze.

Emily came around the corner a second later, looking at some piece of paper she was carrying. She saw him, and she screamed.

CHAPTER TWENTY-NINE

In the spring and early summer, the roads were often dirty. Brett knew highway workers who drove plows throughout the winter to salt and sand the roads. Spring rains pushed the dirt into patches, frequently gathering at intersections.

Brett drove the Savage off the interstate, came to the stop too fast, and the tires went out from under him. The bike went down, and he went with it.

He jumped away and rolled towards the grass as the bike skidded to a stop. The engine revved once and then quit.

Brett got to his feet. He wasn't wearing leather pants or chaps – his jeans were torn up on his left leg, and he could see his skin, the blood welling. He hobbled towards the bike as a truck pulled up behind him.

The driver got out. "Hey, I saw that. You okay?"

"Yeah." Brett tried to pick up the bike.

The driver jogged over and helped him. "Lot of sand on the road."

"Yeah, I know. Thanks for the help."

They got the bike standing and Brett lowered the kickstand. His backpack was still on, his helmet secure, so he mounted the Suzuki and tried to turn the engine over. No luck.

"Well, carburetor is wet now," the driver said, hands on his hips. "You'll have to give it a few minutes, at least."

Great.

"Okay, yeah. I'll wait. Thanks again."

"Alright. Be careful."

The driver returned to his truck and drove around Brett. More cars had queued up and moved along, passengers rubbernecking.

Brett removed his helmet, took out his phone. Still intact. He dialed Emily and waited. He knew she had her yoga class, but maybe she was getting done early. No answer. He left a message.

"Hey babe, it's me. Listen I got some crazy news about this whole thing. I don't want you to get worried, just… maybe just stay out of the house; wait for me before you come home. I'm, ah, just getting off of 87 now. So about a half hour away. Okay. Love you."

He decided to send her a text, too. She'd be more apt to see a text than listen to a message.

After he sent it he checked his log and saw a missed call from Morales. He returned the call and again recorded a message. "Investigator Morales, Brett Larson. Really hoping to talk to you. Maybe you can meet me at my house today if you're available? Or just call me back. I'm on the road now, on the bike. But I'll check messages as soon as I get home. Thanks."

He put the phone away and tried the engine.

Mercifully, the bike started up. He slipped back into his helmet and drove away. He needed to be careful now, but he had to get home.

CHAPTER THIRTY

The woman screamed and then she turned and ran straight for the front door.

She was little and she was quick but he was bigger and had longer strides.

Russo grabbed her around the chest, clamped a hand over her mouth, and pulled her back deeper into the house.

He didn't want to hurt her, but he couldn't have Shelly seeing the woman coming screaming out of the place.

He dragged her, kicking and writhing, back into the kitchen. She was strong, but he held tight.

The clock in the kitchen read twelve thirty. Right on the nose. That was bad, because now Shelly was going to see the damned car parked out in front and drive right on by.

Shelly was afraid of the house, afraid of the cops – Russo had never really seen anything like it. But then, he'd grown up in the city during a time when cops were as dirty as the crooks and you only cared they might hurt you. Maybe Shelly had a lot to lose, but Russo thought the CO was anxious about more than he was letting on.

Still, Russo wanted to go outside and try flagging Shelly down. He just needed to do something with the wild and crazy woman first, and fast.

He looked around the kitchen for something he could use. He backed up until his ass bumped the counter by the sink. She was screaming the whole time, howling bloody murder right through his hand – and then she bit him.

Russo jerked his hand away and the gardening glove tore off in her mouth.

She spit it out. "Get off! Get off meeee!"

He yanked open the drawer beside him, found forks and knives. He slid his butt along, still holding her around the ribs while she flailed with her legs and clawed at his arm, and pulled a second drawer open.

Bingo. There was a roll of masking tape.

He yanked off the second glove with his teeth. He balled it up and stuffed it in her mouth. It would be easier than all this to just knock her out, but he couldn't do it. Fifi would never forgive him if she ever found out.

If the woman was acting crazy before, she was positively batshit now with the dirty glove in. She kicked her bag off the kitchen island. It hit the linoleum and barfed out its contents.

Russo struggled to get a piece of tape unwound with just one hand. He had to use his mouth again and this woman was acting electrocuted, jerking him all over with her frantic movements. He thought he heard a truck out on the road.

"Help!" Her scream was blood-curdling. She'd spit out the glove. He finally managed to tear some tape loose and then ripped it with his teeth. He slapped the tape over her mouth, gag or no gag. But now he needed to tie her up with something.

He looked at the basement door. That made more sense. He lifted her off the ground and walked her over, got the door open, shoved her in. She started to fall forward down the stairs but he caught her by the shirt. She regained her balance, stared up at him with terrified eyes – and anger, he saw something feral there he hadn't expected – and then he shut the door, slid the lock closed.

She pounded on the door, her screams barely muffled. What a botched job this was. She screamed again, more loudly – she'd easily ripped the tape from her mouth.

Russo ignored her for now and jogged to the front door, jumped out onto the porch just in time to see Shelly's big-ass truck go bye-bye down the road.

Fuck.

Shelly was gone.

Russo stood in the driveway, the afternoon sun blasting. The rumbling engine faded and the world fell silent save for some insects buzzing. They buzzed all around, the kind of sound you heard in movies when the characters walked out into the long grass in high summer. He didn't belong here. He felt completely out of place and out of shape – he was making mistakes. All he could think about was getting home.

Thump thump thump thump.

Emily was really working the door. He headed back into the house, glancing at the Prius. He saw his reflection in the glass, distorted, his big face wide and pale-looking. Then he stepped up onto the porch and went back inside.

She was yelling to be let out. Relentlessly pounding the door.

Russo looked down at the bags of cash. He picked up his gloves, jammed them back on. Then he quickly left the room, trying to block out her screams.

Why did she want to get out? She didn't know who he was. She was better off down there.

He found a dining room that had been converted into some kind of office. There were papers scattered around, a couple yellow legal pads, and several newspapers. One of them was the same publication that Nate Reuter had been getting at Rikers, the *Press-Republican.*

Suddenly his chest tightened, his vision blurred. Shelly had come and gone. Right now the CO could be calling Richard, the psycho. The girls were in immediate danger. Russo saw a landline phone sitting by the laptop, picked it up, and listened for a dial tone. He started to punch in the number for Jockey, realized he didn't have it memorized. It was in his phone, which Shelly still had.

Russo tried different combinations and said, "Sorry, wrong number," three times in a row. He felt the heat rising in his head and neck, the panic squeezing his breath. Time was running out, the woman was yelling and pounding. He tried one more combination, knowing that these calls might become evidence, no longer caring.

"Hello? Who is this?"

"Jockey! Jesus. It's me. Where are the girls?"

"Jimmy? The fuck are you?"

"Did you do what I asked, Jock? Yesterday, did you keep your eye on the girls all day?"

"Yeah, bro, sure. I mean, not *all* day…"

Russo closed his eyes, sucked air through his nostrils.

"… I mean, it's the middle of the week, bro. You know how it is. I gotta keep that job, Jimmy. It's all I got."

Russo's eyes flew open. He'd had enough of Jockey and his idiocy. "Jock, *I'm* all you got, okay? Me and Felicia and the baby… Did you see anyone yesterday? Did you see the guy on the bicycle?"

"Look, Jimmy, I'm sorry. I just…"

"Forget it. Do you hear what I'm asking you?"

"Yeah, yeah. I hear you. Look, I thought maybe something was up."

"What're you talking about?"

"I went by, Jim. Just like you asked. I went by on my lunch break, I went by after work. After work I seen this guy there, seen him in the window. Holding the baby."

The thought of someone holding onto Zoe made Russo want to scream and vomit at the same time. "The guy with the leg? The bicycle guy?"

"No, Jimmy. Another fella. A black guy. I thought, maybe…"

"A black…" But Russo trailed off, remembering the ex-con who'd ridden with him to Port Authority and made sure he got on the bus.

Two men at home with his wife and daughter. Not just Richard. The both of them.

Russo took the cordless phone and walked back into the kitchen. It was five minutes to one.

"Jockey, where are you?"

"The fuck is that noise, Jimmy? Where are *you*?"

Russo struck the basement door with his fist. He hit it so hard he smashed the wood in.

"Shut *up!*" he bellowed.

The woman fell silent.

Then he spoke very carefully into the phone, enunciating each word: "Jockey. You have to go to my house *right now*. If you don't, that black guy you think was banging Felicia – he's going to kill her and the baby. Or the other one, on the bike."

"What? Jim, you're freakin' me out over here."

"Go, right now. Forget your job, *leave*. On your way, call the cops. Ask for Barbieri. Tell her you're my friend, and someone is going to try to kill my wife. Do it *right now*, Jock. This is as serious as it gets."

Emily began banging on the basement door again. The pounding overwhelmed Jockey's voice, Russo couldn't hear the response.

"What? Jock – do you hear me? *Get over to my house!*"

"Alright, Jimmy!" Jockey spoke louder. "You got it."

"Call me as soon as you find out what's going on. Call me from my house. You got the number I just called you from in your phone, right? Just call back this number when you get there."

Russo hung up. He squeezed his eyes shut again. He couldn't think with all the racket the woman was making. He didn't want to hurt her, but he felt like his mind was being torn in half.

Russo jerked the lock back and threw open the door. "Hey! You gotta stop the—"

She hit him with something, he didn't know what, but the phone went flying from his grip and down he went. *Boom* on the kitchen floor.

CHAPTER THIRTY-ONE

When Russo opened his eyes, the world was blurry, like something was blocking his eyesight. He wiped with his fingers and saw blood.

The woman.

Emily.

He sat up, everything flooding back. He heard a car door slam shut in the driveway and he scrambled to his feet. Maybe it was Shelly out there, making a getaway. Russo ran out the front of the house. He stopped and locked eyes with Emily behind the wheel of the Prius. Shelly wasn't in sight.

Russo approached cautiously, the way you might an unfamiliar animal. He didn't want to make any sudden moves.

Her gaze fell away. She was looking around for something, acting frantic. Maybe she didn't have the keys?

Then the car started up – she'd located them.

He broke into a run, grabbed the door handle, found it locked. He yanked on it as she continued to reverse towards the road, accelerating, and then he lost his grip.

She was going to get away. Maybe it was for the best, at this point.

A truck was barreling down the road towards them. Shelly's truck. Before the woman could reach the end of the driveway Shelly plowed right in, cutting off her exit.

She didn't brake fast enough and slammed into his passenger-side door with a loud crunch. Then the Prius came to a rest.

Russo caught up to it and tried the door once again. She reached for something and he saw she'd grabbed her cell phone. As Russo went around to try the other door, she was keying in a number.

Shelly jumped out of his monstrous pickup but didn't come round to the driveway just yet. Emily screamed inside the Prius and threw her phone after a few seconds – she couldn't get a signal, Russo thought. He wondered how people lived like this. And it was supposed to be the good life up here. God's country.

God needed to erect more cell phone towers.

Shelly appeared at last, holding the shotgun. He strode up to the driver's side door and leveled the gun at her. He was going to shoot her through the glass.

"No!" Russo ran to the front of the small car. Shelly gave him a nasty look, furious. But maybe desperate, too. Desperate because the plan was falling apart and whatever he was paranoid about was closer. Furious and scared was a lethal combination.

Russo waved his arms. "No, no…" He lunged for the weapon.

Shelly stepped back, gave Russo another knock upside the head with the back of the gun, and Russo stumbled.

Holding his pained head, he watched Shelly aim the weapon through the window at the woman again. She cried out and covered up with her arms.

"Get out of the car."

He tapped the business end of the shotgun against the glass.

"I said get up, get the fuck out of the car. I'm not going to tell you again."

Russo's head was throbbing. Two blows right in a row. It felt like a rock had permanently lodged in his brain, pulsing hot. Still holding his skull, as if trying to keep his brains in, he moved towards Shelly, attempting to ward the man off with his other hand.

"Shelly, easy…"

"Shut up," he said to Russo. "Get out *now*, bitch."

She was trying not to cry. Through the storm in his head, Russo thought Felicia would admire Emily, tough as shit. But she did as she was told and stepped out into the dry, hot afternoon.

The dust was settling from the vehicle derby and it had gotten dead quiet. Even those buzzing insects had shut up.

"Move," Shelly said.

She started towards the house. Russo had never seen anything quite like it on a person's face. Not for years, maybe. Fear, pride, and something else.

Shelly marched her up the stairs and Russo followed them.

Shelly jammed a set of car keys in Russo's hand. "Put the vehicles right – get them out of sight. Open the toolbox in the back of my truck."

Russo squinted at Shelly through the bright sun and pain, tempted to rip that shotgun out of his hands and take care of him the old-fashioned way – beat him half to death with it.

"Tell me they're alright. Did you hurt my girls?"

"They're fine as long as you do what you're told. Where's the money?"

"Inside. In the kitchen."

Shelly shoved Emily back in the house and stepped in after, pulling the door closed behind him.

Russo was tempted to follow. To ask for proof that Felicia and the baby were unharmed. But he realized he was hanging on by a thread – Shelly had overcome whatever made him paranoid and was handling things on his own now, making Russo more disposable. This was only going to end with Russo dead and the two of them subject to whatever horrific shit Richard was capable of unless he made the right moves.

He turned and lumbered towards the vehicles.

The little bell was chiming inside the Prius, the door opened, the keys still in the ignition. Russo squeezed in, barely able to fit behind the wheel.

Why had Shelly doubled back? The man was clearly risk-averse – he'd gone to all this trouble, him and Kim Delahunt, roping someone like Russo in to their mess to do their dirty work. Shelly hadn't wanted to set foot in this house, and now here he was, showing his face. Russo had a guess as to why. Money did that to people – he'd seen it before. Money could take just about anyone and turn loose the animal inside them.

He drove the Prius around to the rear of the house, which he'd wanted to do in the first place, shimmied out and went back for the truck, listening for what was going on inside the house, but heard nothing.

In the truck he tumbled over some rough spots on the lawn – oops, maybe that was a lawn mower or something, sorry Shelly – and then he parked it out of sight from the road, angling it nose-out so he could make a hasty getaway, either with Shelly or without him.

Russo searched for his phone. Checked the glove box, the messy console, the back seat – nothing. Maybe Shelly had just destroyed it. It was what Russo would've done.

He got out and peered into the open truck bed where a large aluminum toolbox was mounted to the back of the truck cab. Russo thought it was called a saddle box, spanning the width of the truck bed, at least fifteen cubic feet of storage capacity.

He flipped through Shelly's keys until he found one marked Master Lock, and used it. Left the lid open and hung the lock on the edge of the box, tossed the keys back onto the driver's seat. Afterward, he looked at the damage done to the side of the pickup and felt a little better about things. At least the man's oversized truck, something he clearly babied from the shiny looks of it, was damaged.

Russo went back inside.

Shelly was standing next to the bags of money.

Emily was stretched out on the floor, face down, her arms over her head. Like an inmate getting her cell searched.

In sight of the money, Shelly's demeanor had grown even darker. A crooked smile touched his thin lips.

But when Russo walked closer the smile faded. Shelly was all nasty-business again. "Get the bags into the truck."

"Don't hurt her."

"I'm not gonna fucking hurt her if she lays there like a good girl."

"Did you really call the guy? Or text him?"

Shelly pointed the gun at Russo and took a menacing step forward. "Motherfucker, what did I just tell you? Do what I say."

"You don't need me anymore. You don't need her, either. Let us go, take the money and be on your way."

Shelly took another step, the anger coming off him in waves. He got nose-to-nose with Russo. The men were the same height, staring into each other's eyes. Russo could smell the honey-cut tobacco on the man's breath riding on the more noxious scent of last night's liquor.

"You're going to see this thing through with me, convict. You and her. When the time is right, maybe I'll let her go. Now get the bags into the truck."

Russo glanced down at the shotgun pointed at his guts. Shelly grinned, bits of brown tobacco stuck in his lower teeth.

"Go for it. Try it again. Two of my associates are at your house now, playing house-husbands. You think you can make a three-hundred mile trip in under an hour? You think I haven't been in touch with them, told them about the shit you pulled at the cabin? Try it and find out."

Russo breathed. Visions of grabbing the gun and splashing Shelly's brains all over this nice farm kitchen faded from his aching mind. The man had a point. He'd been sitting out there in his truck the whole time. He could have revised the signal that meant all was status quo.

Russo picked up two of the bags for now. Emily was still on the ground, unmoving. He started for the front door.

That's when he heard another vehicle slow down and pull in the driveway.

To Russo, it looked like an unmarked cop car. Sleek, navy-blue sedan with featureless rims and balding tires.

The guy behind the wheel definitely looked like a cop, too – the glass reflected the bright afternoon but Russo could see enough. Buzz cut hairdo, shirt and tie.

"Get the fuck away from the window," Shelly growled.

Russo stayed where he was, thinking this could be it. If the guy who'd just pulled in was a cop, maybe it was time to end this whole thing. Russo would have to answer for everything illegal he'd done so far – but it would be worth it. He'd explain to the cop that his wife and daughter were being held by a couple of maniacs at his home on Staten Island. *Send the cavalry, save my girls.*

He put his hand on the doorknob as the cop stepped out of the vehicle.

The guy looked Latino, even. Bonus – this was a fellow hot-blooded man.

"Russo, get away now or I blow her head off."

Russo looked over his shoulder. Shelly was standing over the woman with the gun aimed at her head. No way was he going to murder someone with a cop outside, even if proximity to the money was liquefying his brain. But Russo let go of the doorknob because he just couldn't say for sure.

There was another vehicle coming. The engine whined like a motorcycle. Sure enough, one came into view, slowed down, and turned into the driveway.

What the hell was this? A party?

The cop had gotten halfway to the house, but when the motorcycle turned in, the cop stopped and walked over to meet the driver.

"What's going on out there?" Shelly asked. He was starting to sound panicked, his new plan to take Emily hostage and abscond with the money disintegrating.

"I don't know. Looks like the husband maybe called the police."

Shelly dropped down beside the woman and got his arms around her, covering her mouth. She had been cooperative until now – she struggled against him, and she screamed.

Russo saw the men in the driveway react – the motorcycle driver had barely gotten his helmet off – his eyes got wide and he charged the house. The cop yelled at him and pulled his gun.

Russo didn't know what to do.

Shelly let go of the woman – she was too much of a hassle. He kicked her, grabbed up the shotgun, and strode towards the front door.

He shoved Russo aside and opened it.

Then he stepped out onto the porch and started blasting away.

CHAPTER THIRTY-TWO

Brett barely had time to say two words to Investigator Morales before he heard the scream from inside. It was Emily, there was no doubt about it. He started running for the house when the front door flew open and a man he'd never seen before was standing there with a shotgun.

There was a flash.

Something hit Brett, caught him right in the waist, by the hip – it felt like he'd run into a metal pole he didn't know was there. He spun halfway around in the air and landed flat on his back.

There was no air in his lungs. He couldn't breathe.

He stared up at the sky, making smacking sounds with his mouth. It felt like his leg was gone.

The guy with the shotgun fired again. Brett heard glass shattering, a high-pitched sound cutting through the thunderous clap of gunfire.

He didn't move. He waited until his chest muscles relaxed and he took in a whooping breath. It sounded like air whistling down a ragged tunnel.

He didn't dare get up or run for cover. But the man was apparently finished shooting and Brett heard the front door slam shut.

Morales was behind his car, crouched down, holding a handgun with the barrel pointed up at the sky. He gave Brett a hard look and then patted the air slowly with one hand. *Stay down.*

Brett listened for Emily. It had definitely been her voice, even though she wasn't supposed to be here and he didn't see her car.

Whoever else was in the house was there for the money. Just one man? Or multiple people in there? Affiliated with the bank robbers, or the other dangerous criminals Parker had warned about?

Everything was dead quiet. No further sounds from the house. Morales wasn't moving. The air, of all things, smelled like firecrackers. Like the Fourth of July.

Brett touched his upper leg and side with a trembling hand. Things felt really messed up down there. His shirt was torn, his work pants shredded, the skin beneath cheesy and numb. He thought he detected little hard bits of metal with his fingertips. He didn't know much about guns, but he thought maybe he'd been hit with buckshot – a blast of steel pellets. The blood was seeping out.

I've been shot. It was the funniest thing, the oddest thing, something he'd never expected in a million years. He'd wondered about it, from time to time, what it would be like. This wasn't what he'd expected. This was scarier.

Emily.

If she was in there, she was in real trouble.

Brett tried to roll over.

Morales made a hissing sound. He was still at the rear of his car, his eyes wide and pleading, his head tilted. He patted the air again, more forcibly. *Stay down! Down!*

Brett didn't want to stay down. His wife was inside. His unborn child was inside. He rolled over on his stomach, and rotated around. The numbness in his abdomen became a burning sensation. From his new position he was able to look directly at the front door. But he couldn't see anything through its window.

Because he wasn't listening to Morales's instruction, perhaps, the investigator got moving.

Morales disappeared around the other side of his vehicle. The driver's-side door opened, but he couldn't see Morales from this angle.

The front door of the house flew open again. Brett dropped his head, instinctively playing dead.

He heard the clump of boots over the wooden planks for a second, then the shotgun blasts, two flat claps of thunder in rapid succession. One of the headlights on Morales's vehicle popped, then the other blast scorched the hood, maybe some of the shot reached the interior.

The man on the porch retreated into the house again.

Brett realized the guy was using a double-barreled shotgun. He could only fire two shots each time, so he was going back into the house to reload. Brett wondered how many shells the shooter had on his person. Maybe his pockets were stuffed; maybe he had a whole bag full of ammo, or maybe he only had a few, and could run out.

Brett started to crawl across the wide dirt driveway, away from the front door. His body felt broken and wrong but his thoughts had gotten remarkably clear. Rushing into the house to save Emily was a bad idea – it might only get her and the baby hurt.

He stopped crawling, reached down to his pocket and felt for his phone. It had been shattered by the buckshot.

Hopefully Morales had made a call from his own phone, if he'd been able to get a signal. Or maybe he would use the radio Brett had seen in his car the other night.

The front door opened again.

Jesus, this was insane.

Brett lay still, listening to the footfalls, waited for the shotgun blasts. Nothing happened.

Then the guy on the porch started yelling.

"Cop in the Ford Mercury. Get away from the radio, and let me see your hands. I got a woman inside here and you don't show me those hands, I'm gonna shoot her in the fuckin' face."

Do what he says, Brett thought at Morales. He could see beneath the car a little bit. He thought he saw one of Morales's feet dangling out of the driver's side. Like the investigator was half in, half out of the car, lying low. Maybe he'd been hit by the last volley of gunfire.

Then Morales's other foot stepped down. Brett saw the investigator's hands rise up above the roof of the vehicle. He was surrendering.

CHAPTER THIRTY-THREE

Shelly's eyes were wild, dully shining, as if he had now fully detached from sensibility. After he went out the first time and shot the kid with the motorcycle (it was the husband, Russo figured, that was the likely explanation), Shelly came back in and stormed around, loaded two more shells into the shotgun from his pants pocket. Then he grabbed Emily by the arm and chucked her in the basement.

She was strangely quiet, and Russo thought maybe she was keeping that way for the safety of the people outside. She hadn't seen who was involved in the firefight in the front yard but she'd probably heard the motorcycle arrive, and knew her husband was out there. It reinforced the idea she was smart and resilient. Instead of wailing like a siren, possibly alarming him to such an extent that he came tearing into the house and got his head blown off, she was silent.

Russo had seen the husband take the shotgun blast in his midsection. It was maybe a survivable wound, if he got to a hospital. Unless his abdominal artery was severed, the bleed-out would take a while. Otherwise, he'd probably get feverish, sleepy despite the pain, and want to close his eyes.

After returning to the porch, blasting the cop car again, Shelly had shouted at the cop to get away from the radio and put his hands up. The cop had complied, setting down his service weapon and kicking it under his car as instructed.

Now Russo watched through the window as Shelly stepped off the porch and walked into the driveway. Shelly glanced at the husband, face down in the dirt, dark blood slowly spreading.

Shelly stopped in front of the cop, ordered him to put his hands on his head, and, once more, the cop did as he was told.

For some reason everyone did what Shelly said.

Nobody moved for a moment. Nothing happened. A terrible feeling threaded into Russo's gut as he watched. The throbbing in his head subsided and a clear thought resonated: Shelly had come completely unhinged. He was going to execute the cop.

Russo stepped forward and banged on the glass, yelling. Shelly's head whipped around.

The cop made a break for it, ducking and running to where he'd tossed his weapon.

Shelly let off a blast with the gun, catching the edge of the porch as the cop disappeared. The corner of the house blew apart in a spray of splintered wood.

Someone had to hear all this shooting. How far was the nearest neighbor?

Russo jogged to the basement and threw the door open. He took the stairs two at a time down into the gloom.

Emily was on the uneven floor. She didn't look good. Her eyes were closed. She looked as though when Shelly shoved her through the door, she'd taken a tumble.

Russo shook her a little bit and her eyelids fluttered. She mumbled something, he didn't know what.

He walked to the steel doors that opened to the side yard, tucked into the egress, and gave the doors a push. They gave a little and then were stopped by the chain.

He heard Shelly re-enter the house, then come pounding across the floor towards the basement.

Russo grabbed the chain through the gap and tried to work it loose.

"Did you lock it?"

She only moaned.

"Did you lock it before? Did you—"

Shelly opened the door from the kitchen. Russo was sure he was going to come down the stairs and finish both of them off, but the CO stayed up where he was, at least for the moment. There was commotion from around the back of the house as the cop did some shouting of his own.

Russo kept working the chain until he was able to get it free, pull it down through the gap, and let it drop. She hadn't engaged the padlock after all.

He shoved and the heavy doors swung open with a crash. He started to leave.

Emily spoke again. This time he caught what she was saying. "I'm pregnant."

Russo stood in the egress, overcome with conflict. The house threw a shadow in the yard beside the open doors. The Prius sat close by, in the sunlight, where he'd parked it.

If he left – if he managed to get in the Prius and haul ass out of there, the men wouldn't get their text from Shelly and they might hurt the girls. Maybe the cops were there by now, maybe Jockey had finally intervened, but Russo had no way of knowing until he talked to Jockey.

And now another person was in trouble, the wife, sitting up on the basement floor, looking at him. She had a baby inside her, for Chrissakes. What he needed to do, what he might be able to manage, was to get her out of there, get her somewhere safe.

Russo walked to the woman and helped her to her feet. She was wary of him and quickly pulled her arm away, eyes glistening in the gloom.

They didn't have time to talk it out. Russo gently pushed her towards the cellar doors and she seemed to understand. He stopped her before they walked up the concrete steps, and ventured out just a ways himself, listening.

Everything was quiet, just those eerie-sounding bugs that had resumed doing their thing in the weeds. He jerked his fingers, indicating she should follow.

They ascended the stairs and stepped onto the grass. The car was a few yards away. The back end was a little banged up, but Russo figured it would run just fine. He moved towards it, crouching like he was leaving a helicopter. The door stuck and he had to give it a yank. Then he turned and held out his hand to her.

Emily hadn't budged from the edge of the steel doors. She had both hands on her stomach, and she was standing there in the shadow of the house, just staring.

Russo scowled and stuck out his chin. *Come on.* What was she doing? Then it dawned on him – she was thinking about her husband again. But she couldn't do anything for him. She needed to worry about herself, and her baby.

Russo summoned with his hand, *Come on come on come on*, but she stayed put. The seconds were draining away.

The sun blared down, everything felt dry as tinder, like a match could set it all ablaze. He thought he caught a whiff of something fruity, like berries, and then it was gone.

There was a crash from inside the house, as if a lamp had toppled, then rapid footsteps. It sounded like the two men fighting – Shelly and the cop. Savage grunts and shouts from the top floor. Another crash. If the cop killed Shelly, Russo was right back in the same position – serious jeopardy for his wife and baby girl.

If Emily wasn't getting in the damned car, so be it. Maybe she'd come to her senses on her own.

He left the car open, bypassed Emily, and reentered the basement. The muffled sounds of the melee continued as Russo crept up the stairs to the door of the kitchen.

He eased it open. The money bags were still right there.

Footsteps thundered down from the floor above. Russo shut the door and braced against it.

Someone came into the kitchen, cursed, and then banged out the back door. It had to be Shelly.

Russo risked cracking the door ajar again and saw that all four of the bags had been taken. He slipped out of the basement, ran to the front entrance, and looked beyond the porch at the dirt driveway. There was a trail of blood there, but no husband. No cop anywhere either. Maybe he was on the upper floor, maybe Shelly had killed him.

Russo hustled to the back door in time to see Shelly humping the bags to his truck, putting them in the toolbox, along with the shotgun.

Shelly slammed the lid and clinched the lock.

He had the money and was making a break for it. Russo couldn't let him get away.

Russo stepped out and edged closer as Shelly climbed up into the truck cab, looking hobbled. Russo charged the vehicle, ready to yank Shelly out.

But then Shelly hollered, "What the fuck?!"

The truck hadn't started. Russo slowed as Shelly clambered out, the truck shaking on its shocks.

He glared at Russo. His face was a ruddy mass of sweat. "The fucking keys – you have them?"

Russo said nothing.

"Give them to me." Shelly put out his hand.

"I don't got 'em."

"Where the hell are my fucking *keys*?"

Russo had seen the look on Shelly's face before. It was a deranged, animal look, one that inmates got when they were fighting for their lives.

"Give me your phone," Russo said.

Shelly came right at Russo, if for no other reason than he was super fucking pissed and needed to hurt something.

This time Russo was ready for him. Shelly swung and Russo easily ducked the punch. He slammed Shelly with a straight shot to his ear, a good, solid punch, and Shelly yelled and grabbed the side of his head as he stumbled back. But he recovered and charged Russo again, coming in low, knocking Russo off balance.

They hit the ground beside the truck. Russo struggled to get the advantage, but Shelly was like a wild bear. Russo thought of Nate Reuter, how in those cage matches just about every fight went to the ground, and that was where it was won. He tried to trap Shelly the way he thought a fighter would, wrapping his legs around the man and twisting until he got on top.

It worked, and he had Shelly pinned beneath him, spitting and grunting and all red-faced with rage.

Russo snapped him in the nose with a short punch and Shelly's head bounced off the ground. His eyelids fluttered and he exhaled with a wheeze. Then he was still.

Russo shook the fresh pain out of his hand and looked around. He saw how the blood trail wound round from the front of the house and led to Shelly's truck. If Shelly hadn't been so hasty and agitated he would've realized that the wounded husband had gotten his keys.

Good for you, buddy.

Russo took Shelly around the armpits and dragged him through the grass. The man was heavier than an ox, but Russo was able to get him in the back door and leave him in the kitchen.

It was almost one thirty. Shelly had to make the call. Russo removed one of the gardening gloves he wore, went through the CO's pockets, and found the phone. His big awkward fingers poked at the buttons until he reached the screen with the texts to Richard.

His heart lifted. Shelly had bluffed. The texts were still the same, just a series of OKs. He was about to punch in the letters when the cop showed up at the bottom of the stairs, pointing his gun.

"Put the phone down," the cop said. He was pale, holding a wounded hand against his chest, but he was dead serious.

Russo swallowed. "I can't. I have to send a message right now."

"I don't care. Put it down."

"I have to do it. You don't understand, man. My wife and daughter."

The cop straightened his gun arm so that Russo was staring into the black hole of the barrel. "You don't drop that phone I'm going to shoot the arm holding it, do you understand?"

"Fine. Then you can take the phone and send the text. I'll tell you what to do."

The cop narrowed his eyes. "What are you doing here? Who are you?"

"Just let me do this."

Shelly moaned on the floor, starting to move. Russo saw a blur of movement out of the corner of his eye.

He and the cop both looked out the front windows at the green Prius coming around the house.

Those hybrid engines were so damned quiet.

Now the cop really didn't know what to do. His eyes jerked back and forth between Russo and the vehicle. He was confused, he was probably in a world of pain, but he made his decision and stayed where he was. They both watched as the Prius turned onto the road and drove off.

Russo saw two shapes inside it. The husband and wife had left.

He typed the two letters and hit send.

CHAPTER THIRTY-FOUR

The phone in the dining room rang a moment later, sounding like something from a doctor's office. Russo and the cop were in a stalemate stare-down.

"I'm gonna answer it," Russo said.

The cop, growing paler by the second, and dripping blood all over the floor from his mangled hand, didn't object.

Russo wriggled back into the glove and answered. "Hello?"

"Jimmy, it's me."

"Jock?" Russo felt a mixture of fear and elation. "I was in the middle of texting the—"

"Jimmy, listen, the cops came."

"The girls are okay?"

"Yeah. The cops showed and the two guys bolted out the back."

"That's great, bro. That's really great." Russo suddenly felt weak in the knees, like he needed to sit down, but he stayed where he was. Felicia and the baby were temporarily out of harm's way. This was way better than just having Shelly's phone to string them along. "Did the cops chase them?"

"Yeah, think so. And you know, Feef is giving her statement to the other one, the woman you mentioned."

"Barbieri?"

"Yeah, right, Barbie doll. She's not half-bad-looking for an older—"

"Jockey, listen to me. You tell Barbieri that they're working with a woman named Kim Delahunt. She's up at Rikers right now. You hear what I'm saying?"

"Jimmy... those're cops, man..."

Russo raised his voice. "Jock, stop it. You're clean, we're both clean, you've been a janitor at the school for years now."

"Jimmy, you know I'm not clean. That thing I got into with Bobby Mars, the night you drove my car..."

"I don't give a shit, Jock! Listen. Yeah, I helped you out. Now you gotta help me out. Okay? I got pulled into something. Okay? Delahunt used those guys to put pressure on me to cooperate. They posted my bail, sent me up here."

"Up where?"

"I don't know. The Adirondacks. It smells like cow shit. You'd love it."

Shelly was stirring, getting to his feet. Russo met eyes with the cop in the room. "I gotta go, Jockey. You do what I said."

Jockey started to protest again and Russo hung up. He stared at the cop, hoping it was all sinking in.

The cop didn't say anything for a minute. He kept the gun aimed at Russo. "Who are you?"

"I couldn't afford bail, I went to Rikers. The rest you just heard me say on the phone."

"You're not connected to these guys in any other way?" The cop made a nod towards Shelly, who was getting to his hands and knees.

"This guy picked me up from the bus station. That's all I know. Who are you?"

"Investigator Morales. State Police." He lowered his gun and holstered it. "I need that cell phone, please."

"You're not getting it." In fact Shelly's phone was buzzing in Russo's pocket. Richard was probably freaking out, wondering how the police had gotten involved.

"Fine. Keep the phone for now." Morales turned his hip towards Russo. "Take these handcuffs and put them on him. Can you do that?"

Russo took the cuffs and knelt beside Shelly, and whispered in his ear. "You hear that? My girls are safe." Then he grabbed Shelly's neck and shoved the man down.

Shelly growled and struggled as Russo mounted him, managed to get his hands around to his backside. Before he could clinch the bracelets home, Shelly bucked, knocking Russo off balance. The big man was quick – he'd been lying in wait, storing up energy.

Shelly scrambled to his feet. He rushed Morales as the cop tried to pull his gun. Shelly rammed into Morales who went sprawling back, bashed his head against the wall, and crumpled to the floor.

Shelly spun around, his stance wide, arms out and hands clutching. He looked like a pro-wrestler standing there, and Russo went after him.

The two men broke through the front door and landed on the porch in a heap. Russo was on top of Shelly again. They were evenly matched, but Shelly seemed to be still reeling from the last crack upside his head. Russo grabbed the man by his ears, lifted, then slammed his skull down. The wooden floorboards cracked, and Shelly's eyes rolled back white.

Enough.

Russo dragged him over the threshold. He rolled Shelly over, found the cuffs on the floor and clamped them on. Now Shelly was lying face down on the floor just like he'd made the woman do.

Russo, sweating from the exertion, moved on to Morales and checked the man's pulse. He was alive but unconscious.

He thought of the money stashed in the back of Shelly's truck – *How much? Half a million bucks? More?* Surely this involved more than local PD. The feds were always nearby when it came to bank robberies. Morales might not have been able to call for backup in time, but Russo could call 911. He just needed to do a few things first, like get that shotgun out of the truck. He'd gotten his prints on it at the cabin, and now it had been used to shoot the husband.

The husband had the keys, but he was gone. Unless he hadn't gotten the keys at all. Russo had just assumed it. Shelly could have taken the keys out of the truck at some point, then lost them while fighting with the cop upstairs. There was a chance at least. He needed to check.

Russo left the two unconscious men and walked up to the next floor.

There was a wide hallway feeding three rooms one way, and a single room the other. He looked through all of the rooms, bathroom last.

He was a mess, blood drying on the side of his face, matting his hair down on one side, one of his ears bleeding. He removed the gloves again, ran the tap and cleaned himself up, watching the water turn red as it circled the drain.

He sat down on the toilet. The bathroom was wrecked. There were shampoo bottles and toothbrushes on the floor. Morales and Shelly must've tussled in here. The bathtub was an old-timey type, with clawed feet. The shower curtain was rumpled and drawn back. Bright red blood was splattered on the white porcelain. He looked everywhere, but no carabiner full of keys.

Russo drew a shuddering breath. Time, events, everything was blurring together. There had been too many hours spent sitting in a subway toll booth, and these past years keeping house with Felicia, changing Zoe's diapers, laughing, forgetting his old life. He didn't have the mind for this anymore, nor the heart.

Shelly's phone vibrated in his pocket, a reminder of the text that had come in two minutes ago. Russo stared at the words, wondering how to respond.

What the hell is going on?

He started to type an answer when a vehicle turned in the driveway, car doors opened and slammed shut. Jesus, this house was like Grand Central goddamn Station. Maybe Morales had called for backup after all, and they were just arriving.

Russo put the phone away, quietly left the bathroom, and tiptoed to the biggest bedroom, which overlooked the porch and driveway.

A black Audi had pulled in next to Morales's vehicle. There was a man in a suit checking it out. Another man circled round the back of the house, out of sight, and two more started for the front door.

Russo carefully crept to one of the rooms with a view of the backyard, wincing as a floorboard creaked beneath his weight. He looked down at Shelly's pickup just as the man who'd walked back found the toolbox, jiggled the locked lid. Then the man leaned into the passenger side of the truck.

Russo felt vibrations as the others moved around below him in the house. Muffled voices came up through the floorboards. Russo couldn't make out exactly what they were saying, but he could imagine they'd discovered Shelly and the cop. Who were these guys? Not more cops, no way. Something else.

The guy at the truck pulled his head out, flipping through some papers now in his hand. His voice carried up through a double-hung window, opened halfway for the fresh air.

"I got a registration! Sheldon Danvers."

After shouting this towards the house, he glanced up at the top floor.

Russo jerked away from the window, his heart suddenly hammering. He didn't know if he'd been seen. He stayed out of sight.

"That's the CO fucker from Cold Brook." The muffled words came from directly below Russo. The kitchen. "And the car out front is an unmarked."

Russo remained crouched and listened as the guy by the truck called back, "You fucking kidding me? There's a fucking cop in there? He alive?"

"Barely."

A new voice joined in. Russo felt as much as heard the booming words. "Hey! Anthony!"

"What?"

"What's in the truck?"

"Bunch of shit. Locked toolbox in the back. What's the matter, Eddie, we ain't happy?"

"Nah. We ain't. It ain't here. Paulie's checking the basement."

Russo sneaked a look back out the window. The man standing by Shelly's truck, Anthony, tried the toolbox again, yanking on the lid as if he could just tear it off by brute strength.

Anthony. Paulie. Eddie. And a fourth guy, now joining Anthony at the truck.

Anthony scowled, wiped his forehead in the heat. "Did you check the CO for keys?"

"Nah. Nothin'."

"Well, what the fuck? Help me get this open, Vic. Don't just stand there."

Anthony, Paulie, Eddie, and Vic. They sounded like guys from Bed-Stuy, or somewhere like it. Could be Jersey, too, who knew. Organized crime guys, muscle. Somehow they knew about the money and were here to collect.

"I'm going after them," someone said from beneath Russo. Russo felt his throat turn dry. They were talking about Emily and her husband, they must've seen the couple leave. That meant they'd been watching, waiting.

"You're gonna go after them? They weren't even supposed to be here. Maybe we need to just let 'em go..."

"No. We need that truck, and they might have taken the keys. We'll just modify the plan a little bit."

"You think that's what he'd want?"

"Yeah I know that's what he'd want... Vic! Meet me in front!"

Russo heard the front door bang open. The house beneath him fell silent. He thought there was one guy left, Paulie, but in the basement. He dared to hurry back to the front side of the house and see Eddie get into the black Audi. Vic joined him a moment later and the car tore out of the driveway in the direction the Prius had gone.

How long had it been since the couple had left? Russo had spent a few seconds talking on the phone, a few more fighting Shelly, a minute or two looking for the keys. Maybe it had been enough time for the couple to have gotten away.

CHAPTER THIRTY-FIVE

Brett was struggling to stay conscious.

Emily kept talking to him. "You're going to be okay, baby. You're going to be okay."

She had blood on the side of her head, and he was worried about her. He was also worried that he was going to die.

The Prius was driving funny, the rear axle shuddering.

"Watch the road…"

"We're going to drive to the hospital. Okay? You just need to stay with me."

Brett used both hands to hold the side of his stomach together. It was burning worse than ever down there, and he had visions of his insides slipping out. He didn't think they would, but it felt like that.

He also had the keys in his hand from the truck. He'd spotted it after Morales was taken inside, and he'd crawled a bit further, seen the chrome grille of it around the edge of the house. He hadn't been able to find any shotgun shells, but he'd yanked the keys from the ignition. Maybe it wouldn't do any good – maybe it would've been better to let the son of a bitch who'd shot him just drive off, leave them alone. But something – pride, maybe – had said, *No, don't let him get away.*

He had to be working with the Fighting Bandits. Possibly a prison guard, maybe even from Cold Brook, in collusion with the woman bandit, Kim Delahunt.

"You still with me?" Emily really sounded worried.

"Still here. How are you?"

"I'm great, I'm super great..."

"What happened to yoga?"

"She cancelled. I just went and got a few groceries. There's some granola bars in the back if you're hungry."

She looked at him with such an affable smile that he had to laugh. And the laughing hurt, and the burning worsened, and again he envisioned the red ropes of his intestines leaking out and piling on the floorboards.

"You're going to make it," she said, serious again. "You're going to be just fine. And what a fucking book this is going to make, huh?"

The darkness was closing in around his vision. Emily must've sensed it because she rolled down her window. The wind blew around inside the car.

"Brett? Baby, keep your eyes open. Brett, you gotta stay awake."

"I'm awake," he slurred. It felt so good to just close his eyes, though. He'd managed to get the seat back to a nice recline. He could sleep all the way to the hospital – what was wrong with that?

"Brett..."

"Mmpf. I'm awake, I'm awake."

"Brett, there's someone behind us."

"What?" He popped his eyes open.

"Behind us." There was a trill of panic in her voice.

"What do you mean?"

"I mean there's a black car behind us, Brett."

Brett tried to sit up and see behind them. Every movement triggered a wave of pain that rolled up from his abdomen and seemed to pulse in his temples. "Keep driving."

They were still in the middle of nowhere. They'd only left the house a few minutes ago. It was another couple miles to the interstate – the county backroad was a winding path through the countryside. There were a few farms around, big rolls of hay sheathed in white plastic, a pen of alpacas in the distance. Nothing else.

"Brett, they're right behind us."

He craned his neck to see, gritting his teeth with the pain. He saw the car and stared in disbelief at its flashing red and blue dash lights.

"Maybe they're cops," he said. "Undercover, or FBI."

But he knew that anyone could buy those types of police lights right off the internet. Sometimes emergency workers used them in their personal vehicles. When you saw lights, it made you want to pull over. Maybe Parker was right after all. Maybe these were bad people.

"Just keep going," he said.

The black car was really on them, swerving back and forth a little. Its driver's side window came down and the driver stuck out a hand, jabbed a finger in the air towards the road shoulder. *Pull over.*

"They can just follow us to the hospital," Brett said. His vision was darkening again. The longer he stared out the rear of the Prius, the more it looked like he was watching things through a tunnel.

"Brett, Jesus, you're bleeding bad, honey…"

They passed an apple orchard, bristling with blossomed trees. The black car veered into the opposite lane and started to overtake them.

It slowed and paced them. The passenger rolled down the window and held up a badge. He yelled, "Pull over up here, okay?"

"Brett, I'm gonna do it. I'm gonna pull over."

Everything was hazy. He felt cold, his legs were tingling like they were losing sensation. He dropped back into the seat, close to passing out.

"Parker talked about other people involved. I don't think you should."

"Did he say who?"

It struck Brett as an odd question. "No. He wouldn't."

"Brett you're bleeding everywhere…" She sounded panicked. "Are you keeping pressure on it? Ah God, Brett. We need help. First aid. Something. We have to stop that bleeding. You also said the FBI could be involved, so maybe it's them."

Emily slowed down. Brett pulled his eyes open and looked in the mirror. The black car dropped further back, lights still flashing. Emily pulled off in front of a red barn with white trim that said *Darby Apples* and stopped the car.

"I have to get you help," she said.

The black car rolled up behind them. The dust from both vehicles rolled through, turning everything grayish-brown for a moment, and then the ostensible cops appeared, one on each side of the Prius. They were dressed in dark suits.

One leaned down through Emily's open window. "Folks, take it easy. We know what happened, we're here to help."

"We need to get him to the hospital," Emily blurted. "Do you have medical supplies?"

"Oh, absolutely," said the one on Brett's side of the car. He opened Brett's door. Brett glimpsed a tattoo just under the cuff of the man's sleeve. "Let's get you there, quick."

He stared down at the keys in Brett's hand.

CHAPTER THIRTY-SIX

Russo sat in the front bedroom.

What the hell is going on?

He typed his response.

Bad cell service. Everything OK.

The two men left behind were making a racket downstairs. Something sounded like it was being dragged across the kitchen floor. A voice drifted up the stairs.

"Hey! The fuck? You just slopped that shit all over my shoe!"

Someone else mumbled, maybe an apology. Then, more dragging.

"Careful! You got bleach on your gloves! Don't get any on him."

Russo lifted the bug screen on the window, set it aside gingerly. The road in front of the house was quiet, empty. If anyone else was around, watching, he didn't see them. He squeezed through and stepped onto the porch roof, then quickly pulled the screen back in place. Crawling on his hands and knees toward the edge, he peered over the lip – about a ten-foot drop down to the ground.

He couldn't think about it for too long or he'd lose the nerve. He lowered half his body, legs dangling, then gave a shove.

A brief freefall and then his feet hit the dirt, his knees buckled.

He lay still, listening, hoping to God no one heard him. Sounds were nominal, and his legs felt okay from the drop. The phone vibrated in his pocket.

He scrambled away from the house, headed for the woods. Then he sprinted like he hadn't done in years, the tall grass and goldenrod slapping against his legs and hands as he pumped his arms and gnashed his teeth.

Safe in the trees, he stopped and looked back. From the angle he could see the house and Shelly's truck.

He waited, gasping for breath, trying to slow the slamming of his heart. He wasn't in the best shape these days.

He didn't see anyone. More importantly, no one seemed to have seen him.

Time to leave. He'd come in through these woods and knew there was a thruway on the other side, not far, which went straight down to New York City. He'd hitch a ride and be home to his girls in a few hours.

He took out the phone again. The message from Richard made him feel cold.

Call.

Fuck. Richard obviously sensed something awry. The cops had run him off, and he wanted answers.

Russo thought for a moment, then checked the signal on the phone. Three out of five bars. Closer to the interstate, he figured, service had improved.

He dialed his own cell phone number. The call went straight to voice mail – either because the phone's battery was dead or it had been damaged. He punched in his password and learned that he had two new voice mails.

The first was from Felicia, explaining what Jockey had said about the police being there, and that she knew he was out of jail. "Whatever you're doing, baby, be careful. Hurry home." Zoe was babbling in the background as usual, and hearing her pierced his heart.

The second message sobered him right up.

"Hello, Mr. Russo, this is Deputy Louisa Barbieri. First of all, your wife and daughter are okay, they're safe. Your wife, of course, is concerned. Your friend, Horatio Peña, doesn't seem to like the police. He's either not saying where you are or doesn't know. Uhm, we've been able to identify Richard Dean and Ernest 'Snake' Montoya as the two men who were at your house. We checked, and Richard Dean is the bondsman who put up your bail, so not sure if he's looking to collect so soon, or what, but there are proper channels for that. Your wife says she's not pressing charges until she speaks to you. At this time we're not taking any further action. If you'd like to discuss the matter, you can give me a call."

She left her number. Russo didn't call it. He immediately went back into the contacts and located the 917 number.

The line rang three times. Then a voice, reedy, ugly-sounding. "Shelly?"

"No. Shelly's dead. This is Russo. Go near my family again and I'll kill you, too. I'm coming."

He ended the call.

He felt strangely calm. His heart rate leveled off.

Things were going to be okay. Skinny, gimpy Richard and his halfwit friend "Snake" would stay away. The police had other things to do. And if they ended up coming around with questions, he was already forming a story, a way to spin this for the cops in order to keep free.

Just needed to get to the interstate now and thumb a ride home.

But he stayed riveted to the spot. For one thing, the shotgun with his prints on it was in Shelly's big toolbox. He wondered why four grown men hadn't just beat the piss out of that toolbox until they got it open. Shelly's bolt cutters had to be around somewhere, too. They didn't really need the keys to get at the money, but they'd said they wanted the truck, they wanted the husband and wife back. None of it sounded too good.

Get the hell out of here.

It was the right choice. It was the only choice. He had his own family to worry about, his own mess to deal with. The four men would likely keep the gun, it wasn't like they were going to turn it in to the police.

They way these guys moved, the way they talked – they were mafia guys, for sure.

Obviously Shelly was working with the bank robbers, he was Kim Delahunt's contact, someone helping her on the outside. And Reuter had been a fighter who went on a run of bank takeovers with Delahunt.

But that money, for some reason these guys were after it, too.

The money probably belonged to someone who'd stuck it in the bank, then had it robbed. Russo knew about outfits using banks to launder money. Maybe that included little banks in the mountains, like the one ripped off by Delahunt's crew. It could've been mob money. And those four guys in the Audi were here to reclaim it.

Why had Delahunt's crew ripped it off in the first place? How did they know about mob money getting cleaned by some bank way the fuck up in the middle of nowhere? Russo thought about Nate, pacing his cell, this kid who was a time bomb, talked a blue streak about what a badass fighter he was. Maybe he'd lost a fight, wanted the money collected by whoever had bet on the other guy. Or – and this happened all the time back in Russo's day – Reuter had agreed to throw a fight, then got it in his head to go after the money he'd lost.

At any rate, a real friggin' mess.

Time to go.

But, he didn't. He waited.

A minute passed.

The black car returned. Russo could just see the roof of it, slipping along above the high grass.

Behind it, the puke-green Prius.

They both disappeared out of his view as they parked in front of the house.

The husband had been shot. Shelly had gotten him right in the gut, and the guy would be in bad shape. The cop, Morales, wasn't too healthy, either. Neither of them would be any good to Emily.

Who was pregnant.

"Dammit," he said under his breath. "Dammit dammit dammit…"

He made fists as he crouched in the buggy underbrush. Since he'd been here, the friggin' insects had been eating him alive. He was starting to hate the countryside. He was safer in New York City, for God's sake.

What was he going to do? Take out four mob guys on his own?

He could call the cops. The signal was weak, but if it had been good enough to get through to his voice mail, he could call 911. They would be here in minutes, surround the place, and maybe the woman and her baby would be saved.

Maybe somebody had already called them. Someone who'd driven past the house, seen some of the terrible things happening. He hadn't exactly been people-watching. He knew it was a rural area, but *someone* had to have been by.

Right?

Cops might be on their way…

And then there would be a violent shootout. The mob idiots would take the woman as a hostage, or worse.

The shotgun might be a moot point, and otherwise he'd been wearing the gloves. But there could be blood, DNA. And the woman, Emily, could identify him. So could the cop.

As soon as the police learned he'd left on foot they'd have dogs out tearing through the woods and would set up roadblocks along the interstate.

He wanted time. He needed time. Time to get home and see his girls before any shit hit the fan.

He had to deal with this on his own.

Still muttering curses, Russo yanked the gloves out of his back pocket and stuffed his hands back into them.

He started out of the woods, then stopped. One of the men appeared and climbed into Shelly's truck. They fired it up and drove it out of sight. Russo waited a few more seconds, then crawled away from the woods. Keeping on his hands and knees, he moved towards the house, concealed by the weeds blowing in the hot breeze.

When he got to the garden, he stopped. There were some tools scattered around, including a shovel with a pointed blade.

Russo picked up the shovel and continued along the edge of the garden where the grass was still tall and thick. He was close enough to hear the men talking. One of them let out a celebratory whoop, the sound coming from the front of the house.

Russo figured they'd gotten Shelly's toolbox unlocked at last.

He thought again about the *Press-Republican* article on human remains found on some old farm. Obviously, he wasn't the only one who'd read it; the mob guys had known the money was here once the remains were found.

Or they'd known someone *else* was going to come for the money once the remains were found. Like the bank robbers, or their goon for hire, Shelly. Or Russo himself.

Either way.

He wasn't sure how it all fit together, but it didn't matter.

The house was still twenty yards away. Happy husband mowed this part, and now Russo was exposed. There was no more time to lose. Gripping the shovel like a spear, he ran for the cellar doors.

They were closed again, but the chain was gone. He left the doors behind and crept to the edge of the house. The porch floor came up to his stomach and he lowered into a crouch.

All the vehicles were still there. The black Audi had its back hatch open. One of the men, who Russo had learned was "Vic," stood next to the Audi. Vic had removed his suit jacket and rolled up his white shirt sleeves, revealing some barbed-wire tattoos. He wore yellow rubber gloves. He took them off and tossed them in the trunk. Then he lit a cigarette.

The guy looked twenty-five, thirty at most. It was just a hunch, but the way he stood there looking smug, Russo figured he didn't have much going on between the ears.

Russo made a sound – his best impression of a squirrel – by sucking a little air through his teeth. Vic looked over just as Russo ducked out of sight.

The dirt crunched beneath Vic's boots as he neared. The rest of the men banged around inside the house. Now that they had the money, if they were going to kill the cop, the husband and wife, they were probably trying to cover their tracks. Russo smelled bleach. They were cleaning the house, wiping out traces of DNA; staging it to appear a certain way for the police when they eventually arrived. It was what Russo would do.

Vic came to the corner of the porch where Russo was hiding. Vic's gun was out, his face one big sweaty scowl. Russo swung the shovel, hitting Vic in the side of the head. The impact made a hollow-sounding *bong!* and Vic dropped like a sack of mail.

Russo grabbed Vic's feet and pulled him closer to the cellar doors. He'd always wondered if something like that would work, just smacking a guy in the head with a shovel. It was now one less mystery in life.

He took Vic's weapon, a tight little Glock 19, ejected the mag, and emptied it. There was one last round left in the chamber and he popped it out. He used Vic's white shirt to wipe his prints from the gun and set it and the empty mag back on Vic's chest. Russo threw the handful of bullets into the yard.

Something caught his eye – the bolt cutters he'd set aside when he'd first entered the basement. He dropped the shovel and picked them up, hefting them, thinking they'd be better in close quarters than the shovel. He slipped around to the back of the house, staying tight against the wall until he came to the door to the kitchen.

The main door was open, just the screen door closed. One of the four men stepped out of the basement and into the kitchen.

The man turned and spoke to someone still apparently down there.

"That's good. Yeah. That's perfect."

Russo pressed against the wall beside the screen door as the guy turned and walked into the kitchen. He was muscular, strongest of the guys Russo had seen so far.

The guy opened the fridge and bent down, probably hunting for a cool drink.

Russo whipped open the screen door and sprang into the kitchen. The muscle-bound guy heard the screen door squawk and lifted his head from the fridge. Russo rammed into the fridge door, knocking the guy off balance.

Then Russo, wielding the bolt cutters like a tomahawk, brought it down on the guy's skull. Not hard enough to kill, him, just enough to brain him good.

Didn't work, though.

The bolt cutter glanced off the man's cranium and, with the downward momentum, bashed him on the shoulder. He grabbed Russo's arm and tore the bolt cutters from his grip.

Russo lunged forward, but the fridge door was still between them, and he failed to get the cutters back. The muscular man backed up. He seemed to need a moment to register what the hell was going on. He looked at the cutters, then at Russo.

"Paulie?"

Someone was coming up from the basement.

Russo left the fridge and ran. Just as one of the guys came up the stairs wondering what the hell was going on, Russo crashed into him. The new guy went sprawling onto the floor, his gun clattering away.

Paulie came around the kitchen island at the same time and charged after Russo.

Russo slammed the basement door closed behind him. His thoughts buzzing, he hoped the fourth and last goon wasn't also in the basement. He started down.

In the pale throw of the single overhead lightbulb lay the married couple.

The husband was passed out, looking real shitty.

Emily was conscious, and she stared up at Russo, face as white as the moon, hands tied behind her back, but alive and untouched.

Russo stepped beside the stairs. Simple wooden stairs, just tread and no risers, space on both sides – real neck-breakers. Paulie came bounding through the basement door a second later. He had the roll of duct tape and some shredded cloth in his hands. "Alright, so this is what we're gonna—"

Russo grabbed him by the ankles. The muscular man went ass over tea kettle down to the hard concrete floor, and Russo heard a crunch. The duct tape rolled away and the strips of cloth slowly fluttered to the ground.

The way Paulie landed, his legs were still half on the stairs, his back bent at a funny angle. He made weird noises, gasping for air like a fish out of water, something in his throat clicking.

Footsteps thumped from above. Someone was coming down from the top floor. Eddie and Anthony were the guys still left. Russo heard them arguing as they neared.

He grabbed up Emily, and for the second time that day brought the woman to the cellar doors and shoved them open.

Daylight poured in. As Eddie and Anthony got their shit together and came down the basement stairs from the kitchen, Russo and Emily ran up the concrete stairs out of the egress and into the sunny afternoon.

Vic was still lying where Russo had left him. Russo ran for the Prius, holding Emily by the elbow. She dug in her heels and shook her head violently back and forth.

"No time," Russo said between heavy breaths. He'd drag her by the hair if he had to. Anthony and Eddie were right on their heels.

Russo got to the Prius and stuffed Emily in the vehicle. He looked back at the corner of the house as he rounded to the driver's side and saw Anthony there.

Everything slowed down.

Russo saw the gun flash and felt the wind of the bullet inches from his face. The gun fired again – it seemed like a long time between rounds, but he knew it wasn't.

He dropped into the driver's seat. He twisted the keys dangling from the ignition, put the shifter in reverse and hit the gas. The Prius silently tore out of the driveway and onto the road.

Eddie and Anthony were running after it. Anthony still had his gun drawn and aimed, but Russo saw Eddie lunge for it, knocking the barrel to the side. Russo wrenched the transmission into drive and buried the accelerator. The car leapt forward, Russo struggling to keep the steering straight.

He watched in the rearview mirror as the men ran into the road. Then the Prius crested a rise, entered a dip, and the men disappeared. Russo kept the gas pedal nailed, their speed hitting seventy miles an hour, eighty.

Only after he'd done another ten seconds of white-knuckle driving did he slow down. He looked over at Emily.

She was scrunched down in the seat, her head buried in her arms.

"It's over, it's okay."

She gradually lowered her arms and sat up straighter. She looked behind them and Russo saw that her face was wet with tears.

"Do you have a phone?" he asked.

She shook her head, still looking out the back window. The wind was louder than the hybrid engine, thundering in the open windows, blowing Emily's hair wildly about. Russo hit the button and closed his window.

"Do you have friends around here?" he asked. "Neighbors?"

She shook her head, *No.*

"Alright. What's up ahead, here? Where does this road lead?"

He'd gone in the opposite direction Emily and her husband had taken earlier. It had been an instinctual move, no time to think.

"To Essex," she said. "Lake Champlain. Please let me go."

"What else is in Essex?"

"There's a ferry to Vermont. But I can't go with you."

He used his teeth to pull off a glove, then dug Shelly's cell phone out of his pocket and handed it to her. "Call the cops. You can tell them about the men at your house, and get your husband some help. I'll drop you at the ferry."

Emily didn't move for a moment. She just held the phone like it was a dead thing, she watched the road rolling away behind them.

"You see them? They following us?" Russo kept his eyes on the mirrors. So far, nothing.

"No."

Emily was listless. She still wasn't dialing. Russo gave her a quick look. "You alright? Are you hurt?"

She was a little banged up, he thought, but nothing major. She was in shock. She didn't respond to his question.

He said, "I had to get you out. I'll let you go, I promise. Just, please, give me this chance. Let me get back home to my wife and little girl."

Finally she faced forward and seemed to register the phone in her hand. The keypad beeped as she dialed 911.

CHAPTER THIRTY-SEVEN

Brett opened his eyes to the sound of gunshots. Everything was dark – he heard voices. A moment later, someone picked him up and carried him up a flight of stairs. Then the world grew lighter and he recognized his kitchen, upside down. Someone had him over their shoulder.

He saw the man who'd shot him, propped against the bottom of the stairs between the kitchen and the living room. He looked dead. One of the men in suits was wiping down a shotgun, then they placed it in his lap.

Morales looked pretty bad, too, lying on his back in the living room. His smaller gun was in his hand.

The way the men were sitting there facing each other, it looked like some Western movie that ended in a shootout with everyone dead.

There was a terrible, funky smell in the air. A mixture of two things – firecrackers and laundry. Not just any laundry, but the way the laundry room smelled after Emily washed her whites.

Then the front door swung open, there were heavy steps on the porch, and he was in the driveway. Blood on the dirt. Maybe his blood, maybe someone else's.

Emily...

The person carrying him walked a few more steps then set Brett on his feet. But his feet didn't want to work, his legs couldn't support his weight.

"Stand up." A powerful hand pinned him against a vehicle. The person opened a door, hoisted Brett, and shoved him into the back of a truck. He lay awkwardly across the rear seats in the extended cab. The door slammed closed.

It was beastly hot, but he was cold and shaking. He saw jumper cables on the floor boards, empty beer cans, tins of chewing tobacco, some newspapers, food wrappers, shotgun shells, a busted cell phone. He worked himself sitting. He couldn't feel his legs – he had to use his arms to do everything, and he struggled to elevate himself enough to see out the back window.

The black car wasn't there. He couldn't see the Prius either, but it was hard to remember what had happened to it. The men had tricked them into pulling over. One guy had taken Brett by gunpoint into the black car, the other guy had ridden passenger in the Prius, holding a gun on Emily. They'd all returned to the yellow farmhouse. Brett had finally blacked out along the way.

Obviously he'd been taken back inside, put in the basement for a time. He had no idea where Emily was, but if the black car was gone, he could only assume one of the men had kidnapped her. Now they were going to take him hostage.

Or kill him.

The passenger door to the truck opened. Brett slumped down and acted passed out. He cracked his eyelids and watched as a guy with a huge red welt on the side of his face crawled into the cab. His sleeves were rolled and he had tattooed arms – it was one of the guys who'd pulled Emily over. His white shirt was covered in blood along the shoulder.

Another man got behind the wheel. It was the second guy who'd stopped them and brought them back to the house, the same one Brett had just seen inside, wiping the shotgun. He turned around and looked at Brett. Brett shut his eyes completely; didn't move.

"Fuck," someone said. "That motherfucker bashed me in the face with a fucking shovel."

"I know, Vic."

The engine rumbled to life. Brett wondered what the hell these guys thought they were going to do, driving around in a beat-up truck with obvious wounds. The truck lurched forward and bounced out onto the road, and the driver made a hard turn.

They got up to cruising speed.

"Who is that fucking guy?"

"Anthony thinks he's working with Delahunt and Danvers. My guess is he's an ex-con; he was inside with Delahunt and Reuter. They got him involved so Danvers wouldn't have to go in the house. They either knew we were watching or something else. We really shouldn't have waited."

"Waited for what?"

"Soon as Sheldon Danvers drove by in his stupid truck, we shoulda moved in. But, we didn't know. We didn't know he'd had this *other* guy sneak into the basement…"

"Little Joey is going to be super fucking pissed."

"I *know*, Vic. Shut the fuck up."

"Where the hell is Paulie?"

"Don't worry about Paulie."

A silence developed. Then Vic said, "You made it look good, right?"

"I made it look best I could. Danvers was getting the money out of the house, the cop showed up, surprised him, there was an exchange of gunfire, both of them went down."

"Yeah, but they were all beat to shit, too."

"Hey! I did the best I fucking could, alright?"

Vic spoke in a small voice. "And we've got Danvers' truck…"

"Listen to me. You gotta stop putting that shit up your nose. Eat some ginkgo biloba, Vic. You're like a fuckin' child. No, *we* don't got Danvers' truck… this piece of shit in the *back* has Danvers' truck. Cops are gonna find *him* in the truck, not us. We're long gone. Get it? We'll drop it, meet with Anthony, get out of the state."

Little Joey. It sounded like a mobster if there ever was one, Brett thought, and had to be who Parker was afraid of. These guys worked for Little Joey. It was his money that had been stolen from the Placid bank.

"Fuck," Eddie muttered.

"What?"

"This thing just got all fucked up. She wasn't supposed to be there. Neither was her husband. Or this other guy, whoever he is."

"Maybe this other guy, the one who hit me with the fuckin' shovel, maybe he's with Oberst or something?"

"No. I don't think so. He's just some guy. Like I said, probably an ex-con – he had the look."

Vic sighed. It sounded like he was in pain. "You know, we never shoulda killed Oberst before we knew where—"

"You think I don't know that? You think I don't know that, Vic? But how hard is it to find four fuckin' bags of money in one house? I *still* don't know where he hid that shit. Must be a fuckin' secret room or something."

Brett stayed down, quiet, listening. He was still bleeding, and the blood terrified him. He didn't know how much more of this he could take.

A secret room in his house? That shit hadn't shown up anywhere in the property appraisal.

When Vic spoke again, he asked the same question forming in Brett's mind.

"But why the note?"

"Hey, it was Little Joey's idea. He likes those – whaddayou call them. Anachronisms."

Anagrams, Brett thought.

Eddie said, "If someone found it and the feds started looking at that place, whatever it was, Hurricane Road or some shit, we could make them out, buy a little time."

And that was it, Brett thought. This whole twisted mess he and Emily had stumbled upon amounted to gambling, theft, and stupidity. He was bleeding to death in the back of a prison guard's truck right now, his wife and unborn baby kidnapped – and for what? All he wanted to do was raise a family. Grow a garden. It made him angry.

He opened his eyes. He didn't know what he could do in his condition – maybe he could wrap his arms around the throat of the dumb one, Vic. He could at least do that. If he was going to die, if he was going to lose everything, he would go down fighting.

He started to push himself sitting when Eddie said, "Shit."

"What?" Vic sounded panicked.

"Fucking state trooper. Coming up on our six."

"Oh fuck," Vic said. "That fucking ex-con emptied my piece."

"Take mine. I'm gonna pull over. When the trooper gets up to the window, you let him have it."

CHAPTER THIRTY-EIGHT

The ferry port was a small place, just a few parking spots, the little village around it like something out of a storybook. Russo sat in the Prius and stared out at the water lapping the shore.

"And this is the quickest route to get downstate?"

She nodded. "Unless you want to go back and get on 87. But you said you wanted to stay off the main roads. This will take you into Vermont, you can pick up route 7, which will take you almost the whole way."

"Okay."

She blinked at him. "Who are you?"

Russo briefly told her his story. He didn't sugarcoat anything and he used few words. It took less than a minute. When Emily got out of the car and walked away, he didn't try to stop her.

A few seconds later, a state trooper pulled in, lights flashing but the siren silent. Emily had honored Russo's request and didn't mention him during the emergency call, but someone was here anyway. He watched her talk to a tall, tough-looking cop. The trooper spoke into a cell phone while looking at the Prius and at Russo. Maybe the men had fled the house and the police were out hunting.

This was it. It was over. No getting home to see the girls. No pinching those tiny little jujube toes on his baby daughter. The next time he got to see her in person, she wouldn't be a baby anymore. If he was lucky, she'd still be a kid. Unlucky, and she'd be a teenager. He'd blown it. He'd completely blown it all – his second chance at life, a family life, and it was gone. Drifting away like the ferry which left the shore, sailing out over the shimmering water.

Another ferry passed it, on its way in to dock.

Russo looked back at the trooper with Emily, surprised to see the trooper getting into his vehicle. Emily stepped away and the trooper did a hasty turnaround and raced off, raising dust.

Emily walked slowly back to the Prius. She had her fingers laced across her belly. Then she opened the passenger door and dropped into the seat.

"You got any money?"

Russo was confused. "Where did the cop go?"

"He got another call. I overheard it – another trooper requesting immediate back-up, and he's the closest, I guess. Do you have any money on you?"

Russo just stared at her. She had light brown eyes, with flecks of green in them. A really beautiful Italian woman. He wondered if Zoe would have eyes like Emily's one day. "I don't have any money, no."

Emily frowned then popped the glove compartment, shuffled around, came out with a couple of loose bills. She opened the console between the seats and scrounged a bit more, counted it up, and handed it all over to him. "That's enough to get you across as a foot passenger."

"I don't get it."

"There will be more cops here soon and they'll want to talk to you. But you can get on that ferry right now and get into Vermont. Just not in this car, okay?"

She nodded out the window and Russo watched the inbound ferry come to rest against the pilings. The gate came down and connected the boat with the parking lot, and a worker removed the rope in between. A few cars were queued and waiting, but a couple foot passengers boarded first.

"Better go," Emily said.

Russo looked at the money in his hand, then gazed into Emily's eyes for another moment before he got out.

He walked to the pillbox, where an attendant gave him a strange look. He'd cleaned his face up but was developing that nice bruise around his eye, and his clothes were dirty, torn, speckled with dried blood.

The attendant didn't ask any questions. She took his money and handed him a ticket with a lopsided smile.

Russo glanced back at Emily one last time and made a small wave.

She raised her hand in return and he boarded the ferry for Vermont.

CHAPTER THIRTY-NINE

Brett stayed low in the back of the truck cab as the men pulled off the road. His heart was pounding now, despite how much blood he'd lost. If his heart pumped any harder, he was going to lose the rest of it in minutes.

"That's a lady cop," Vic said.

"I can see that."

"Black, too."

"I said I can fuckin' *see.*"

"She's not getting out of the car. Eddie, what if the ex-con called the cops?"

"That ex-con ain't gonna call the cops."

"Well, there's a fucking state trooper bitch behind us. We gotta just *go.*"

"Shut up."

Brett was torn – if he popped up right now and revealed himself, banged on the glass, hollered for help, it was going to touch things off like a match. They might kill him at last, they might shoot at the trooper. It was a black woman, they said – Brett wondered if it was the same female trooper who'd showed up after he and Emily had first called the police about the bones in the backyard.

He got ready, tensing for the opportunity to rise up and make himself seen and heard.

"Alright. She's getting out," Eddie said.

"Shit, shit, shit. Eddie, I never shot a cop."

"Stop whining."

"She's going to see the guy, Eddie!"

"Here she comes…"

Brett got his hands underneath him. There was only one gun between the thugs, and whiny Vic had it. Forget making himself seen to get saved by the trooper – he needed to get that gun. He got himself ready, listening as Eddie whispered, "Hang on…"

Suddenly the truck lurched forward as Eddie stomped the gas. Brett heard the tires spinning in the soft shoulder and shearing rubber when they hit the pavement. The truck roared forward, then stopped.

"Eddie! Eddie!"

"Shut *up*!"

Eddie put the truck in reverse, the tires squalled and they backed up, then shot forward again. They had turned around, apparently.

"She's running." Eddie sounded like he was enjoying it. "She's getting back in the car. Brace yourself, bitch."

Brett saw Vic grab the handle above the door and put his palm on the dashboard. The engine thundered – Eddie was going to ram her.

The impact was loud and violent, throwing Brett hard against the backs of the seats. Eddie whooped like a cowboy at a rodeo.

Then he backed the truck up and jerked forward again. The truck bounced over uneven terrain – they were off-road.

"Did you see that? Did you see that shit?" Eddie was ecstatic. Vic wasn't saying anything.

Brett, with fresh pain racking his body, managed to get a look between the seats. Vic's head was lolling, blood running from his scalp. His eyes were closed. Despite having braced himself, it looked like Vic had smashed his head on the dashboard.

Brett hoped the trooper was okay.

The truck bucked over furrows of earth. Up and down, up and over, it felt like his bones were coming apart, blood squirting from his wounds with each successive impact.

"Vic? Vic, you with me?"

Vic didn't respond.

Brett got up. He had trouble moving, everything hurt, and there wasn't a lot of room in the back of the truck, but he was able to reach over the passenger seat and grab the gun in Vic's lap.

Eddie saw him, his eyes went wide, and he made a grab for the gun.

Brett was quick with the trigger. He'd never shot a gun before in his life, but this was close range, a small handgun, and he did it without thinking.

The round exploded out of the barrel. Eddie's face contorted in pain and he let go of the steering wheel.

The truck bounced a few more times and then came to rest.

Brett had shot Eddie through the ribs. Eddie put his hands on the wound, then made another move for Brett, who had shrunk back into the rear of the cab. When Eddie came after him, Brett fired again. The shot took Eddie in the chest and he stopped. His mouth opened and closed a couple times and he stared down at his torso in disbelief.

Brett kept the gun aimed, this time at Eddie's head.

Eddie backed away. He got himself turned around and scrambled for the door handle, got the door opened and then fell out of the truck.

Everything was silent except for the pinging of the engine.

Then Brett heard Eddie grunting. He saw the man rise to his feet and hobble away from the truck, holding himself around the ribs.

They were in the middle of a cornfield, the vegetables just sprouting. Brett climbed through the seats and got behind the wheel. There was so much blood everywhere – he didn't know what was his blood and what was Eddie's. Eddie was a few yards away, stumbling along. Eddie glanced back at the truck, lost his footing and went down. He didn't move.

Still gripping the handgun, Brett got out of the truck. He felt the sun on his skin – it had to be ninety degrees – but he was still cold inside. Freezing.

Brett looked back at the diagonal path Eddie had cut through the cornfield, really making a mess of things. He saw the trooper car on the road in the distance, the front end all smashed in. He didn't see the trooper anywhere.

No one was around. The nearest house – a big, white, rambling farmhouse – was ensconced in a grove of maples a few hundred yards away. He recognized where they were – just about a mile from Essex. Someone had to come along eventually, see the trooper, and have a phone. Or, he would figure out how to use the radio in the cop's car. He started that way and stopped.

In the back of the truck, the toolbox was unlocked. Whoever had opened it when they'd gotten the keys back from him hadn't bothered to lock it back up. And all the jostling as they'd bounded over the corn furrows had sprung the lid.

There were tools in there, a winch and some rope, but no bags of money. Brett searched the bed but it was empty. There was no money in the truck.

Then he looked down at his legs, the jeans soaked and dark with his blood. He hadn't been able to use his legs a few minutes ago, now he was standing on them. All the adrenaline was overriding his system.

He felt short of breath. He clutched the side of the truck, dropping the gun into the soil, holding himself up. But his strength was ebbing. It had taken the last of what he had to get the gun and shoot Eddie.

I shot someone.

He sank to the dirt and leaned against the pickup's rear tire. He watched the quicksilver dance over the road. He thought someone was coming, but it could've been a mirage.

CHAPTER FORTY

The boat was smaller than the ferries to Staten Island. This one only held about twenty cars. The upper deck featured a small café. Two sets of stairs ascended.

The vehicles were still queuing for the ferry when Russo climbed to the second level. He kept an eye on the ferry parking lot, the road beyond it, expecting the police. He saw a black car pull past the pillbox and roll slowly aboard.

You've got to be kidding me…

The black car was an Audi.

Russo slipped into the café. A plastic menu board hung behind the counter, advertising sandwiches, potato chips, soda.

He had a few bucks left from the money Emily had turned up in the car and was able to buy something to eat and drink. He moved to the window and continued to watch the cars below as he ate. He could no longer see the Audi – it must've parked beneath the overhang off the upper deck.

A ferry worker hooked a thick chain across the rear of the boat. The water burbled and the vessel started across the lake.

Russo waited by the window until he saw the man coming up the aft stairs. He was the one called Anthony.

Russo faded back from the window and left the café on the fore side.

He calmly descended to the main deck, smiling at some passengers who'd gotten out of their car to watch the prow of the ship cut through the water. The ferry gently rocked, and the water sprayed white over the deck.

He eased into the shade of the overhang and spied the black car. No one else was in it. Anthony was here alone. He must've had the same idea about getting out of the state and sticking to lesser routes.

Russo finished his sandwich and licked his fingers, then wiped his hands on his pants. He glanced around before trying the door. It was unlocked. Anthony had let his guard down, thinking he was in the clear.

Russo slipped into the back of the car.

Brown leather interior, spacious, a nice car for sure. It was dark inside, the sun blocked by the overhang. Russo nestled down into the footwells behind the front seats and waited.

It was a fantasy to think he was coming through this unscathed. The woman may have done something wildly kind and unexpected – after hearing his story, she'd helped him to escape. But the cops would still want to talk to him. The trooper at the ferry had seen him in the Prius.

Even if the cop from the farmhouse – Morales – hadn't made it, the trooper was at least one member of law enforcement who could provide a physical description of Russo.

After everything came out in the wash, there was no way investigators would believe whatever story Emily had given the trooper. She'd probably catch hell for it, too – obstruction of justice.

But, she'd bought him a little time. Just like Anthony, he was on his way to another state, so he had a chance. Even if the feds were involved, Russo had a head start. Having wheels would be even better. He'd take the car from Anthony, and the first chance he got, he'd switch plates.

By now they were halfway across the lake. The ferry would arrive in Charlotte, Vermont. It was a nice, short little jaunt.

The driver side door opened and Anthony got behind the wheel.

CHAPTER FORTY-ONE

The state trooper came limping over the rows of corn, her gun out. Brett tried to speak, but nothing came out.

The trooper shouted, "In the truck, come out with your hands up!"

Another state trooper pulled up on the road in the distance. The officer hopped out and began to jog towards them.

The first trooper, the woman, called to the second trooper, "There's one in the truck, one on the ground, and this one is armed."

Brett was still holding the handgun he'd taken from Vic. He pushed it off his lap. He didn't want to get shot again after all that had happened. Once more he tried to speak but could only produce a wheezing grunt.

"Out of the truck, now!"

The door groaned as it opened. Brett couldn't see around to the other side but he imagined Vic stepping out into the bright day. The first trooper held her spot near the back bumper, her stance wide, solid grip on her weapon. She looked hurt but not too bad.

"Hands on your head," she said to Vic. "Down on the ground. On your knees."

The second trooper had arrived and dealt with Vic while the first trooper checked on Brett. She was still wary because she'd seen him with a weapon, and kept hers aimed. But then she seemed to recognize him. Her nametag flashed in the light – Soames. She was the same state trooper who'd first come out to the house to take the report on the bones.

"I'll be right back."

Brett watched her jog to where Eddie lay fallen. She came upon him slow, gun still drawn, and then took a knee, felt for his pulse. When she took her hand away she looked back at Brett.

A siren warbled in the distance, drawing closer. Brett lost consciousness.

When he opened his eyes again, the ambulance had parked alongside the road and EMTs were running over, carrying a stretcher. The two state troopers were close by, Soames getting some medical attention for a gash on her leg and a potentially cracked femur, Brett overheard.

As the EMTs worked on him, he marveled at how the whole thing had begun with him digging up a leg. This guy's leg; Oberst's leg. A man linked to organized crime who'd double-crossed his people, stolen money from this Little Joey guy, then cut a deal with the prosecutors to get into witness protection. And then he'd gone after the money. What a story. Emily had to hear it.

"My wife…" Brett moaned.

The second trooper came closer.

"Is she Emily Larson?"

Brett nodded. The EMTs were talking to each other about his wounds, but he wasn't listening. He stared up at the state trooper, waiting.

"She was at the Essex Ferry," the trooper said. "She'd placed an emergency call. Another unit just picked her up. She's okay."

Brett closed his eyes as something warm filled him up. Maybe it was whatever the medics were doing, maybe it was because his wife was alive. It was music to his ears.

He let the EMTs work on him. They seemed frantic, but he didn't mind. There was some shouting and then he was being moved. He thought he heard a helicopter, and when he looked up, he saw the blades chopping through the sky as one landed. Apparently it was for him.

The darkness was thick and cool. It felt like a pool in a cave, like something deep underground, a special place. He saw Emily there, on the other side of it. Even though it was below ground, the air was iridescent. A tiny figure emerged from behind Emily on shore, holding her legs. A little boy.

Brett waded into the pitch-black water, smooth as glass, soft as silk. He swam out to the middle, he waved to them. Then he slipped beneath the surface.

CHAPTER FORTY-TWO

As soon as Anthony sat down, Russo rose from the back seat and clamped a hand around the man's mouth. With his other hand he dipped into the suit jacket Anthony was wearing and pulled his weapon.

It was amazing how the skills were still there now that he'd shaken off the rust. Not to mention, he thought, now that Fifi and Zoe were safe.

He dug the gun into Anthony's ribs. "Take it easy," Russo said. "Let me see those hands. Put them on the steering wheel."

Anthony said something, muffled by Russo's big paw of a hand. But he did what Russo asked.

"Good boy."

"You're a dead man," Anthony managed.

"Yeah, that's the line. Now, I want you to keep calm, Anthony. We're going to drive off this ferry together, alright?"

The ferry was pulling into the Vermont side. It was another charming little port, a few cars waiting. The surrounding shore was craggy with rocks and evergreen trees. The vessel bumped the pilings gently and the workers prepared for the passengers to disembark. Anthony was breathing heavily. Russo burrowed the nose of the gun deeper into Anthony's side.

"Did you get a sandwich up there?" Russo asked. "I had a turkey on rye."

"Little Joey will have you fucking hunted down and killed."

"Little Joey, huh? You know, you try to fix a fight, then someone else steps into the pie. You can't trust fighters. Too much ego at stake. That's all gambling is – odds and stakes. I used to be part of this kind of life, you know. I've seen this before."

"Then you know how fucked you are."

"Well, I never had much choice. About being fucked, I mean."

Russo left it at that and watched as the foot passengers crossed onto dry land. The vehicles surrounding the black car fired up their engines.

"Start the car."

"No."

Russo leaned close, stuck the gun in even deeper. "Start the fucking car."

"No. You're going to have to shoot me. G'ahead. Shoot me and see how far you get. You stupid f—"

Russo hit Anthony in the head with the gun. In the movies, you might do that and a guy would be instantly knocked out cold. But Anthony moaned, took his hands off the steering wheel, tried to turn around. So Russo hit him again. This time Anthony went limp.

Russo jammed the gun in the waistband of his pants and quickly grabbed Anthony under the armpits and hauled him into the back seat. It was a monstrous effort and Russo was sweating and grunting. He looked up at one point and froze. A little kid, sitting in a minivan beside the Audi, was watching. But then Russo remembered the tinted windows. The kid may have heard something but couldn't see in. Then the minivan rolled forward.

Russo riffled through Anthony's pockets in the tight space. Finally he got the keys, climbed into the driver's seat, and started the engine. He dropped the driver's side window down a bit as he got the car moving. When he passed one of the ferry workers he branded a big smile on his face and the worker waved.

He was in Vermont.

He followed the cars out from the ferry to a narrow county road. The road wound through the countryside – Vermont was even prettier than upstate New York. Christ, it looked like a fantasy, with little white houses and red barns and a church with a perfect little steeple.

Fifi would've hated it.

The line of vehicles spread out, some people turned away, and when Russo thought it was safe enough, he pulled over.

Off the road was a sprawling field. Not a farm or an orchard, just an old pasture.

Russo stepped out of the Audi and took in the view. The field looked damned familiar. There was a distant line of rocks and then more field beyond, rolling up and away into a hill. It looked identical to his memories, the place his father had taken him as a boy.

Taken him to show him what life could be. Russo remembered now. His father, so sick he was jaundiced, purple rinds underscoring his dark brown eyes, taking his only son into the countryside to say, *See? There is another way.*

Don't be like me.

Russo snapped out of the daydream. Anthony was down, but not out. He was going to have to put the guy in the trunk for now. But not right here – it was the country, but vehicles were still cruising through on the road, and someone would see him. All the same, he reached in beside the steering wheel and hit the lever to pop the trunk. He walked around back to see how much room there was inside and found himself staring down at a dead body and the four bags of money.

CHAPTER FORTY-THREE

Emily wondered if she was in shock. There were so many police and paramedics on the scene that it felt like a circus, something staged. As if at any moment they were all going to stop pretending and have a laugh.

A state trooper escorted her from the back of a cruiser to where responders prepped Brett to be airlifted to a trauma center in Albany.

He was a complete wreck, his lower body covered in blood. His shirt and part of his pants cut away, his midsection wrapped in a large bandage already dark with blood. He was pale, his jaw slack, lips parted. They folded his arms over and strapped him to the gurney.

She waited for the tears to come, but they didn't. Hard to shake that feeling of unreality.

The helicopter thundered on the ground.

She started towards it when the trooper caught her by the arm. "Miss. We need you to stay here."

"He's my husband." The word had never carried so much weight. They'd been together for two years, married for three months. This was her *husband*, this was the man she'd decided to have children with, to grow old with. None of the rest mattered.

The trooper, gently but firmly, held her back.

Paramedics lifted the gurney into the belly of the rescue copter, then climbed aboard. The helicopter rose straight up and then banked south, towards Albany.

She noticed a man in a suit smoking a cigarette and standing by the pickup truck deeper in the cornfield. He started walking towards her and she saw him stick the cigarette in his pocket. She was overwhelmed, but she had enough wits about her to realize he'd been smoking an electronic cigarette.

He came stepping over the rows of green corn sprouts and stuck out his hand.

"I'm Detective Stokes," he said. "You must be Emily Larson."

Stokes took her from the trooper, led her to the road, away from the hubbub. She watched as people in white jumpsuits arrived, carried expensive-looking gear towards the pickup truck. More personnel were down the road where the trooper car had been damaged, taking pictures.

Stokes stood by another state trooper and the detective mumbled something in the trooper's ear. The trooper looked at her – he was the same officer who'd been at the Essex Ferry – then walked away to join the rest of the group. It was a kind of law enforcement galaxy between the trooper car on the road and the pickup truck which had come to rest in the burgeoning cornfield.

They continued on their way to an unmarked vehicle and Stokes opened the passenger door.

She didn't feel like getting in another car. She didn't feel like answering any questions. She just stood there, searching the sky for the helicopter. The sound of it had faded almost to nothing, but she saw it, just a speck now, in the southern sky.

"Ma'am?"

She got into the car.

At least it was quieter, and cool – the engine was running and the AC was blasting. The sweat began to evaporate from her skin. She put her hands over her stomach.

Oh Brett... Oh God, honey...

The tears finally stung the backs of her eyes, threatening to spill. She pursed her lips and took a deep breath through her nose.

She felt the detective watching her closely.

"What a day." He was attempting levity.

She offered a pained smile. "Yeah."

"He's going to be alright."

The tears felt hot on her skin, and she wiped them with the back of her hand. "You think so? He didn't look too good."

"He's going to get the best care. Emily, I'll take you to Albany myself to see him. This thing… what's happened here, this is pretty raw right now. We're all just struggling to make sense of it. There are other officers at your house – they just got there and I heard from one of them and it's not looking too good over there. Anything you can tell me right now… so we can get the guys who did this, who did this to your husband, and to you. Did you know any of these men?"

She wiped more tears and pulled herself together. "No."

"Tell me what happened. Can you do that?"

She could, and she did. The numbness was gone and her mind was clear. She explained everything to Stokes starting from the discovery of the bones. She went through that part quickly, figuring he was already up to speed. She then talked about how Brett was interested in the whole thing, and how he'd been trying to find out more on his own, planning to write a book.

She paused to fight back fresh tears, then pressed on, relating what she knew about Brett's discoveries, including talking to the cop at the Hurricane Road property.

"That's Daniel Morales," Stokes said.

"Is he… okay?"

Stokes said he didn't know, but the look in his eyes suggested he didn't think so.

"My husband said he was drinking. Acting a bit unstable."

"Morales has been going through some stuff. Upset about how things have played out with this case, and having some personal issues. I think that's what your husband was witnessing."

She continued her timeline of events and got to that morning, finding out that her yoga class was canceled, returning home, and then being attacked.

"Do you know who the man in my house was?" Her lip trembled as she thought of him putting her face down on the floor in her own kitchen. She felt angry, sad, and confused at the same time. Humiliated.

"We think so, yeah, we know him. Listen, we're going to go to your house now, alright? I'll be with you the whole time…"

Someone appeared at the car window, making Emily jump. It was another plain-clothes cop, a few years younger than Stokes, heavier, like a football player. He and Stokes gestured to each other through the glass, then Stokes nodded and put the car in gear.

"That's Detective King. He's going to accompany us on the way, and we're going to ask you a few more questions as we go. Listen, you just need to keep doing like you're doing, okay? You're sure you're not hurt? Do you want the paramedics to have another look at you?"

"I'm fine. I just want to get this over with and go see my husband."

The rear door opened and Detective King slipped into the back seat.

"Okay. Ready." There was a metal grate between him and Emily. "Hi," he said to her.

"Hello."

Outside their vehicle, it seemed like a hundred people had gathered. The firemen were setting out cones in the road. People in white jumpsuits were roping off the trooper vehicle with crime scene tape.

Someone stepped in front of the car and directed Stokes where to drive. Emily felt like everyone was looking in the car at her, watching as she and the two detectives slowly rolled through the chaos.

*

Her house was nearly unrecognizable. Swarmed with more law enforcement, including people wearing breathing masks, taking pictures of the two men sprawled out between the stairs and the living room. Their quiet lives had been overrun by the outside world.

Emily stood on the porch near the busted front door, the screen hanging off one hinge. The two detectives protectively flanked her. She saw someone cross the doorway with a cell phone in a bag.

"Hey, that's mine…"

The tech stopped, gave each detective a glance. Emily held out her hand and Detective Stokes nodded. The tech handed over the bag and Stokes intercepted before Emily could grab it.

"Hang on, just one sec, Emily." She watched him examine the phone, and he spoke quietly to King behind her back before handing it to her. "We just need to keep track of everything." Stokes wrote something down in a small red notebook jammed with scribbly handwriting.

She checked her phone – there were a dozen text messages, mostly from her mother, but also from her friend, Lori. There was one from the yoga instructor, Tilly, offering a belated apology for canceling class at the last minute.

You have no idea, Tilly.

She also had several missed calls, including one from Brett, and even Brett's mother. Emily figured the word had gotten out. Brett's father was still a volunteer fireman in Saranac Lake and regularly listened to the police scanner. Brett's parents were probably a wreck right now, his father doubtlessly hearing the police talk about an accident on Brett and Emily's road, maybe something about a Prius at the Essex Ferry.

There was also a text from Brett. The detectives were unabashedly reading over her shoulder as she opened the message from her husband. It had come in over two hours ago, right about the time she'd arrived home from cancelled class to find the man – Shelly – inside her house.

Babe, headed home. Think there could be something in our house. Stay away until you hear from me. Love you.

She handed the phone to Stokes who was leaning so close she could feel his breath.

He raised his eyebrows. "Okay? May I?"

She nodded, and he began scrolling through the messages.

Emily faced the driveway. She looked at Brett's motorcycle. Seeing the bike, having just read her husband's text, she felt a fresh pang of emotion – a hot, tight bunch in her chest. More people in white jumpsuits were analyzing the blood in the driveway. She watched them for a moment.

"I don't know much about law enforcement," she said to the detectives, "but your forensic investigators got here really fast."

"Mrs. Larson," Stokes said, "let's have a seat right over here, shall we?" He motioned to a set of wicker furniture, like it was his own. Suddenly the situation felt bizarre again, like this was no longer her home, but belonged to the cops, and she was just a guest.

Had the house ever even been hers? It felt like an alien place now, hostile, full of dangerous secrets. She wished she'd never laid eyes on it, never accepted her brother's offer to help.

Her legs were wooden as she walked across the porch. King sat down on the loveseat beside her; Stokes took the chair where he could face her and the front door at the same time, people coming and going.

Emily read Stokes' expression carefully. "We found a note," she said. "With the bones. You know about it, I'm sure."

Stokes traded a quick glance with King and put on a half-smile for Emily's benefit. "We do, yes, of course. Mrs. Larson, while it's still fresh in your mind, I need you to tell us exactly what happened when you came home this morning."

"Didn't I just do that?"

"One more time, please. If you would."

She looked between them. "Do I need a lawyer?"

"That's certainly your right. But you're a witness, Mrs. Larson, not a suspect."

He set a small audio recorder on the wicker table between them. She glanced at it, then looked at Stokes again.

"The note was an anagram. Brett got excited because he figured it out. Investigator Morales was there, so obviously the police figured it out, too. But then Brett thought the money was here, at our house, instead."

"Can you tell me, again, what happened when you walked in? Was there someone already in the house?"

She continued to ignore the questions, maintaining level eye contact with him. "Did you suspect there was something in our house? Did someone involved in this have ties to the property here? It was a real challenge to close on this house. There were reluctant family members. One in particular. Susan Resnick."

Stokes blinked. Then he shared another look with Detective King. He opened his mouth but was interrupted as another car pulled into the already vehicle-choked driveway. "That's the coroner." Stokes stood. "Excuse me."

He left the porch to greet the elderly man stepping out into the darkening day. Emily saw a storm coming from the direction of Vermont, gray pillows of clouds on a slow march.

She watched Stokes and the coroner walk together towards the house, Stokes giving her a quick look as they went inside.

Detective King spoke quietly. "You're not entirely off-base, ma'am," he said. "But this wasn't our investigation. It probably still isn't. We're with the county, so we're just hitting the ground running on this. A deputy checked the house here after your call for service came in, and Trooper Soames' distress call, and found the two men inside. We're here for the death investigation, but we're just the opening act. Does that make sense?"

"Yes," she said, feeling some of her tension easing. "So who is the main act?"

"They'll be here any minute. You're probably going to be talking to Investigators Tambor and Reed with the state police."

"Have they found anything on Hurricane Road? Did they find money from the robberies?"

"Not that I know of," King admitted.

"Why didn't they want to search this house? After my husband found the bones – why not look here if they knew there was unrecovered money?"

He looked away, seemingly avoiding her eyes. "I don't know."

But she thought he did. She thought maybe they hadn't known for sure, but could have suspected the money was at her house. And they'd waited, to see what would happen. To see if the money drew people out of hiding.

The thought made her sick to her stomach. It was only speculation, she really had no idea. She wanted somewhere to put the blame, and she decided to put it where it belonged, one way or the other – on the men who'd shot her husband, shot Morales, the cop inside the house.

"Detective King?"

He turned back to face her, kindness in his eyes. She held her phone in the air. "I need to call my mother. Can I do that, please? Before all these other people you're talking about get here?"

"Absolutely." He rose from the wicker chair and stepped away to give her some privacy. She saw him fold his arms and stand between her and the front door in a protective way.

Emily walked to the corner of the porch and called her mother. Her mother answered on the first ring.

"Hi mom…" Emily choked up again, unable to stop the tears.

CHAPTER FORTY-FOUR

Russo closed the lid on the body and money and got back into the car. He drove a ways until he found a dirt road that went back into the woods. The Audi had GPS and he switched it on, located himself on a map of the area.

The dead body in the trunk was Paulie, the one who Russo had tripped as he'd come down the basement stairs. Russo hadn't meant to kill the guy. Shit.

He took the windy, dusty road, his breathing shallow, hands clammy. No, for God's sake, he hadn't meant to kill him.

Maybe he *hadn't* killed Paulie. Maybe Paulie had just been injured and had become a liability. Russo knew about organized crime, knew how brutal it could be. A wounded guy in the heat of battle was like a lame member of the herd. The herd didn't hesitate to stampede the wounded party to death. Anthony could have finished Paulie off.

But whether he'd killed Paulie or not, Anthony got the body out of there, not wanting their outfit linked to the scene. And now Russo was driving around in this flashy stolen car with that body in the trunk. The situation needed a fix.

He watched the GPS, aiming for a small pond that showed up on the map. There were a couple of houses out here, and a big, sprawling ranch that seemed to take forever to get beyond, the post-rail fence running alongside the road interminably.

There was a lot of money in the back of this car, too. An eyeball guesstimate, over half a million, at least. That much money would go a long, long way. He and the girls could be set up for life. If he was careful, contacted the right people – it had been years – invested some of it, saved some more, and spread it around carefully to avoid the prying eyes of the IRS, he and the girls would be sitting pretty.

Of course, the first thing he'd have to do was hire good lawyers for when the police came knocking.

Anthony moaned in the back seat. He was coming around.

Russo stopped the car. One thing was sure, when all this was over, he would be glad to be back in the city. The countryside was nice, but it just went on forever. *Sorry, Pop. The country life is not for me.* No landmarks, no bridges, no subways, no direction. Just these rambling properties, middle of nowhere, like this one, sitting back from the road by a quarter mile. Never seemed to be anyone around. Where did the people go?

Anthony grunted again. He was trying to sit up. "You mother-fucker…"

Russo popped the door open. He stepped out into the arid, scorching day and pulled the gun from his pants. He opened the rear door, grabbed Anthony by his feet, and yanked him out.

Anthony landed smack on the hard, dirt road, the wind knocked out of him. He gasped for breath and kicked his legs in the air. Russo stayed back, holding the gun on him.

After Anthony had his little fit and sucked in a whooping breath, he flipped himself over and gained his feet.

He glared at Russo, one of his eyes squinty in the sun. "Where the fuck did you come from, anyway?"

"Queens," Russo said without really thinking about it. His mind was elsewhere. He noticed the hazy, cumulus clouds low in the eastern sky. There was a tumble of thunder from that direction, a storm still a ways off.

He thought of his baby, Zoe. How far he'd come since the old days, what a struggle it had been to stay on the straight and narrow.

But it had been worth it. He never would have had a woman like Felicia, or a daughter like Zoe, if he'd kept going the way he had been.

Russo looked at the brown and red house in the other direction, a nice place with cathedral-style windows on the face of it, a huge wrap-around porch with cedar posts. It looked like a speculative home, a place built by some rich entrepreneur that no one lived in yet. He spoke while his thoughts carried him off. "Nate Reuter was my cellmate at Rikers."

"Ohhh…" Anthony nodded his head, like they were just two guys chewing the fat, having a beer. He leaned against the Audi and ran his hands through his thinning hair. "Well I'll be a son of a bitch. What are the fucking odds?"

"It's got nothing to do with odds. I was just there."

"Well, it's fuckin' *something*, that's what."

Russo really sized Anthony up for the first time. The guy had a wide face and high cheekbones, spiky black hair receding towards the top of his head. Around forty years old, six feet, two hundred pounds – including the spare tire around his waist. He was wearing a white shirt, black slacks, and black loafers on his feet. A giant gold ring on one hand, a gold bracelet, and a thin gold chain around his neck, the chest hair tufting out of his shirt.

"You work for Little Joey?" Russo asked.

"Me? I'm self-employed."

"Cut the shit. You're with the Straccali family, aren't you? Back on the ferry, you said Little Joey. You're talking about Joey Esposito. Maybe I know a little bit about him."

It seemed to throw Anthony, and the pretense dropped. "How do you know about Esposito? No way. You're a spic, ain't you?"

"My mother was Latina. My father was Italian. 'Russo,' you idiot."

Anthony blinked, putting it together.

"Esposito is from Long Island," Russo said. "Depending on who you ask, he's got three houses, or four. One of them is a ritzy palace on the beach out on Montauk. He's worth multiple millions, at least. Is this his money?"

Anthony was grinning now. He turned and spat blood on the asphalt. "You bet your ass it's his money."

"How much is in the trunk?"

This time Anthony didn't bother to act ignorant. "Little over eight hundred grand."

Eight hundred thousand dollars. Not chump change, but also not a hell of a lot in the scheme of things. When Russo thought about these guys working for Esposito, about their mistakes – and the more he looked at Anthony with his big jewels and wide face – the more he thought that these guys were the B team. Expendable types, the equivalent of Esposito sticking up a hat on a stick to see if it got blown off. Maybe the feds were too close for comfort, and Esposito was wary.

"Get undressed," Russo said.

Anthony grimaced. He had a dark welt forming on the side of his head from where Russo had hit him with the gun. He must've had an excruciating headache. "You fuckin' kidding me?"

"Take your clothes off, put them in the back seat." Russo aimed the gun between Anthony's eyes.

"Alright, alright." Anthony started to strip. He looked around, as if expecting someone to show, and his words echoed Russo's thoughts. "Jesus, doesn't anybody live around here?"

"Less than a million people in the whole state of Vermont," Russo said.

Anthony peeled off his clothes down to the underwear. "I'm not taking off my jewelry."

"I don't care about your jewelry."

"You gonna fuckin' shoot me?" Anthony looked serious for a moment, then he cracked a maniac grin and started giggling.

"The fuck you think you're going to do, convict? G'ahead. Like I said, g'ahead. See how far you get before Little Joey finds you with his money." He lost the grin at the mention of the loot, somber again.

The thunder rumbled, closer this time, the clouds shouldering up on the horizon, drawing nearer.

Russo stared at Anthony, who was watching the weather. "What were you going to do with the woman?"

"The woman? You're fuckin' outta your mind..."

"What were you gonna do to her?"

"You tryin' to psych yourself up? Huh? Big guy? Big ex-convict? Jail make you tough, you think? Put down that fucking burner. We'll see how tough you are. What do you care about that bitch for, huh? She's a pain in everyone's ass. Joey ought to have her whacked and be done with it."

"She's pregnant."

Anthony spit some air. "Fuck her. Fuck her kid. I'd make it a stillborn."

Russo tossed the gun in the open car and slammed the door. He walked toward Anthony so quickly Anthony barely had a chance to protect himself.

Russo beat him senseless, giving him a few solid kicks for good measure once Anthony was already on the ground. Then he dragged him off to the side of the road, into the bushes.

He returned to the car and popped the trunk. Paulie was almost too heavy to lift, and Russo felt something give way in his back as he hefted the big man over the back bumper. Paulie's body crumpled onto the pavement. Russo dragged it, too, and let it tumble into the bushes beside Anthony.

Someone was coming, an old pickup rattling down the dirt road, forming a cloud of dust.

Russo hopped into the Audi, hidden behind its tinted windows while the vehicle rolled past. When it was gone he stepped out again. He dumped the money out of one of the bags in the trunk and kept the bag.

The pond was set back from the road a couple hundred yards. The humidity gathered, and the clothes clung to his skin as he dragged Anthony through the bushes and trees. They were clothes Shelly had given Russo to wear. Shelly hadn't wanted anyone to notice an MTA worker riding around in his truck.

He left Anthony by the edge of the pond and went back for Paulie. Another car drove by on the road – Russo hid, waited, then dragged Paulie. He picked up every large stone he could find along the way, placing them in the garbage bag.

The pond looked fake, like it was man-made. At least that would mean it was deep. It would be best to bury the bodies, but he didn't have a shovel. He gave the big house near the pond another appraisal, deciding it had definitely been built by some developer and no one currently resided there. New owners might find corpses in the depths of their little pond someday, but by then…

Russo removed his clothes, bloody and torn. Dressing Anthony was the worst part. Russo was sweating and cursing, bitten by the hovering insects as he painstakingly worked the man into the outdoorsy clothes from Shelly.

Then he dumped the stones. He weighted down the two men, stuffing their pockets, their shirts. Dead people tended to sink in water. But then their bodies filled up with gasses, they'd start to float. The stones would keep them down.

Russo waded in, taking Paulie first. He got out to where he could just barely touch and gave Paulie a shove. Bubbles popped on the surface as the big man slipped below.

Then Anthony next.

Russo said a prayer as the man went under. Anthony's arm was the last to sink, the white tips of his fingers just breaking the dark surface of the water a moment, then they vanished.

He returned to the shore and gave himself a few minutes to air dry. Anthony's suit was almost a perfect fit, the pants just a half an inch too long, the waistline a bit loose. Russo cinched the belt tight and slipped into the loafers.

CHAPTER FORTY-FIVE

"Investigator Tambor," said the slim man in the black suit. He looked hot standing there on the porch, his forehead beaded with perspiration.

Emily shook his hand and glanced around at the other law enforcement looming behind him. One woman wore a tight expression and seemed to regard Emily with skepticism.

"Investigator Reed," she said. "We'd like to speak to you for a bit, will you come with us?"

They led her back out to the road where three dark SUVs were parked on the shoulder. Once inside, the vents blowing ice-cold air, Emily was introduced to the other parties.

Tambor and Reed were with the state police robbery division. To date, they had recovered all the heist money from the Fighting Bandits takeover spree except for Center Bank in Lake Placid.

One of the bandits was Jerry Oberst, who'd been cooperating with federal investigators after his arrest. But Oberst was a double-crosser who'd fled witness security and tried to get back the money.

He'd been intercepted by "thugs" along the way, men operating on behalf of someone who claimed the money belonged to him in the first place.

A mafia figure known as Joey Esposito.

Emily felt her stomach clench.

"We believe Esposito himself may have pulled the trigger on Oberst," Tambor said. "Then told his thugs to bury him. That was probably Eddie Marks and Victor Ricci, the men who crashed the pickup truck. They did a poor job, buried the body shallowly, searched the premises for the money, but were unable to locate it."

Susan Resnick fit into the scheme because her daughter, Heather, worked at the bank. Heather had been seeing Nate Reuter, the fighter, and agreed to help the robbers. Heather was being held for questioning. She had a young daughter named Chastity, just a little girl.

The investigators believed Heather had been promised a cut of the take, and had urged her mother not to sell the property. It was unclear whether Susan Resnick or any of the other Cobb family members knew about the money in the basement, but the police doubted it.

"The whole thing looks like one bad move after another," Tambor said.

They were able to sit facing one another because the middle seats in the spacious SUV swiveled backwards. Emily sat beside Tambor and faced Reed, who was still giving her the stink-eye.

"Yeah, well, they knew enough to denature the crime scene," Investigator Reed said. "The house is covered in OB."

"What's that mean?" Emily asked, though she thought she might already know.

"They used oxidation bleach, sodium hypochlorite. It gets rid of blood evidence, can even break down hydrogen bonds between DNA base pairs. It's the cleanest your kitchen will ever be." Reed's lips cracked in a humorless smile.

Tambor jumped back to the original point. "You've got the Fighting Bandits, and then who they corrupted, and then the thugs working for Esposito to try and take the money back. A total clusterfuck, excuse my French."

Reed spoke to Emily again. "One of these people, 'corrupted,' as Investigator Tambor describes, was a correctional officer with the Cold Brook State Correctional Institution. Sheldon Danvers.

That's one of the men inside your house. He was the one who was here when you got home?"

They had Emily tell her story yet again, and she explained it the same way she had explained it to the county detectives, omitting the parts about the man she'd helped get away. She knew, despite their kind words, the detectives were waiting to see if she'd trip up and change her story during the retellings.

Reed seemed to scrutinize her throughout. "You told one of our troopers that you were picked up by a man who drove you to the ferry. But that vehicle, a Prius, that's your own car, registered in your name. Can you explain that?"

Emily swallowed, and took a breath. This was the moment. She'd given the man a head start – it had been spontaneous, an impulse to return a favor. It needed to stop there. If she continued trying to protect someone she'd never met before that morning, she would be breaking the law, impeding a major investigation.

But he'd done more than just do her a *favor*, she thought. Here was some guy, roped into this thing and just wanted to get clear of it, get home, and he'd gone out of his way to protect her from Sheldon Danvers. He'd lent her his phone so she could call emergency services, get an ambulance for Brett.

And, honestly, she just didn't like the way Reed was looking at her.

"I was confused. I meant to say I picked *him* up."

Reed blinked. She traded looks with Tambor. "You mean to say you left your house, you were fleeing for your life, and you stopped to pick someone up?"

"I didn't have my phone. I was just driving, trying to get away, probably in shock. I saw him hitch-hiking. I slowed down and asked him if he had a phone. He did, he let me use it. I called 911, explained what happened, said I'd be at the ferry."

"The man was seen in the driver's seat." Reed cocked an eyebrow.

"Yes. I had him drive so I could make the call."

Reed sighed and sat back. She didn't buy it. Nobody in their right minds would. Emily figured she wouldn't have taken the story at face value, either. She added, with a touch of emotion, "I was in shock, ma'am. My husband was shot. You said I was fleeing for my life. You're right. I hate to sound like the damsel in distress, but I saw someone, asked for their phone, and he was very concerned for me. He asked if he could help. I said I needed to call the police. It all happened very fast. I asked him to drive – I was just… I was so… everything was…"

She lowered her head and closed her eyes. She felt Tambor put his hand on her back. A moment later he removed the hand, probably because Reed was glaring at him.

Emily knew she had just stepped through a certain door, and there was no turning back. But she didn't regret her decision. She got a feeling about people, and the person who'd helped her was a good man. Maybe he hadn't always been, but he was trying.

The cops in the car with her were good people, too. But he had potentially saved her life, and the life of her child.

"Ma'am," Reed said. "We have the incoming 911 call originating as a prepaid cellular. We're searching for the person who bought that phone. And your entire house will be searched. Fingerprints, blood, DNA…"

"Fine." Emily lifted her head. "I'd like to see my husband now, please."

The investigators exchanged more looks and then Tambor spoke. "Alright. Let's get Mrs. Larson on her way to Albany."

CHAPTER FORTY-SIX

Russo stopped at a gas station and took out Shelly's phone. He removed the battery and threw it in the trash beside the gas pumps. When he was finished fueling the Audi, he got rid of the phone itself in another trash bin beside the lone pay phone at the edge of the convenience store.

Jockey's number was burned into his brain now.

"Jock, I need one last favor from you."

"Jesus, bro."

"I know, I know. Put it on my tab. I need you to contact Bobby Mars."

"Bobby? You crazy? What do you want to talk to that garbage-peddling shithead about?"

"Just call him. Tell him it's for me – ask him to talk to his contact at Rikers. Bobby's been pushing bug juice there for ten years. He knows everybody."

"Jimmy… I gotta say something here…"

"Save it, Jock. I appreciate it, but I know what I'm doing. For one thing, I want to know about the woman, Delahunt, and anything going on with her."

"Delahunt? There's already word, bro."

Russo felt the hairs on his neck stand up. "Oh yeah?"

"Yeah, bro. She's toast, that's what I heard. Straccali, they got to her now that she landed on the island. Yesterday, she got shanked in the yard."

"How did you hear it? Bobby told you?"

"Hey, I didn't hear it from him, you didn't hear it from me. You know how it goes."

Russo left it at that. It was fortunate news. Too bad for Delahunt, but good for him. There was a chance she'd told someone about her deal with him – nothing he could do about that. But, if she hadn't, that meant the connection between him and the Fighting Bandits was almost dead. Just the man in black, Richard, and the other one, Snake, left to deal with.

"Any sign of our friends?"

"Nah, bro. Not since I moved in. Hey, you oughtta think about doin' a little redecorating around here. I mean, all these little friggin' ceramic cats and whatnot? You got something to tell me, Jimmy?"

"They're Fifi's grandma's porcelain figurines. Put Fifi on the line."

"Alright, alright. You friggin' homo."

Russo waited for Felicia. He lost his smile as soon as she started talking, ranting away at him, the words coming so fast he could barely understand her. Questions and accusations all in one Puerto-Rican-accented torrent.

"I'm coming home, baby. I'll see you soon. Four hours or less."

"Yeah?" At last she eased up. "Dammit, Jimmy…"

"I know. I'm sorry. I love you."

"I love you too, for God's sake. Just get home."

He hung up and walked back to the Audi. Slipping behind the wheel, he thought of his wife's expression when he showed her the money. Gambling money stolen from a bank stolen back by the gamblers and then by Russo himself.

It would make a good book for someone to write.

CHAPTER FORTY-SEVEN

Her husband was covered in tubes and surrounded by machines. Mostly, the doctors said, he'd lost a lot of blood, and the buckshot burrowed into his gut had sat too long and he'd gotten an infection. It all amounted to his needing a blood transfusion, which he'd already had, and a strong course of antibiotics. But he was going to make it.

The police were still with her, but they gave her some privacy as she visited with Brett, first rousing him from sedation with a few kisses on his lips and forehead.

His eyes opened and cleared when he saw her, and he stretched to embrace her.

She cried in his arms, overwhelmed with gratitude. They stayed like that for a good while before she pulled up a chair and sat beside the hospital bed.

"How you doing, honey?" Brett asked.

"I'm fine. Paramedic already checked me out but I'm going to see the obstetrician, just make sure everything is normal."

"The little pinhead is okay?"

"I think the little pinhead is okay."

He looked over her shoulder. "Who's with you?"

She glanced at the door, saw the figures through the narrow window. She told him about the police, and their questions. Brett didn't know a thing about the mystery man, and he didn't need to. She recapped for her husband the same story of her escape she'd given the investigators. Someday, further down the road, she'd tell him what really happened.

"So where did the money go?" he wanted to know.

"That's the question." She didn't know either. She figured one of the other men had made off with it; it hadn't been in the pickup truck, according to the cops.

"I think we should move," Emily said, staring at her husband.

"Yeah? Whatever you want, babe."

"Let's get a nice little apartment somewhere. With lots of people around. I'll plant some herbs on the fire escape for our garden."

She laughed at her own joke, and it sounded louder than she would've wanted. She stood and walked to the window. The rain had come and the city of Albany looked dark, almost smoky in the downpour.

She put her hands over her stomach. She could sense Brett watching her, wanting to say something. She turned around and looked at the door to the room, to the police on the other side of it.

A federal agent was standing there, pushing Investigator Morales in a wheelchair.

"Oh, shit," she said.

CHAPTER FORTY-EIGHT

The rain came when he was more than halfway home, just about to cross another border, this one into Massachusetts.

Russo listened to music from area radio stations, tapping his fingers on the steering wheel, keeping an easy pace. One station broke for weather, talked about a big front that had moved in, rain expected all throughout the northeast.

At one point he thought he heard the sound of a helicopter, but it could've been thunder. He stuck mainly to route 7 but occasionally veered off to lesser-known roads. He was anxious, half-expecting a roadblock to show up at any minute; cops with guns aimed over the hoods of their cars.

In Connecticut, he finally dared to merge onto I-95, a major artery. He sped along with the traffic through Stamford, anxiety replaced by excitement as the many miles between him and home shrunk away.

The rain came, furious and frothy.

After Stamford he entered Westchester County, back in New York.

He changed states again, taking the George Washington Bridge over the Hudson and into Fort Lee, New Jersey. Over the past seven hours he'd seen more of the country than at any other time in his life, and it was just the northeast. He thought it was time to take the girls and go traveling. They said New Yorkers were mostly afraid of the rest of the U.S., and he understood that. But it was time for a change.

Maybe out west somewhere.

He picked up I-278 and took the Goethals Bridge to Staten Island, the wipers working overtime in the deluge. At least he was back in familiar territory, and he exited the freeway on Targee Street, headed for St. George, his neighborhood.

Jockey's old beater Ford was parked out in front of the house, looking sad in the downpour. Russo parked behind it and bounded up the steps through the rain, his stiff back really giving him trouble, but he didn't care.

He opened the door to his home.

"Feef? You here? Jockey?"

No one answered. It took just a few moments, standing in the gloom, his clothes dripping, to realize something was wrong. There was a cat figurine smashed on the ground. The rest of the living room didn't look right either, a couple of pillows on the floor, a newspaper scattered.

The clock in the living room – a cat with eyes that twitched back and forth – ticked away, too loud.

He rushed upstairs, bent over a bit because of his lower back, but oblivious to the pain.

He stopped at the landing, his breath catching in his throat.

Jockey was on the floor of the upstairs hallway, sprawled out face-down, blood everywhere, mostly coming from his neck.

Russo heard the creak of a floorboard behind him and saw a shadow slip over the wall. The shadow was reaching in the air. On instinct, Russo covered his face. The gag wire someone was trying to get over his neck caught on one of his hands. It was a steel wire, razor-thin, and it cut into his flesh.

The man behind him pulled on Russo with all his weight, and Russo struggled to get free of the wire. He took a few steps back and pivoted, slamming into the wall, pinning the man. He snapped his head back and connected.

The man let go of the gag wire and Russo was free. He spun around on Snake Montoya, grabbed his shoulders, and threw him down the stairs.

Snake tumbled head over heels and landed in a broken heap at the bottom. That was two guys who'd taken the quick way down today, Russo thought. But his attention was diverted when someone whistled from the back bedroom. Russo leapt over Jockey and stopped short in the bedroom doorway.

A man sat in the rocking chair, and he had Zoe in his arms.

It was Felicia's parents' old room, which Russo and his wife had turned into the nursery. And the man sat in the middle of it, in the very chair where Felicia had spent a year breastfeeding their baby. This painfully thin man in black jeans and a grubby black suit coat holding Zoe, who was passed out in his lap.

The streetlights shone through the rain streaking down the windows, forming serpentine shadows in the room.

Russo didn't know what to do. It was after Zoe's bed time, and she was a deep sleeper for the first few hours before she invariably woke up and demanded something to eat and someone to feed it to her. Felicia was nowhere to be seen.

Russo took a cautious step forward, his stomach clutching, reaching for his child, his bloody hand dripping on the peach-colored carpet.

"Hey, hey…" said the man in a soft voice. "No no."

He had a knife, and he lay it across Zoe's soft midriff. She was in her footie pajamas, powder-blue. Her head was back – she was well past needing head support like when she was an infant, but it still looked wrong, the way she was splayed out like that. So defenseless.

Russo felt his temperature rising, but he stopped moving toward the man. "Give her to me."

"She's cute, huh?"

"Give her to me."

They both whispered, like adults duly respectful of a child's slumber.

"In a minute, just relax."

Russo heard something downstairs. A thump, then a gagging noise.

"Where's my wife?"

The man in black just smiled and kept rocking. His eyes glinted in the shifting light. His face was gaunt, peppered with uneven beard stubble. But he wasn't a junkie, Russo didn't think. Russo had known a lot of junkies. He was too calm, his hands weren't shaking, his gaze was level.

Richard.

Another noise. This time from the master bedroom. It sounded like it could be Felicia, trying to talk through a gag. Russo wanted to go to her, but he was afraid to leave Richard with his baby girl.

He took a short step back just so he could see down the hall to the top of the stairs. The bathroom door was closed, the master bedroom door was slightly ajar. The sounds of his wife were definitely coming from that room.

Richard was looking Russo over. "Nice suit."

"I'll give you the money," Russo said. "It's downstairs, in the car. Give me the baby, and I'll go get it."

Zoe stirred for a moment. She was lying on her back across Richard's bony legs. Her arm twitched, and her little fingers went to her face, then the arm flopped back and she sighed. Still asleep. Russo prayed she stayed that way. Richard and Snake had killed Jockey, done something to Felicia, then come in here and picked Zoe up out of her crib. He couldn't have been waiting long.

So much for the cops scaring them off. They had just come right back, like roaches.

"We got a deal or what?" Russo asked.

"How'd you get the money?"

More thumping from downstairs. Like Snake was trying to get up, but falling over.

Richard continued rocking, using the tips of his ragged boots to push the chair back over and over again. It was unnerving. He kept one hand resting on the handle of the knife, still resting on Zoe's stomach.

Russo didn't answer him.

"You really have a way about you, don't you, Russo? I know about you."

"You don't know anything about me."

"Not too many people left now. No Shelly, no Delahunt, no Reuter. Sad about Nate Reuter. You could say the money was really his. Well, fifty grand in prize money, anyway. Terrible to get forced into something like that, then to die in prison before you can take back what was yours."

Russo didn't know that Reuter had died. He'd been shanked pretty bad, and inmates died in Rikers far too often, but he'd been hoping the kid had pulled through.

"And me, well, I guess you could say I'm owed the five thousand and change put up to bail you out. Right? You know what I was before I was a bondsman? Bounty hunter. I went after the people who didn't pay back their bonds. Then my leg got messed up, changed things. You're sort of like Reuter, you know? Abused by the system. You've got a past too, don't ya?"

"Give me the baby. I'll go get the money. Last chance."

"We've got an epidemic, Russo. We've got New York City prosecutors subverting speedy trial rules in order to extract guilty pleas from poor defendants like yourself who can't afford to make bail. It's a sad situation. And it's been lucrative for a guy like me. But not lucrative enough."

Richard was stalling. Waiting for Snake to recover.

Meeting the devil in person was never as scary as he was in your mind. Richard was just some wannabe, a greedy scumbag, horning in on a deal that had nothing to do with him.

And he was still sitting with Zoe in his lap, holding a knife on her.

"And while all us little guys get fucked," Richard said in that airy voice, "there's been outrageous leniency toward 'systemically important' companies. These so-called too-big-to-fail banks that get away with murder. Did you know that every time the unemployment rate goes up a point, forty thousand people die?"

Russo pulled Anthony's gun from the small of his back. He aimed at Richard's head and squeezed the trigger, putting a bullet between his eyes.

"I hear ya," Russo said.

CHAPTER FORTY-NINE

The federal agent wheeled Morales into the hospital room. Emily thought the detective looked terrible – his face was bruised, his arm in a sling, his head and hand wrapped in massive bandages – but he was alive.

"It's by some miracle they didn't execute me," Morales said after a few moments.

Emily had finally been able to piece it all together: Esposito's men had tried to frame the crime scene to look a certain way. They'd used powerful cleaners to remove any traces which didn't fit the narrative they wanted the cops to believe. Morales had been unconscious, beat to hell. They'd luckily assumed him already dead.

"These guys may not be the brightest bunch working for Esposito," Morales said. "Thank God." Then he grew serious, looking at Emily and Brett with sober eyes.

The federal agent stepped forward. "Roger T. Wilshire." He was square-jawed and handsome with a brush cut, maybe forty-five years old. The look in his eyes told Emily that the jig was up. Tambor and Reed stood behind him, Reed furious. "We found another phone," she said. "This one in the pickup truck. It's broken, but we were able to pull some data."

"We know there was another man at the scene," Wilshire added.

Emily was sitting on Brett's bed, her arm around him, and she withdrew it now, unable to bear the look her husband was giving her.

But Wilshire kept going before she could say anything. "Listen, I understand this man helped you. But you don't know who he is. His name is James Alonzo Russo. He's got DUIs and a burglary on his record, and suspected associations within various organized crime syndicates. We were never able to prove it, but we spent a few years trying to link him to murders in the Five Boroughs from the late nineties and early aughts, as a contract killer. He went to prison for the burglary, though, did a year. After that he disappeared. Tried to live the quiet life, I guess."

Reed picked up the thread. "The money is gone. If Russo has this money, Esposito's money, it could be very bad. On all sides. Esposito will try to get it back. Who knows what Russo might do to defend himself."

Emily straightened her spine and looked Wilshire in the eyes. "I met him. Yeah. He helped me, and that's why I wanted to help him get back to his family. I don't think he's a bad man. And he doesn't have the money, I saw him walk away… Where is he now?"

"We don't know," Wilshire answered. "He lives on Staten Island. We spoke to police there. They responded to complaints that some men were harassing Russo's wife. Hired hands, I think, part of this scheme the Fighting Bandits cooked up to get back the money."

Wilshire came even closer, and held out his hand. "Mrs. Larson, I'm going to need you to come with me now."

Emily sighed. She kissed her husband on the lips and let Wilshire lead her toward the door.

Brett called out before they left. "What's going to happen to Emily?" He strained to sit up in the bed, wincing in pain.

Wilshire raised a hand. "We'll take good care of her. Mr. Larson, your wife obstructed a federal investigation. And there is something very critical she didn't tell the state investigators."

Brett swung his legs out of the bed. He was trying to come after them. The other officers in the room subdued him.

"What are they talking about?"

"Brett," Emily said, tears sheeting her vision. "It's okay. I love you."

He fought against them. She turned to Wilshire and spoke rapidly in his ear. "Please get me out of here. Don't do this in front of my husband."

And he led her away.

CHAPTER FIFTY

Zoe was screeching, just totally pissed off, and Russo bounced her on his hip and tried to shush her.

"Shhh. Hey, Ikey-Ikey, shhh. Papa's here."

The gunshot had been loud, but the storm outside was frenzied. Hopefully any neighbors would consider it thunder. This was a quiet area, gun violence didn't usually happen here – people wouldn't expect it.

Felicia was okay. Somehow, she was alive. She wasn't even bleeding. She had a gag in her mouth and was tied cruciform to the bed, but she was alive and well.

Russo set Zoe down beside the bed. She immediately pulled herself up and tried to climb up, wailing all the while.

Russo undid his wife's bonds, listening to her immediate stream of questions and curses. He smiled through the tears pouring down his face.

Felicia picked up Zoe and looked her over. "There's blood on her. Jimmy, there's blood…"

"It's mine. She's not hurt."

Felicia put the squalling baby to her breast. Zoe hadn't suckled from her mother in more than three months but they fell back into the routine like they hadn't missed a day. Even if there wasn't any milk and she was shuddering the way she did after a hard cry, Zoe was soothed.

Russo fawned over his wife. "What did they do to you? Did they hurt you?"

"They broke my grandma's cats, is what they did."

Russo laughed through more tears. He climbed up onto the bed and spooned his wife as she clutched Zoe tight against her chest.

"I'm serious. She will not be happy."

"I know."

"You need to bandage your hands."

"I will."

"So you didn't come right home after getting out, I take it."

"No. I took a little trip upstate." He was trying to keep it light, but the emotion broke over him again, like a wave. He buried his face in his wife's hair.

But he couldn't stay long.

He left them and descended the stairs. Snake Montoya was on the first floor. He'd managed to crawl most of the way to the front door. One of his feet was twisted at a funny angle and blood was pouring from his mouth. It looked like he'd bitten off his tongue.

The wire Snake had used to try and strangle Russo was lying at the foot of the stairs. Russo got it, climbed onto Snake's back, and slipped it around his neck.

He watched out the front windows as the storm whipped the trees on the street.

When Snake was dead, he stuck the razor wire into his pocket and went outside.

The windows of the surrounding buildings were dark. Many of the neighbors were old and retired, but there was one young family a few doors down. The man worked the Staten Island ferry and the woman was a school teacher, and they both got up early. Russo liked them, very nice people. Their lights were off, too.

He hustled down the front steps and out to the street where he'd parked Anthony's black Audi, soaked to his skin in a matter of moments.

Russo opened the trunk and stared down at the bags.

Just go.

The thought came out of nowhere, so simple, so terrible.

Just go. Put the girls in the car and go. Drive until you get to California then make a left into Mexico.

Even Little Joey had limits, didn't he?

Joey Esposito had come out of the Straccali family, originally a bootlegging crew, operating out of northern New Jersey, smuggling alcohol into New York during prohibition.

Joey's father had pined to take over the New York faction, but was never officially inducted into the Straccali family due to what they called "closed books." Still, he controlled much of the loansharking, narcotics, money laundering, and extortion operations in New York. Gambling was always a part, but it had never been the biggest slice of the pie – too much chasing around after lost money. Eventually, he settled in Long Island, where he raised his family, including a son, Little Joey.

It seemed Little Joey hadn't learned from his father and was the one chasing money.

Maybe Joey would just cut his losses. He knew the feds were close. Maybe he would let it go.

Get the girls. Get in the car.

But what if Joey Esposito *didn't* let it go? It was, after all, over eight hundred grand.

Russo closed the trunk, hustled up the steps and back into the house. His lower back was seizing, his sciatica flaring – he almost didn't make it.

Jockey was dead. His friend of more than thirty years.

Russo dragged the huge man into the nursery, where Richard was still sitting in the rocking chair, slumped over, dark blood oozing from the hole in his forehead.

The upstairs hallway was carpeted, a big maroon stain where Jockey had died. There would be no getting out the stain tonight.

He checked in on Felicia and Zoe. It pained him to see the red marks around Felicia's wrists, but it was a joy to see Zoe happy again, jumping up and down on the bed like it was Christmas morning.

"Ah-da!" She held her arms out to him. But he hesitated, because he was dirty, still bloody.

Felicia gave him a look. "Stop looming in the doorway."

She got up from the bed and crossed the room to him. He blocked her from leaving.

"Jimmy. Outta my way."

"Feef, you don't want to go out there."

"Jockey is dead. I know. You killed the other two, I know that too. I knew when I married you that you had a whole life before me. I'm not stupid, Jimmy. Forty-year-old man, no kids, never married, ex-convict. Do I look stupid?"

"No."

"Let me help you."

"What about Zoe?"

Their daughter was bouncing on the bed, throwing her head back, having a ball.

"I'll put a show on for her."

Felicia took a baby gate and wedged it in the door frame. She turned the TV on in the corner and flipped to a children's program called *Yo Gabba Gabba*. Russo watched, baffled. "You said no TV until she was two, I thought."

Felicia stepped over the gate. "We'll make this one exception."

Downstairs they hauled Snake Montoya into the kitchen and cleaned the blood from the wood floors at the bottom of the stairs. Felicia foraged in the bathroom for bandages and wrapped both of Russo's hands, mostly about the wrists. When it was over, Russo used Jockey's cell phone and called Bobby Mars.

"Russy? Oh my God, bro. Been a long time. I talked to Jockey tonight. What're you two fuckin' nut jobs up to?"

"I don't have time to explain. I've got a problem, though. I got three problems. You still in that business?"

Mars was silent for a moment. "I'll give you friend prices. For old time's sake. Grand a piece."

"Done. One of them is a special case. You'll understand when you get here."

"Alright, bro. I'm an hour away."

Russo hung up and kept cleaning. The storm raged outside, and he wished he could just tear the roof off the house, let the rain sweep through.

Mars was even earlier than promised. He came equipped with body bags and industrial cleaning products, but by then Russo and Felicia had already made good headway.

Felicia had shifted gears and was in the master bedroom with the door shut, getting Zoe back to sleep for the night.

In the nursery, Mars stood looking down at Jockey and grew emotional. "Goddammit." He wiped a tear.

"That's the special case. I don't want him in the landfill."

"I know what to do."

Poor Jockey. The only saving grace was that the big lug had never married or had kids. He was survived by his mother, a tiny woman who people could hardly believe gave birth to the behemoth who'd come to be ironically known as Jockey, and she would be devastated, but at least those collateral casualties were limited to her and a few friends. Maybe the kids at the school would miss Janitor Horatio "Jockey" Peña, though.

Russo helped Mars get the bodies into the bags. Mars drove a garbage truck, part of a private outfit that serviced Staten Island, and the two men carried the bodies outside and set them in the back of the huge vehicle. Russo kept an eye on the surrounding windows. If someone was watching from a dark room, he couldn't see them.

He spied something beside the house, walked over, and rounded up Richard's bicycle. In the rain, excited to be home,

Russo hadn't seen it there when he'd first arrived. They threw it into the dump truck.

Back inside, Mars wanted answers. Normally he was a no-questions-asked kind of hire, but seeing Jockey had rattled him.

"That car out front ain't yours, Russy. What did you get into? You back in the business?"

"No."

"The way bodies are piling up, I'd say you were back to your old line of work."

"The less you know the better."

"Well I already know about Delahunt, and Reuter. I know about the money. Chances are you're going to pay me with some of that money. Esposito's money. So, I'm already in this thing, ain't I?"

"Yeah. I'm sorry Bobby. I'll take care of it."

"How you gonna take care of it? Don't fool yourself, Russy. Esposito will follow you to the ends of the earth. You gotta make this right."

"I know I do. I know. That's why I'm going to have you make a call for me."

CHAPTER FIFTY-ONE

The storm was still raging as Russo made the drive to Long Island.

It was going on one in the morning as he drove the rain-slicked streets of an upscale neighborhood, homes fortified and gated like castles.

He lowered the window and leaned out into the downpour to press the button on the intercom. Mars had called ahead and Esposito's people were expecting him.

The gates swung open and Russo rolled up a long driveway to a porch with massive pillars.

Men with guns stood waiting. One opened the door. Russo stepped out, holding up his arms.

One guard patted him down while the other kept a gun on him. Russo was unarmed. He'd left Anthony's gun with Felicia. He'd changed out of Anthony's clothes into his own tracksuit; the kind of outfit he'd wear around the house on the weekends.

The guards showed him in. The first room was immense, a clerestory, with two staircases cascading down from a balconied second floor. They led Russo through a door and down a flight of stairs, into a finished basement.

There was a mammoth flat-screen TV, a full bar, a pool table, couches. Two more guards were in the room, sleeves rolled up, shoulder holsters and pistols, having a pool game. Baseball played on the TV, the sound turned down.

Little Joey was at the bar, sitting on a stool. He waved like Russo was an old friend.

"Come on in, come on in."

The guards flanked Russo as he walked to the bar and stood in front of Esposito.

Esposito looked him up and down, then grabbed a towel from the bar and threw it.

Russo caught it and blotted at his face and neck, never taking his eyes off the man.

"Siddown, siddown."

Russo took a seat on the stool beside Esposito.

Esposito was on the small side with pointy features, balding black hair slicked back. They were about the same age. Russo had never met him in person, but something in his eyes looked familiar. "Cocktail? Something to warm you up?"

"No thanks, I don't drink."

Esposito smiled, revealing a gold-capped tooth. Then he turned to the guards who'd escorted Russo in. "Money?"

"It's in the car."

"Well what is it doing in the car? Bring it in, bring it in."

One of the guards left.

Russo said, "Not all of it is there."

Esposito took a sip of his drink. "Oh no?"

"I had to pay someone to get rid of two men working with Delahunt."

"You killed them, huh?" Esposito raised his eyebrows in appraisal.

Russo said nothing.

"You also killed *my* men," Esposito said.

"Just one. Well, maybe two."

Esposito stared a moment, then broke out in another toothy grin. He wheezed a laugh and looked at the men playing pool. "'Maybe two.' I love it. 'Maybe two.' That's good."

Russo carefully folded the damp towel and placed it back on the bar. "I also used a little money for gas."

Esposito threw back his head and howled with delight. The laughter turned into a coughing fit and he curled over, gagging into his fist. After he'd comported himself he said, "You really are broke, huh?"

"I'm asking you to let me go. Forgive the money I took. Forgive me for what happened to Anthony and Paulie. Know that I just got caught up in something to protect my family."

"Hey, hey," Esposito said, and patted Russo on the knee. "Slow down, slow down."

Little Joey apparently liked to repeat everything he said.

The guard who'd left came back down the stairs with the four bags, grunting and red-faced with the effort. He dropped them at Esposito's feet. This cued the rest of the men to start taking out the money in stacks. There was a money-counting machine on a table beyond the couches and they started to run it through. "Let's just see," Esposito said. "Let's just see."

He got up and walked to the other side of the bar, fixed himself a fresh drink, a Jack and Coke.

"You sure I can't interest you?"

"I'm fine."

"Your old man drank, huh?"

Russo was silent, his eyes fixing on the big silver gun hanging from Esposito's holster. "Benicio Russo," Esposito said, swirling the drink with a red straw. "Meanest fucking guy I ever met. You mean like that, Russo?"

Russo stayed quiet.

Esposito sucked his finger. "Maybe you do some work for me, pay it off."

"I can't."

"You can't, huh?" Esposito came back round, sat beside Russo.

Russo took a breath. "Maybe another way to look at it is that you have your money now. Most of it. And you probably would've gotten none of it the way your B team was fumbling around and fucking everything up."

Esposito's eyes got wide and he looked at the three men working the money-counting and the one standing by, gun in hand. "Whoa-ho. Listen to this guy."

"You've got a lot," Russo said.

Little Joey grew serious. "Well I didn't *get* a lot without being careful. Pinching my pennies. I start throwing this 'oh fucking well' attitude around, I won't have anything anymore. Besides, it's the principle of the thing."

The silver gun was snug in the holster, held by a thong strap. Getting the strap unsnapped was the kind of thing that could cost vital seconds.

"Hey," Esposito said. "I got something to show you."

Russo figured the gun was loaded. It was a revolver. No safety. He could pull back the hammer and aim it right into Esposito's ribs. Then, using Esposito as a human shield, turn the gun still in the holster on the closest guard. By the time the three bean-counters in the corner got their shit together, Russo could have freed the silver gun and shot the rest of them.

Maybe.

Or maybe it would all go horribly wrong and he'd leave Zoe fatherless, Felicia a widow.

Esposito got up and went to the other side of the bar again before Russo even had a chance to make a move. Esposito dipped his head out of sight a moment, then stood back up.

He put a small tin, like a cookie tin, on the bar.

"You like anagrams, Russo?"

"What?"

"Anagrams. You know what they are, right?"

"No. I don't think so."

"Oh come on. You're a bright guy, ain't you?"

"I don't know."

"Anagrams are like… well, they're when something is hidden inside something else."

He pushed the tin towards Russo.

"Open it up."

The cover had a flowery, ornate pattern.

"Come on, take the top off. It ain't gonna bite ya."

Russo pried the top and looked inside. There was a bunch of photographs, but the one right on top grabbed his attention.

He plucked it out and held it up in front of his face.

Esposito was giddy. "Huh? Bet you never saw that coming."

Russo set the photo down on the bar, unsure of what to say, picturing Emily's light brown eyes as she'd let him go at the ferry.

Esposito returned to the stool and grew solemn. "We're not super close. You know, I regret that. She sorta condemns the life, and, you know, who can blame her? She married some real sweetheart guy. They're pregnant."

Esposito locked eyes with Russo. "We may not be close, but I know my sister. She wouldn't tell nobody she was pregnant until she was far enough along, but she told me, today, just a couple hours before you showed up."

He suddenly reached for Russo and Russo jumped. But Little Joey wound up putting a hand on Russo's shoulder. His eyes were glistening with emotion. "Emily told me what you did. How you coulda ran outta there, but you came back for her. When that big shithead CO was going to take her, maybe kill her, you messed him up. You saved their lives, her and the baby."

Russo broke away from Esposito's stare and looked at the photograph again. It looked like Christmas, Esposito standing arm-in-arm with Emily.

Emily Larson.

The thoughts were racing faster than Russo could keep up.

"And my guys…" Esposito began wistfully, "you know, it's hard to get good help. You're right, you know, they're not my best guys. Anthony… let's just say Anthony was on my shit list anyway. Emily wasn't supposed to be there. She still coulda gotten hurt with that limp dick around. Emily takes yoga, you know? Had a class get canceled, came back. But you came back then, too."

"I came back hoping to wipe down my prints. Cover my tracks."

"Bullshit. You saw my guys doing clean-up. You're no stranger to how this life works. You used to be for hire, you did your own clean-up. You were good, too, from what I hear. You went back because you knew she was preggo. Alright? Don't fucking spoil my good mood."

Russo kept his mouth shut.

"I helped them buy that house," Esposito said, growing nostalgic. "She didn't want to take my money, but, in the end, you know, my sister wanted a family, wanted to settle down. It took a while but I convinced her to let me help her." He raised his hands up suddenly in a gesture of innocence. "Money from legitimate businesses. I showed her the documentation, I even showed her my tax returns!"

Esposito wheezed through another bout of laughing.

The men in the corner finished counting.

"Eight hundred thirteen thousand four hundred and two," one announced.

Esposito studied the ceiling a moment, then looked at Russo. "Is that right? You spend a little? About how much did you spend?"

"Three thousand forty-nine."

Esposito's eyes were shining. "That's precise. Had a few things to take care of?"

Russo nodded, still astonished by the turn of the tables. Here he'd been moments away from killing everyone in the room. "I'm sorry."

The sheen over Esposito's eyes, Russo saw, was wet emotion. "That's alright, my friend," Esposito said, "because you… well…

one benevolent act." He touched Russo's shoulder again. "You see? One benevolent act."

Then he hopped off the bar stool and crossed to the pile of money. "Count out a hundred grand," he said to the men. He scowled, put his hands on his hips. "Nah, make it fifty. Let's not get crazy." He turned and called across the room to Russo. "Sound good to you? Fifty grand? Probably more than you make in a year now, right?"

Russo slowly dismounted the stool, grimacing at the pain in his back. His heart was resuming a normal rhythm, though, his mind clearing. He felt lighter than he had in years.

"I'll take it."

CHAPTER FIFTY-TWO

SIX MONTHS LATER

The new apartment in Ithaca wasn't as spacious as the farmhouse in the Adirondacks, but Emily loved it.

She stroked her round belly as she finished up work at her desk. She missed the wide open space – that she could admit – but Ithaca had local farms where they could get their produce, and not gardening had left Brett extra time to finish his book.

They were on a shoestring budget and had been for the past six months. The yellow farmhouse was back on the market. Their realtor was trying clever ways to distract from the property's twisted legacy, but selling prospects looked grim. Even if it did sell, it would be at a substantially reduced price, and they would owe more than they got back out of it. They continued to make the mortgage payments on top of the rent, and were close to being financially sunk.

Brett was back on a road crew and had taken a job bartending three nights a week, but he spent every available moment writing. She'd never seen him so motivated. He was even up before she was, coffee made (though she wasn't drinking any, not with the baby pinhead – now baby beach ball – growing inside her) and he hadn't stopped writing for weeks.

He'd gone up to Troy and met with Gentry Parker two more times. Parker had been won over by Brett's persistence and had agreed to be used as a source for the book.

And then, miracle of all miracles, he'd gotten an email two weeks ago from an agent willing to represent him.

It was fantastic news. It was also the first time he'd really been able to look his wife in the eyes since the day Agent Wilshire had removed her from the hospital where Brett had been recovering from his wounds.

The ensuing months had been painful, a test of their nascent marriage that Emily thought might not survive. The truth of her family came tumbling out of the closet, and Brett needed time to process it.

He'd known she was from Long Island. He'd known that her family had some money – her brother in particular. And he'd known that she had a tenuous relationship with her father and brother, but never knew why.

When Joey called her, it was a Saturday afternoon, the first she'd heard from him since everything had happened.

"Hi, sis. Long time no talk. How's the baby coming along?"

"Fine, Joe. How's Lisa and little Alexa?"

"Hey, all good here. Lisa got into yoga, following your lead, ya know? She's a little self-conscious, still thinks she carries that baby weight. I told her, right, 'You look dynamite.' But she's all… well, you know how it gets."

"That's great, Joe. Glad you guys are doing well."

"Yeah. Hey, you get my package?"

Joey had sent a cookie tin filled with money. It was ostensibly to help pay the mortgage. Emily had thrown the tin out and hid the money in her underwear drawer. She'd considered burning it. But she hadn't.

"Yeah, thanks, I got it."

"And how's hubby doing? I heard a rumor that he's working on a book?"

Emily could just see Brett through the doorway in his office. He'd taken the walk-in closet and converted it into his writing space. He was in there now, furiously pecking away at the keys.

What was the saying he was fond of?

Never miss an opportunity to shut up.

"Sis," Joey said. "You there?"

"I'm here. Yeah. Sorry."

"So, this book…"

"Oh it's nothing, Joe. Just keeps him busy. He had a pretty scary experience, you know? It's just his way of working it all out."

"Yeah, yeah, right…"

"He's able to get around now without his crutch. He's bartending."

"Good, good. And, ah, you know, I figure he knows a little more about you now, huh?"

"Hey, Joe? You think it's safe to be talking on the phone?"

"Not to worry. They ain't lookin' at you. They got no reason."

She closed her eyes a moment. "You put me in danger, Joe. I can't believe what you did."

He was quiet. Joey couldn't stand any kind of disapproval – he was just like their father. She knew she'd struck a nerve.

"Listen, Em. We had an agreement…"

"I didn't *know*," Emily hissed, opening her eyes. "You suggested that house – I thought you were being nice. Trying to help. I can't believe you. I might only be alive right now because of… because of him."

They both knew who she meant – the man who had gotten her out of there after Brett got shot.

"Yeah, and I took care of him. Gave him a nice little chunk of change. Okay?"

"The FBI knew I was your sister all along, Joe. They just waited to see what would happen. Waited for you to poke your head out. And you send those four… *morons*."

"Hey. I got my shit back. You're fine, your little hubby is fine…"

"He was *shot*, Joe! He nearly *died*. And I could have been hurt. My baby could have been hurt."

"Look, you handled it. You're an Esposito, Em. You're one of us."

She brushed damp hair from her forehead. She wanted to scream at him, *No I'm not,* and hang up the phone. She wanted to tell him never to call her again.

But that wouldn't be smart.

It was only by the narrowest margin she'd gotten through any of it. Her defense lawyer had mounted a passionate argument – she'd been a frightened woman, carrying a child, in the midst of a harrowing crime. A man had helped her, and she'd helped him in return. She never did anything intentionally to obstruct or impede the flow of justice. And you couldn't prosecute someone because of who their family was – no one had a choice about things like that. There wasn't a federal judge who would oversee the case, and the obstruction charges against her had been dropped.

But Wilshire and the rest of the federal investigators knew who she was. They'd only temporarily backed off to regroup. They almost certainly would try to rope her in again, cajole her into helping them take down her brother.

And maybe, this time, she would let them.

"Babe!" It was Brett, shouting from the other room.

"I gotta go, Joe," she said quietly.

"Alright. You stay you."

"And you stay you."

She found Brett jumping up and down at his own desk. He jammed a finger at the screen. "Kensington! Kensington is going to publish it!" He grabbed her and peppered her with kisses.

She smiled. "That's good? They're a good publisher?"

"They're *huge* true crime publishers." He was beside himself, his eyes bright, grin stretching ear to ear.

"We did it." He hugged her again.

"We did."

She looked over his shoulder, out the window as a light snow danced in the open air.

He pulled back and searched her eyes. "Who was that on the phone?"

"That was Joe."

Brett's forehead creased with a frown. "Yeah?"

"Uh-huh."

"You tell him about the book?"

"I did."

"He's not going to like it."

"So what. This is *our* life, not his. We're free to do whatever we want."

Brett put his hand on her stomach, and she put her hand on his.

CHAPTER FIFTY-THREE

Central Booking again, New York City.

Russo waited until he was called to the windows at the rear of the cell, sat down across from the lawyer, and spoke through the small hole in the glass.

"Long time no see," Bloustein deadpanned. He flipped through the file in front of him. "Everything good?"

"I got a new job."

"Oh yeah?"

"Yeah. Ferry worker. Get to be outside every day, under the open skies, breeze on my face."

Bloustein glanced up and frowned. "It's the middle of winter."

Russo shrugged.

Bloustein closed the file. He looked at Russo with the first spark of life Russo had seen in the lawyer. Bloustein leaned toward the hole and spoke in a low voice. "Is it true you had a sit-down with Joey Esposito a few months ago?"

"Are you asking me as my lawyer?"

"Look, as your lawyer, I don't care, I don't need to know. The charges we're dealing with today are that you left the state while out on bail. The court gave you direct instructions not to, and you didn't get permission. We can try to say you left the state under duress, but, from what you told me, it sounds like you traveled to Vermont of your own accord. It's a misdemeanor."

"And that's it?"

"That's it as far as we're concerned. I'm your public defender. Whatever happens next to you, that's beyond me. That's federal."

"Have you heard something? You know something?"

Bloustein sniffed. He seemed to enjoy the moment, the brush with darkness. "I know a guy at the Bureau, yeah."

"And?"

"Just that there were some calls placed, apparently, from the Larson's home phone to someone named Horatio Peña. And received from the same number. But this Peña is missing, presumed dead. That, and they don't seem to have any witnesses who'll say what exactly you were up to. There's the woman, who just says you helped her, and there's the cop, Morales, who has no recollection of you taking the money or shooting anyone. Honestly, I don't think the feds are pushing it; they're more interested in Little Joey. They've superseded all authority on this, and want him on racketeering, money laundering, and all the rest."

Bloustein gave Russo a long look, his mouth forming a slight, crooked smile. "That said, I'm sure they'll be knocking on your door at some point."

Yeah, the feds would be in touch, they'd try to rope him into something. In addition to Emily and Morales, there was the trooper who'd seen him, if at a distance, and they'd likely found his phone in Shelly's truck and could link it to him through the serial numbers. Maybe they'd even found evidence of his time driving Emily's vehicle.

Maybe prints on the shotgun.

But he doubted it. Joey's men had cleaned up after themselves, and they could have scrubbed away his own traces. At least from the house. The Prius… who knew? And did it matter?

All any of it proved was that he'd been there. That he'd helped out Emily Larson. Otherwise, they had nothing and weren't pushing it, like the lawyer said.

"Hey," Bloustein went on, "If the feds look you up, be straight with them. Cooperate, let them put you in witness relocation.

You saw the devil and you lived to tell about it. I doubt you'll get that chance again. You've got your wife and son to think about."

"Daughter."

"Right."

"Zoe."

"Yeah, okay, Zoe." Bloustein glanced away, then their eyes reconnected. "Off the record, though, between you and me – what happened up there? Can you tell me that?"

Russo thought of the bodies that had piled up. Shelly, Paulie, Anthony, Jockey, Richard, Snake. Not all were on his hands. Richard and Snake were self-defense. But Anthony – that had been pure murder. A thing that was supposed to be in his distant past, not his present.

"What happened was survival," Russo said.

He doubted the feds would ever find any of the bodies, at least there was that. Bobby Mars was damned good at what he did. Staten Island sat on layers of landfill, and Mars knew where to dig and drop. Anthony and Paulie were deep in a Vermont pond. Not cold or deep enough to freeze and preserve them, they'd be fish food before anyone ever knew better. And Esposito's boys had arranged things to look like Shelly died from fighting with Morales. Morales had been unconscious, so he wouldn't know any better.

The most regrettable death was Jockey. Russo had been paying visits to Jockey's mother in her rent-controlled Brooklyn apartment when he could. The previous weekend, Felicia had made her legendary *asopao* and he'd brought it along. It was a small condolence given that her only son was gone and would never be found, but it was something.

Now all that was left was to deal with the misdemeanor for leaving the state.

"So how do I get out of this place?" Russo asked.

"Well, you're all paid up on your other fines. You just have this one." Bloustein raised his thick eyebrows. "You got any money left?"

"Yeah," Russo said. "I got a little."

A LETTER FROM T.J. BREARTON

Hi. Thank you so much for reading. I gotta tell you, James Russo is one of my favorite people who ever showed up in my head one day. He didn't do it with any sort of fuss, either – he was just sitting there, quietly eating his breakfast, and then the cops rolled up on the street out front. I bet Russo had no idea where the day was going to take him. I hope you've enjoyed the ride.

If you did, and want to keep up-to-date with all my latest releases, just sign up at the following link. Your email address will never be shared and you can unsubscribe at any time.

www.bookouture.com/tj-brearton/?title=buried-secrets

And if you've come this far, then maybe you'd like to go a little bit further and post a review. As another author, James Carol, put it: "As a reader, one of the things I like most is discovering new books and new writers, and the way I do that is through word of mouth. Someone tells me they love a book, I just have to go and check it out." So please consider sharing your own words with others.

I love hearing from readers, too; drop me a line any time. The easiest way is through my website. Stephen King said writing is telepathy, so we're connected now, you and I, by all the chaos that touched the lives of Emily and Brett Larson.

See you again real soon.

tjbrearton.com

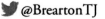 @BreartonTJ

 tjbreartonauthor/

ACKNOWLEDGEMENTS

First, I need to thank Kristy Wilson for letting me bother her with law enforcement questions and for being invaluably helpful to me, all while she's busy being a New York State Trooper, plus a mom to young children. Please award her your thanks for police procedural accuracies; for any mistakes, blame me.

Thank you to Geoff Pierce, who read an early draft, and, as usual, knew exactly how to nose out the good stuff and wasn't afraid to shine the light on the bad. You couldn't ask for a better guy to throw you into paroxysms of despair.

Thank you to the rest of my amazing crew of readers, including Bob Sirrine, John Ramirez, Lee Clark Smith, Wanda Downs, Sandra Hill Elam, and Jeanni Richmond. It ain't easy pointing out mistakes and offering criticism, but these people have the knack to offer insight with humor and grace.

Huge thanks to my editor, Abigail Fenton. It cannot be overstated how important the relationship between writer and editor can be, and Abi is the entire package. Having someone who knows your work so thoroughly, who can cleave through the cloud of mental confusion like a samurai… this is good stuff.

Thank you to Kim Nash, who lovingly introduced me to the Bookouture family of authors, and to those authors, who keep me inspired. (And by "inspired" I mean filled with competitive rapaciousness.) Thank you to Jasper Joffe, who has been monumental in shaping my writing. Thank you to DeAndra Lupu for her laser-like precision as copyeditor and to Bookouture Managing Editor Lauren Finger for pulling it all together. And thanks to my brother, Lane Buzzell, an accomplished martial artist who not only inspired a big part of this book and helped me with the details, but continues to impress me with his soulful and unconventional life.

Finally, thank you to my wife, Dava. Dava listens to me go on and on about stories I'm writing, waits patiently while I thunder around or sulk with a problem, smiles when I've had a good day, discerns when I'm willing to listen to reason and tells me what I need to hear, and has recently been offering her own cracking ideas for stories and story bits. She's been with me since this all was just a pipe dream.

Without these folks, this book would not have been possible.